MARGET POW

FROM A WATER-COLOUR SKETCH   BY HENRY W. KERR, R.S.A.

MARGET POW

MARGET POW

BY

CATHERINE PONTON SLATER

THE MORAY PRESS
EDINBURGH & LONDON

ORIGINALLY PUBLISHED IN THREE PARTS

NINTH EDITION COMPLETING 27,500 COPIES 1943
REPRINTED . . 1944
REPRINTED . . 1946
REPRINTED . . 1947

PUBLISHED AT THE MORAY PRESS
57 GEORGE STREET EDINBURGH
AND PRINTED IN SCOTLAND BY
THE DARIEN PRESS LTD.
EDINBURGH

LONDON: FREDERICK MALLER LTD., 29 GREAT JAMES STREET,
BEDFORD ROW, W.C. 1

TO

MY SISTER

JESSY

THE DEAR FELLOW-TRAVELLER

WHO HAS OVER-PASSED ME IN THE WAY

AND NOW RESTS

CONTENTS

IT was gratifying to be able, even with an effort, to make people laugh, . . . especially as laughter, like mercy, is twice blest : and he who presents it, even the smallest smile, among the overpowering sorrow of the world, is lifted out of sorrow too.

ETHEL SIDGWICK

MARGET POW
IN FOREIGN PARTS

I

CAVENDISH SQUARE, LONDON
January 190–

DEAR CHRISTINA,—I now put pen to paper to send
you all parteeclars of our grand trip.

The new cook here is a Mrs M'Clumpha, and you
will be dumbfoundered when you hear what Mrs
M'Clumpha she is. Well, if you will believe me, her
man was good-brother to Mr Borthwick—she's a
Haddington woman hersel', and so is he—and her
lassie is married on Alec Wilson's John, him that's
the game-keeper up at Burnie, and many a time have
I seen her sittin' in Dunbar Free Kirk in the summer-
time, with a thing in her best bonnet for all the world
like a sweep's besom. And here she is in Lady
Lindesay's kitchen, very near as broad as she's long.
It's a big kitchen, and ill to keep clean. The kitchen-
maid is just a lassie, and figure her speakin' high
English as if she was a lady! I hope I know my
place better than to speak either French or English:
but the sairvants here are terrible upsettin'.

See and no' let the sweeps stramp over the new-
vairnished floors with their muckle feet, and be
canny when it comes to washing the best china.
What for our ladies were so set to go to Italy exackly
at the cleaning-time, it beats me to tell. I understand the Pope is settled in Rome now, poor old
gentleman, so there was no siccan a hurry to see *him*.
But if I am spared to get back to my own town, it's

the first and the last the Pope will see of me, and that I'll certifee.

Would you believe that I never knew when we crossed the Border, and me no' been further south than Galashiels before !

Miss Jean says to me, " You're over the Border now, Margaret," says she. I never let on that I hadn't notticed the difference, but I jaloused that something had happened, for the train gave an awfu' bounce, and very near upset the man that was nippin' our tickets all to nonsense. I saw a field of turnips in England the very same as the one next Oldhamstocks Church ; but, when you think on it, one neep is very like another at the green end.

We were all on the queevee when we got near London, and what with the cabs, and the porters, and the luggage, and Lady Lindesay's grand footman, my head was in a creel till we were all safe landed in Cavendish Square. A very genteel locality. Lady Lindesay is keepin' fine, and I never can get out of my head that she's just Miss Murray still, she's that young and fresh-looking. I felt like to greet when she kissed me, and called me " dear old Margaret," her that was the first bairn I brought up, and thankit me for makin' up my mind to go all the way to Rome with the young ladies. I am sure a month at Peebles or the Bridge of Allan would have been far wiser-like for a dalicate young lady like Miss Jean, but the doctor said Italy, and Italy I suppose it mun be. If I can get her and Miss Celandine safe home without turning nuns or marrying Italian blagyards, I am sure I'll be thankful, so no more at present from your affectionate friend,

MARGET POW

II

CAVENDISH SQUARE, LONDON
January 190–

DEAR CHRISTINA,—I didna forget that I promised
to tell you all about the bairns at Cavendish Square,
but I've been real busy, what with winding up my
watch, and one thing and another. You'll mind the
watch Miss Celandine gave me to take with me on
my traivels ? She bought it in a bicycle shop, and
she's had to buy me a bag to carry it in, it's that big.
It takes very near two minutes to wind it up, and
Miss Celandine says she can hear the racket it makes
down in the drawing-room. It's a good watch,
though, loud in the tick, and plain in the face. It
aye minds me of one I saw in a shop-window in
Dunbar High Street in the summer-time. Two wee
bairns were lookin' in, and the one says, " My faither
has a watch as big as that " ; " Yer a leear," says
the other, and away they toddled as friendly as you
like. Bairns are no' parteeclar.

Master Johneen is four now, and Miss Cielle is six.
The first I saw of them they were carryin' a black-
and-white cat and two wee kitlings betwixt them.
They both held up their bonny wee faces for a kiss,
and then Master Johneen says, " Our cat is a widow
with two young children." " Dearie me," says I,
astonished-like, and 'deed I couldna but wonder what
had put it into their heads. They said their Mother
had told them, and they were so taken up with
petting the poor beasties that they could think about
nothing else. Master Johneen is grown, and Miss
Jean is lamenting sore that there's no baby for her
to cuddle now. I never saw any young lady so set
on infants as she is. I mind fine when she was a wee
lassie, no' any older than Miss Cielle, she used to coax
her poor Mamaw to get a real baby for her to play

with; and one day when Mrs Murray put her off
with " How can I get a baby for you, Jean ? " she
said, " Couldn't you *pray* for one, Mother ? " Poor
wee lassie; she little thought what the baby, (that
was Miss Celandine,) was to cost. The loss of their
Mamaw has been a fearfu' miss to the young ladies;
and the Colonel might have been some use too for
takin' the tickets, and seein' after the luggage : but
a sojer is a handless character away from the guns;
and what with the loss of his head through going too
near the enemy, and one thing and another, he never
come home to his orphan weans.

Look in the top drawer of the chest-of-drawers
in the back spare-room. There's six blue-and-white
checked ones in the left hand corner, near the front;
that's no' them; but they're farther back.—Yours
affectionately,

MARGET POW

III

CAVENDISH SQUARE, LONDON
January 190–

DEAR CHRISTINA,—Our young ladies has decided to
stop here a whilie, so I'll can tell you all about the
strange and manifold sights of London.

Firstly, the colour of the washings is beyond the
power of pen to describe; and, unless you were to
see it with the naked eye, you would never believe
the drumlie, grey, dirty colour poor Lady Lindesay's
napery is now ! I would be black-affronted to see
such awfu-like things hanging out in our back-green.
But everything is sent out to the Lady's Lilywhite
Laundry, so what can ye expeck ? Mrs M'Clumpha
says the gairden is too dirty for bleaching in—fair
black wi' soot—and nobody takes a daunder in it
except the cat.

I have been away seeing Westminster Abbey the day, it being considered one of the foremost sights of London. Miss Celandine took me.

Appearingly there's been a deal of mortality among the high faimlies in England since it was built, for it's fair crammed with tombstones, Kings and Queens being included. We paid sixpence each to be let through an iron gate, and when once we were through, a tall genteel-looking gentleman in a black gown attended upon us to tell us all about the monuments, tombs, sepulchres, graves, and other objecks of interest. There was a good few ladies and gentlemen kept company with Miss Celandine and me, and they were aye askin' questions about one thing and another, and pittin' off the gentleman's time : he was a Verger, it appeared, and he said he would be needed to verge at three in the efternoon : he was gey short in the temper, too, and couldna abide the folk no keepin' close to his heels :—" Keep near me, ladies and gentlemen," says he, " if you wish to hear what I have to say." But, if you'll believe me, he spoke such high English that I couldna understan' the half he said—and him no more than a Minister's man ! He showed us tomb upon tomb till I was fair wearied : a lot of the graven images on the monuments was lying flat on their backs with their feet on their pet lions—poor beasties ! (I wouldna care to keep one mysel'.) Some of them had dogs to stick their soles against. A very stylish tombstone represented a family group :—the old gentleman and his lady were lying side by side on the top floor, like, and the six young gentlemen were kneeling down below, three and three, on six hassocks with tossels at the corners. They were all dressed the same — knickerbockers, awfu full in the legs, and armour on the top—warmish, I'm thinkin'. The hassocks with the tossels were as like as life, mind you, and all made of stone ! I was thinkin' I would mebbe make one for my seat in the

Kirk; a bit carpet on the top, and worsit tossels would look fine : I never saw that style in Edinburgh, but ye need to traivel to find out the new fashions.

The best thing we saw was near the last—no less than the Coronating chair. And what do you think it is made of ? Naething more nor less than a stone the English took from the Scotch folk ! Dear peety me ! could they no' hae gotten a stone to theirsels ? They call it the stone of Destiny, but I'm no' sure where that is; down the West Coast, mebbe. I couldna see that it was onyway wonderfu ; I had a first cousin that was a sculpterer down Leith Walk, and, if you'll believe me, I've seen dizens of stones the very same in his yaird. It must have been a heavy carry ; but, no doubt, it was long afore the days of chairging for extry luggage—a perfeck imposeetion. There's four gold lions, wi' long curly tails, for feet, and they've put a bit wood over the stone for fear the Kings and Queens that sit on it might catch the cold ; " Them that sit on stane, are twice fain " ; fain to sit down, and fain to rise up again, as many a day I've felt mysel', sittin' on the rocks at Dunbar, with the bairns diggin' holes in the beach by the hour thegither.

There's forty poor widows gets something to theirsels once a week in the Presinks ; it will be what the lawyers call a " mortification " in Scotland, viz. when folks leaves their money to the poor, and no' to their own relations. Every one of them gets $1\frac{1}{2}$ lbs. of the best beef ; a 4-lb. loaf of bread ; and tuppence in coppers : my certy !

The very last thing we saw was the monument to Sir John Franklin, who was conneckit, more or less, with the North. The gentleman read the Hepitawph (that'll be what they call the text in London), and it sounded real bonny. Miss Celandine has written it down the way he said it ; she is an obliging young lady, when she's not on the nonsense. It is poetry; viz.—

> Not 'ere ; the wite Nawth 'olds thy bones,
> An' thou, 'eroic sailor soul !
> Hart passin' on thy nappier voyage now
> Towards no hearthly goal.

With which solemn words I must conclude.

The young ladies sends their kind regairds to you and Merran.—Yours sincerely,

MARGET POW

IV

CAVENDISH SQUARE, LONDON
January 190–

DEAR CHRISTINA,—Me and the lady's-maid has been away seeing Madam Tooso's Wax-works : Lady Lindesay sent us : you pay a shilling to get in, and stay as long as you like. But Thomson had to be back at seven o'clock to dress her ladyship for a pairty, so we were just a jimp four hours at the exhibeetion. Susan is the lady's-maid's name, but she aye gets " Thomson " ; it's the fashion in high faimlies appearingly. She's a nice, douce, young woman, but pure English, poor thing.

And who do you think we met in the bus but a Scotchman ! A real decent old body, fresh-coloured, and well put on. " Hoo much dae ye chairge to Madam Tooso's ? " says he, real canny-like ; and I'm thinkin' that, if it had been more than a penny, he would have got out and walked. But there's many an Englisher that would have gotten in and never asked the fare—so they would : no wonder London is just filled with beggars.

The wax-works are numerous :—Kings and Queens by the dizen ; old and young, black and white, as

like as life. It made me fair dizzy to see such a lot
of folk at once, and no' a few of them the very same
as we had seen lying on their graves at Westminster
Abbey, parteeclarly Mary Queen of Scots : there she
sat in a black velvet gown, with Mr J. Knox standin'
beside her. Little thought she, poor lady, that she
would end in a wax-work, and him too.

There was a French lady (I dinna mind on her
name) that had a bonny pink silk tea-gown on : it
would take fourteen yairds to make one the same to
Miss Jean ; Thomson said you would need fourteen
and a half, or mebbe fifteen, but lady's-maids are
aye wasterfu'. It was thinnish—8s. 11d. a yaird, I
would jalouse ; you would likely get the dress-piece
for 50s.

Downstairs we saw a grand tablow of Queen
Victoria receiving the two gentlemen that came to
tell her that her Uncle was dead. They were kneeling in front of her, and, comin' away in the middle
of the night, it was mebbe no wonder that their boots
hadna been blacked. The poor young lady was gey
sleepy-looking ; she had on a white shawl that should
have been in the wash-tub lang syne ; it would be the
first she could find. Many's the time I've told you
and Merran never to wait to be told to wash the
young ladies' shawls ; everything that is dirty is
ready to be washed, and I'm sure you would have
been affronted if you had seen one of *our* young
ladies in sic a like shawl as poor Queen Victoria is
being handed down to prosperity in.

We saw André in a balloon, seeking for the North
Pole ; it must be an awfu height.

Then we saw General Gordon being shot ; and
the two wee Princes in the Tower that was murdered ; and the execution of Mary Queen of Scots ;
it's a very enjoyable exhibeetion.

Finally we had our teas in the Restorong, at a table
wi' as many legs as a centipede, and came away home.

Do you mind of Miss M'Neil that was at the school with Lady Lindesay? Well, she's dead. But they've ereckit a window to her memory in St Album's Church, where she worshipped. It's a great big window with a picture of Noah's Ark on it: (she was aye fond of animals—parteeclarly cats:) the birds and beasts are comin' out two by two, very neat and reglar-like: there's a stag and a roe prancin' over the door-step, and bears, elephants, geese, giraffes, swans, and camels comin' down the hill; glad to get out, poor beasties.

It'll no be long now till we set sail for France! if ever we get safe back again, I'm thinkin' it will be more by good luck than good guidin'! If I'm spared I'll need new flannen petticoats next winter: the way they've shrunk mine's at the Lady's Lily-white Laundry is a perfeck disgrace. I was tellin' Miss Celandine about them, and she says, "The trials that afflict the just, in number many are." She's aye for the poetry, but that's in a psalm.

My kind regairds to all inquirin' friends,

MARGET POW

V

HOTEL VICTORIA, PISA
February 190–

DEAR CHRISTINA,—At long and at last we've crossed the English Channel. What a work folk make about nothing! You might just as well get into a pavee when you were takin' the boat to Burntisland —it is no' that much further—and when I keeked out half-roads the water looked the very same as the Firth of Forth; I must say I was disappointed. Then, when we set foot on a foreign shore, and went birlin' away to Paris, the very first station I read up was Creil, and 'deed the whole country was just as

B

like Fife as need be. But there's an awfu odds on
the language; that's a fack. There was a woman
came to my room-door at a place they call Deeshong,
and she rapped and cried, " Say lo shode, Madame."
Thinks I to mysel', " I'll say naething of the sort—
not without I ken what it means "; so I lay quiet.
In a meenit she rapped again and cried louder, " Say
lo shode." " Havers ! " says I, and in she came with
a jug of hot water, and stood smiling, appearingly
waiting for me to say something. Then I minded
that Miss Jean told me always to say " Mercy "
when I didna ken what folk said : so " Mercy," says
I, loud and plain, and away she went quite pleased.
Daft, mebbe, but I'm no' sure.

Paris is a big town, and there's a great big church
in it. Of course Miss Jean was set to go to it,
and nothing would halt her, although it wasna
the Sabbath-Day nor anything like it, and me in
my every-day bonnet, and the skirt on that I got
dyed black for efternoons. The minister was a
stoutish gentleman, about fifty or thereaway, and
the sermon was a good length ; but I couldna make
out what the subjeck of the discourse was, what
with the language, and one thing and another.

Many a mile we've travelled syne. It's a long
hurl from Paris to Pisa, and we stopped at three
towns in the by-going. What hills for height we
saw on the road here ! all ice and snow on the top
—no use whatever : and we went through an awfu
length of a tunnel they call it the Mong Snee
tunnel.

It was at a place called Tureen that we saw the
two Miss Duffs that worship in the East Church.
You'll mind the old ladies that Mary Campbell's
sister's niece was housemaid to ? It was them.
They were sittin' at a nasty shoogly wee table takin'
their breakfasts, or as much breakfast as they could
get, anyway. I wasna sure at first that it was them,

for I never saw them afore wantin' their bonnets;
but one of them was readin' the *Scotsman*, and she
lookit over the paper at the other one, and, says she,
" Charlotte, guess who's dead ? " The minute she
spoke I knew her; there's something about the
language that makes ye ken the Edinburgh folk fine.

I'm glad to hear you're both keepin' well. See
and no' loss the cat the time we're away : Miss Jean
is aye askin' about it.—Your affectionate friend,

MARGET POW

VI

VEEBABONY STREET, ROME
February 190–

DEAR CHRISTINA,—Figure me in Rome! " The
Infernal City," as they call it ; doomed to destruc-
tion on account of being seetiated on seven hills, and
filled cram-full (as I understan') of idolators and
other Bedevilments. I've been expeckin' an earthquake very near every day, and I aye keep my
flannen petticoat on a chair next my bed at night,
ready to flee in. I've let down one of the tucks, no'
being wishfu to look like a ballet-dancer at my latter
end ; I'll need to put a false hem, though (if I'm
spared), and I'll no' soon forget the Lady's Lily-
white Laundry—set them up !

What do you think was the first name I saw over
a door in the town ? No less than Colonna Ciceri !
You'll mind Andrea Ciceri, who keepit the High-
class ice-cream Saloon in Dunbar High Street, with
" Fried Potatoes " above the left-hand window ?
He'll be a friend of he's—mebbe a first cousin : it's
a queer thing, but go where you like, you'll aye fall
in with somebody that you ken something about.

Miss Jean says we're livin' in a palace. It is the
first time I ever heard tell of a palace up a common

stair. No doubt the steps are marble, and there's a good few of them ; but I've been up a stair in the High Street with seventeen mair.

We landed in the middle of the night, and the folk that keep the pension were all in their beds except a laddie no' above sixteen year old, in a black dress-coat rideeclously long in the waist, and a white tie. He gave us our suppers, and, for all there was to eat, he might just as well have been in his bed too, instead of standin' glowerin' at us like a wull-cat :— cold roast mutton, bread and cheese, and soddy-water in a sighfone—nesty things ; naething but a whiffle of wind, or else squirkin' all over the cloth and making a mess.

Yes : we saw the leaning tower the day we were at Pisa ; it's no' straight, I must say that. The folk at the hotel were real set to know if the man that built it meant it to lean. I would think no' ! if it had been *meant* to lean, it wouldna have leant—no' it. I was tellin' Miss Celandine that, and she says the Tower is a notable instance of the innate cussed-ness of matter ; she'll have got that out of the Guide-book, I'm thinking.

We were shown the gasoliery that made a man called Gallyleeo invent a clock. It is in the church that Mr and Mrs Gallyleeo attended, and it seems that the gasoliery used to swee like a pendulum ; there must have been an awfu draught ; but a knock's a useful thing too, so it is.

Miss Celandine's real ill about the way the folk in the hotels cleans her boots. She says I am to send you the directions, and you are to mind and *never* follow them. This is what she has written down :— " To clean ladies' boots. Remove carefully all traces of polish with a damp cloth, smearing the leather as completely as possible. Then, with a piece of clean flannel, apply the blacking freely to the boot-laces only, and deliver at the bedroom door."

They're tellin' me the Pope's no' a married gentleman; he's just what they call a celebrate, like. I heard a deal about him yon time the Rev. Mr MacTavish was preachin' about graven images in the Established Church. I dinna mind of seeing any mysel'; but they are unchancy things, and I hope they'll no' get creepin' into the Auld Kirk.

See you and Merran take your Sundays out reglar; a Continental Sabbath is no much better nor a Setterday.

With kind regairds.—Your old friend,

MARGET POW

VII

VEEABONE COMPANY STREET, ROME
February 190–

DEAR CHRISTINA,—We flitted on Monday to a top flat in a place they call Veeabone Company Street— fine and open. It's a queer thing what a lot of the names of the streets here begins with a " V." It'll be owing to some peculiarity of the Italian language, I'm thinkin'.

We came here on account of a lift there is to save Miss Jean the long climb; and much need, for there's a hundred and forty-eight steps up—marble every one of them, as sure as I'm here, and it just a common stair! But they'll no' get me to go into yon thing; I'm no' the kind of a woman to go sweein' up like a canary-bird in a cage, thank ye! and the man that pulls the string is an awfu down-lookin' chiel, with both eyes gleyed, and a mouth like the de'il pu'in heather.

It's a big flat when you get up to it, and the three ladies it belongs to take in six paying guests and one terrier dog. They keep two servants forbye a stout young mairrit woman that comes in by the day; I

don't know what her right name is; she aye gets
" Linda." The cook is an auld body, and the table-
maid is a widow-woman. Strange to say, none of
them can speak a word of English : it's an awfu
drawback to the conversation.

There's queer things goes on here, and the very
dog has been away to the church to be blessed, and
me with him. His name is James, and he's no' a
bonny dog, but real respectable-lookin' : I don't
know exackly what kind of a dog he is; Miss Celandine
is real fond of dogs, but she says she never saw one
the same shape before. He belongs to an English
lady—Miss Thomson. She's free and pleasant, and
she says she likes fine to hear me speaking; I'm
sure it's a cheap treat for her, decent body. So
away I went with her and James, although, mind you,
I was raither uneasy about encouraging such a
carry-on.

It was one of the days they call a Feastable, and a
feck of folks was on the same business as us. The
big beasts, such as horses, cows, calves, cuddies,
pownies, and other quadrupeds, were outside the
Church, but the wee animals was admitted. Up
came the priest in full dress, and an anchorite with
him, carrying the holy water. They stopped in
•front of James, but the poor beastie turned his back,
and when he felt the water squirtin' over him he
lookit up at his mistress as much as to say, " I doubt
we'll hae rain," and was in an unco hurry to be off.
It was as much as we could do to get him to bide till
the prayer was said, and by the time it was done, he
had the string Miss Thomson was holdin' him by
wound about her feet like to trip her; she had on
elastic-sided boots with patent leather toes and white
cotton stockings, so you and Merran needna laugh at
me. I wished I had had Tatty with me ; she's such
a meek cat, she would have acted it fine.

Cover comfortably with water and rejuce to a

pulp ; but I can easy see that it will just need to be all done over again once I get back.—Yours sincerely, MARGET POW

VIII

Via Bon Compagni, Roma
March 190—

DEAR CHRISTINA,—See and no' affront yourself with sending such a daft-like address again. Just you copy what I put at the head of my letter. " *Via* " means a street—anybody might have jaloused that —but no doubt it's easier to learn the language when you're in the place.

We have been greatly blessed in the weather the time we've been in Rome—not a single earthquake ! I'm thinkin' Italy is no' near so shoogly as what folks try to make out ; and, speakin' about shoogly, would you believe that I've never seen more than one drunk man in Rome ? and he was not exackly what you would call drunk, but just a wee thing tozy-mozy like, as Mansie would say. Mind you that's a queer thing, for the folk are aye drinkin' wine !

I'll be glad when the young ladies have seen all the picturs and the churches in Rome, for I'm fair *sick* of them. I'll warrant there are twice as many picturs as what there is in the National Picture Gallery in Edinburgh, and mebbe more. There's hundreds of picturs of the Virgin, and no two of them alike ; I canna understan' that. There's a good few saints and martyrs has had their picturs painted too, puir things ; I daursay we've seen five oil paintins, in broad gold frames, of the same thin, old gentleman glowrin' at a scull (I dinna mind his name) ; he must have been set on gettin' hissel' taken. I never had my caird done but once, at

Portobella on the Queen's Birthday; it was like, all except the face.

It was a portrait of a young lady we were away seein' to-day, and Miss Celandine gave me her history. Chenchy was her last name—a high family in Rome. It seems that her poor Papaw was a very difficult gentleman to get on with, and a fair torment in the house. Mebbe her Mamaw was a bad manager, and changed her sairvants every six months like the folk next door: I wouldna wonder: but, any way, they were not a comfortable family. At long and at last, after an extry rippat, the old gentleman was found dead in his bed, and it was easy seen that it was by no wish of he's. Well, they sent for the pollis-officers, and if they didna take up the puir innocent lassie, and off with her head. Nasty, cruel fellies! I couldna bear to look at the pictur—such a bonny bit thing she was, with a waesome look on her face that very near garred me greet.

I was thankfu' to get home again; I was that tired I went up the stair in the lift. Miss Jean gave the Konserge a *bête-noir*, as the French call it, to take extry care of me, and I took a good grip of the seat with both hands; but I was in a trem'le the whole way up, and glad to get a sit-down and my tea when I landed.

The young ladies are keepin' well, but I dinna think Miss Jean's sight is just right, and I'm kind of uneasy about it. When we were lookin' at the picturs to-day she called one of them an " old Master," and, as sure as I'm here, it was a woman in a low-bodied gown, tight in the waist, with long sleeves and starched frills at the hands, sittin' at an open windy, and a shower comin' on! She canna be seeing right.

Miss Celandine is fine. She says she would like to be married on a Cardinal, but she's doubting if she will get the chance; I hope no'; she would make a daft-like Minister's wife. My best respecks to Mr M'Duigald.—Your affectionate friend,

MARGET POW

P.S.—We were away seeing a celebrated church this morning, round-shaped, with a hole in the roof, I canna mind the name of it. The most remarkable featur about the edifice is the number of cats in the vicinity, viz. inside and out. We counted seven airing themselves round about the church, and there was other five inside. The most of them was young married ladies appearingly, so I doubt it will be a while before they'll can get them exterminated. There was a bonny black one asleep on one of the altars. Miss Jean says she thinks she has heard of cats being worshipped :—

> The heathen in his blindness
> Bows down to wood and stone.

See and no forget to put a wee drop of hot water in Tatty's milk at night : it is lighter for the stomach. —M. P.

IX

VIA BON COMPAGNI, ROMA
March 190–

DEAR CHRISTINA,—The weather is much the same as what it is in Edinburgh, Portobella and district at this time of year :—whiles it keeps fair ; and whiles it pours with rain ; but as long as the earthquakes keep off, I'm no' caring. There was a good shower this morning, but it faired up sudden-like, and out blinked the sun as hot as summer. I stuck my head out at the windy to smell the rain (the windy-sole is pure marble), and I got a fine view far and near. Not so bonny as what we see from the top-windy in

the Terrace, away over the Firth to the green hills
of Fife—I'm no' saying that—but bonny for a foreign
land. The Principe Bon Compagni's Villa is exackly
opposeet; a self-contained house, with eight statutory
figures on the top with nothing on, but clean—I will
say that—Rome is a clean place in the way of smoke-
reek. The gairden round about the villa is just over-
grown with trees, and you never saw the like of the
flourish on them, parteeclarly the lily-oaks ! and the
camelias are full out under the trees ; and the rain-
drops were prap-prappin' on them like diamonds
from the sky, as the poet says. Away west there's
a hill they call Monte Cavo, a very neat shape, like
North Berwick Law ; but it is mebbe higher, because
there's snow on the top yet.

Our ladies were away seein' the Pope on Monday
afternoon, dressed all in pure blacks, with black lace
veils over their heads, like nuns ; it set them no'
bad.

I went down to the chapel too, for the sake of the
hurl, and there was a Popish lady with us carryin'
dizens of wee images and a good few rosemaries to be
blessed by the Pope. They're awfu folk for gettin'
theirselves blessed. Miss Jean says you'll never can
get any ill from the blessing of a good man, but the
way that beast James has been carryin' on ever since
he was blessed is no chancy—mind you, the cratur
understan's French—he does that !

Last night at the back of eight, I heard Miss
Thomson crying " Prommeny, James, prommeny ! "
which means " Away you go for a walk," and sure
enough away he goes down the stair with Gemma, to
get a bit run : she's the housemaid. It was nearly
half an hour before they came back, and Gemma said
she had had a job seekin' for James ; and little wonder,
for, when I went out to the post, the dog was sittin'
waitin' at the door on the bass-mat, and Gemma was
seekin' him in the arms of the lift-man—no' a very

likely place, for the poor beast canna abide Joe
Vanny—no him.

There was a terrible crowd getting in to see the
Pope, and it was everybody for hisself, and de'il
tak' the hindmost. The sojers were the queerest
tickets you ever saw, with bunchy red and yellow
breeks, cut in strips. I am told their uniforms were
designed by a gentleman that was something in the
pictur line : dear peety me ! could he no' have stuck
to the pentin' ! Mitchell-Angelo was his name : no'
an Edinburgh gentleman : so no more at present,
from—Yours truly,

MARGET POW

X

VIA BON COMPAGNI, ROMA
March 190–

DEAR CHRISTINA,—I got a fright to-day with Miss
Celandine tellin' me that she was sure my tendency
to ombongpong was increasing. Mercy me ! I was
feared I had got a hidden disease in my inside that I
had never notticed ! but she said that she only
meant that I was getting fatter.

Rome is a healthy locality, but there is a deal of
a queer disease they call tonsures going about ; it
generally attacks the head—men's heads parteeclarly
—it must be a sore trouble. It's queer that none of
the folk in Scotland has it. Castor oil is a grand
thing for the hair. When I was a bairn at Carldoddie, my mother used to put castor oil on our
heads every Sabbath morning (there were seven of
us) ; it was a general custom in the village, and the
grand folks that used to bide with the Laird for the
shooting said they were kept away from public
worship on the Sabbath-Day because they could
not abide the smell of it. " What various hindrances
we meet, in coming to the mercy-seat."

We have been to see St Peter's, which is the principal Established Church in the place : but it is a Catholic Church, mind you ; fair rideeclous ! Miss Jean says it is not very old, any way they've not got the pews putten in yet. It is a goodish-sized place, bigger than St Giles's, I will say that ; but there's no' much comfort about it. They were singing in what they call the Gregorium chapel, and no' a few of the priests were as ombongpongy as me. Miss Jean told me that they were singing the Psalms in Latin—such a carry-on ! When I thought on the folk in Carldoddie Church singing " O send Thy light forth and Thy truth " (Psalm 43, verse 3) on a Sacrament Sunday, to the tune of " Invoca-tion " ; the men first—" My harp," and then the women—" My harp," and then all the folk together loud—" My harp I will employ, I *will* employ," I wondered that Italians would put off their time singing Psalms that nobody could understan' ; but " ye mun hing as ye grow."

I will not attempt to enumerate the tombs we saw. Although not so plentiful as in Westminster Abbey, still there's a good few of them, all the choicest saints being, appearingly, in their graves. The last of the Stuarts lies cold and dead in a strange land, and John Knox is buried somewhere too—I canna mind where.

After we came out of St Peter's, Miss Celandine was set to go and get her new gown tried on, and nothing would serve her but that Miss Jean would go with her. After Miss Celandine was tried on, Miss Jean was tired, and wanted away home, so I went with her in a carotska. Miss Celandine bade me come for her to a Church near hand that she wished to see ; (I'll wager there's a Church in very near every street in Rome !) she said I was to come to the West door, and she would meet me there. Well, away I went my lea-lane, after I saw Miss

Jean settled for a rest, but, by the time I had got to
the appointed Church, I couldna mind which was
North, South, East, nor West, and there was doors
round and round. First I stood a whilie at the
front door. Then up came a grand gentleman in a
cocked hat and a sword danglin' at his side, and says
he in some foreign language, (I suppose) for I didna
ken the words, " You're no' allowed to stand here
more than one hour at a time." " Mercy ! " says
I : " You're welcome," says he, and away I went to
the back-door. I hadna stood there long before
anither gentleman came by and looked at me : back
he came again, and says he, " Ye better either gang
in or come out." " I'm waitin' on a lady," says I
to him, but he lifted the curtain at the door, and
waved his hand, and bade me go in to the body of
the Kirk. I went in a wee bittie, but when I saw
the smoking insecks, I fled like a brand snatched
from the burning. Once I was safe out, I thought
I would try another door, and no sooner was I
settled than Miss Celandine came fleeing round the
corner like an antelope, real glad to see me. She
said she had stooden *hours* at the West door, like the
boy on the burning deck, and she gave me his whole
history on the road home. Puir young gentleman ;
if he had fled like me when he felt the smell of the
burning he would mebbe have been drowned.

See and screw down the gas tight when you go to
your beds ; the wastry of gas that I see going on in
some folk's houses is lamentable.—Believe me, yours
truly,

                                        MARGET POW

XI

Via Bon Compagni, Roma
April 190–

Dear Christina,—They have been busy thorough-cleanin' here, and no' afore it was wanted : but what do you think for ? because the priest was expeckit to bless every room in the house ; did ever you hear tell of such a set-away ! I am thankfu' to say that I was out when he came, no' being habitted with siccan popish plots. Miss Jean told me when I came in that he had strinkled my room with holy water. There was a kind of a damp smell, but I've not taken the cold—no' *yet*, anyway.

The house is not half cleaned : the fuff under the beds is a fair disgrace, and I canna keep my hands off it, although I'm no' expeckit to do more than attend on the young ladies ; and the carpet in the drawing-room is just thick with thrums. Would you believe that dust-pans are made with long shanks in Italy, to save the servant-lassies bendin' their backs ! I hope they'll no' be introjuced into Scotland. You needna think that I'll bring one home to you and Merran—no' likely !

Miss Celandine says I am to be sure and tell you about the eight-legged chickens of Italy. That's just her joke. The chickens have no more legs here nor what they have in Scotland, England, and elsewhere ; but, when the dish gets the length of Miss Celandine she says there is aye nothing but legs in it—and mebbe it's true enough, for it's the very same way when it comes to the kitchen.

This is what they call Holy Week, the same as the Episcopalians keeps in Edinburgh, but totally different : I am sure I hope our young ladies will never take up with any of the rideeclous capers we've seen this very day. It was in a great big Church they call

San Giovanni Laterano, and a priest sat in a confessional-box, no' unlike the box the watchman sits in when the street is being mended, and touched the folks' heads with a thing like a fishing-rod; them kneeling a wee bit forrit. Miss Jean said he was giving them absolution; anyway he very near raised an old lady's bonnet off of her head, his stick becoming entangled in the trimming. It was a plain bonnet too; her last summer's one done up for every-days, I would jalouse, with gauze strings, and a flower at the left-hand side, all black.

We saw three bairns—wee tots, no' above six year old—two wee lassies and a laddie, playing themselves at the same thing. Down they plumped on their knees in a row, in front of a confessional-box; but they were ower far off, and the priest inside told them to come nearer. They warstled on their knees till he could get at them, and then he touched their heads one by one. Up they got quite pleased, and slipped away behind a great big pillar; we saw them keekin' round to see if anybody was notticing them, and away they went to another confessional to play the same game! Poor wee things, it was a fair divert to see them: but the next priest suspeckit what they were after, and he wagged his finger to them to come and speak, and told them no' to do that again; he was a cheery-lookin' gentleman—stout and ruddy—it will likely be an easy life. It must take a deal of faith to lippen to yon rod-thing, but every herring must hang by its own head.

The bonniest place I have seen yet in the antique city of Rome is the Protestant Cementery. They say there's no treat that Scotch folk enjoy better than a funeral; and I'll admit that they are fond of a daunder in a cemetery, and what for no'?

Miss Celandine went with me last Sabbath-Day. It's a fine large place, and many a stranger is lying fremd and forsaken under the shade of the Cypress-trees ; and fine large funeral-lookin' trees they are, very well suited to their poseetion. I notticed the name of John Smith, Sculpterer ; Smith is a well-known name in Edinburgh. If folk had the sense to bide at hame, there would be no call for them to lie lonesome in a foreign cementery. Miss Celandine read out of the guide-book that the Poet Shelley said " It might make one in love with death, to think that one should be buried in so sweet a place." It minded me of the man that went to see the new addeetion to Kilmun kirkyard, and when he saw the green brae, and the flowers, and the Holy Loch shinin' down below, and heard the robins singing, and the lapper of the tide on the shore, his heart melted within him, and he said, " I would like fine to be buried here, if I'm spared."

Another poet had on his grave, "Here lies one whose name was writ in water" ; nae doubt it would be before ink was invented ; I dinna mind his name.

We had a sit-down for a whilie on a wooden seat, and Miss Celandine took the opportunity to cast up to me that when she was a bairn she aye thought that Warriston cementery was Heaven, and that it was all my fault ! It seems that, when her poor Grandpapaw died, I told her that he had gone to Heaven (as was only respeckful to the family), and then, appearingly, I took her a walk to the cementery, and showed her the big monument, and told her he was *there* : she says it gave her a perfect scunner at Heaven.

Cover *comfortably* doesna mean drowned : no wonder it's thin : I wish I was home in my own kitchen.—Yours,

MARGET POW

P.S.—A telegram has come from Sir Ian to inform the young ladies that the Baby has duly arrived in

Cavendish Square, mother and child doing well. It
was born the day before yesterday.

> Few are thy days and full of woe,
> Oh man of woman born.

It is a girl. Name " Jean," after our Miss Murray.
Gentlemen are terrible wasterfu' with telegrams, but
it seems that you get the words cheaper when you take
them by the dizen. There was twenty-seven.—M. P.

XII

VIA BON COMPAGNI, ROMA
April 190–

DEAR CHRISTINA,—If we're spared, we purpose to
shift next week to a town they call Florence. Miss
Jean was set to board with nuns in a convent there
—seven francs a day, real cheap—but I'm thankfu'
to say Miss Celandine put her off it : she said a
monastery at the same price might do, but a house-
fu' of women she couldna abide, she's had enough
of it here : so we have got rooms near the Dwamo.
It will be the river, no doubt. " Florence seetiated
at the mouth of the River Dwamo " ; I think I mind
something about it in the Jography-book we had at
the school. I hope it will no' be damp.

Miss Celandine has lifted her love; she's not
thinkin' of marryin' on a Cardinal now, it's to be a
Bassaleery. That's what they call one of the regiments here ; and a daft-like squad they are, their
hats fleein' with cock's feathers, and wide blue cloaks
hangin' round about them—pale blue, mind you, a
colour that would spot easy—no' the thing at all
for rushin' into battle, what with gettin' between
their legs, and haudin' in their arms, and hangin'
round their necks fit to choke them : the Hielanders

C

would make short work of them I'm thinkin', if they were gettin' near-hand.

I'll be thankfu' when we get the parcel delivered that Mrs Scott gave us to take to her good-brother in Florence, for it's been a fair torment. There's woolly things in it, and the paper burstit before ever we got the length of London : and by the time we lighted down out of the carriage at Cavendish Square, a long knitted leg had cruppen through, and was hangin' down very near to the pavement. Mr Scott is a tall man. We've put a brown paper over the outside of the parcel now, and tied it up with twine, but I wouldna wonder if it burst again ; wool's an explosive thing, mind you.

Miss Celandine's been at me with what they call "The Visitors' Book," and she told me I was to write down my name, age, address, occupation, and remarks. Allow them ! they're no feared ! if I was to put down all the remarks I've made to mysel', and whiles to the dog, James, I wouldna need to come back here in a hurry. Miss Celandine told me to take a look through the book, and I would see the way to do it. Her own name is the very last. She has put " Celandine Murray " ; and, down below, like a text, "Purr when you're pleased"; it's no' in the Scripturs. The one above was just " Miss Murray," and the address in Edinburgh. There was a terrible grumblie lady here for a two-three days—they called her Miss Villars. She was aye findin' fau't with one thing or another. I looked up the book to see what she had putten down, and I was dumb-foundered to see "Miss Villars, London. 'I have learned in whatsoever state I am, therewith to be content.'" My certy ! Philippians iv. 11, and a neat hand-of-write too. There was no age to any of the folk I read, so I didna put mine's. The American ladies put down a very nice prescription, viz.—" We have spent nearly three days in Rome, and have no

hesitation in saying that it is the most elegant city
we have seen yet." But they've no' been in Edinburgh. So at long and at last I tried the pen on
an old envelope ; then I put a piece of paper under
my hand and wrote down, " Mistress Marget Pow,
maid to the aboves, address do." So there's me,
likely to be known far and wide through writin' my
name in Visitors' Books ! Little did I think when
I got my first place at Mrs Murray's (£10 a year, and
find your own tea and sugar), that I would end by
towering through the world as a kind of lady's maid :
but it's a waesome job to be far from your ain
country, and I'm fain to get away home again.
This will be the last letter you'll get from Rome,
so see and no' loss it.—Yours sincerely,

Marget Pow

XIII

Hotel, Florence
April 190–

Dear Christina,—You will see by the address that
we have moved from Rome, and glad was I to see
the last of it. The town was just cram-full of edifices,
and I'm perfeckly worn-out, and thankfu' to get
away to a place where there will be nothing to see.
The packing was a job that I'm no' likely to forget
in a hurry. The young ladies has collected as muckle
trash as would fill a kist, and Miss Celandine was aye
bringin' me one thing and another that she couldna
get into her own box. The last thing was a stone
sculpter of a person wantin' both the head and the
tail, and the weight of I dinna ken what. Says Miss
Celandine, " Take great care of that, Marget, please,
for it is mebbe two thousand years old." " It's
more, I would think, by the dirt o't," says I, very
short-like, and I was just going to plump it into the

basin when Miss Celandine let fly such a squeal that
I stopped in terror. She was feared it would spoil
in the washing, but I dinna think that even the
Lady's Lily-white Laundry could hurt *it*. For peace
sake I wrapped it round with a flannen petticoat,
and put it in my box beside a green china dish, a
bust of a sheep's head, and a pictur of Saint Sebastium that Miss Jean couldna squeeze in.

I had to take out Mr Scott's parcel to let the bust
in, and carry it in my hand the whole way to Florence.
We'll hand it in to-morrow, if we're spared ; we have
not been out-bye yet.

I didna buy anything in Rome mysel' except a
pirn of cotton, No. 30 white.

You will no doubt be surprised to hear that there
was a Scotch lady in the train belonging to Edinburgh : we had a fine collogue together. There was
a terrible crowd at Rome station, and I couldna get
a seat beside the young ladies, so I just ascended the
first carriage I could see. There was only three
ladies in it and a blackaviced-looking man that never
spoke a word. He was mainly occupied with eating
oranges all the road from Rome to Florence. At
first I was feared it was a smoking-carriage by the
smell, but there was nobody smoking when I got in.
No sooner were we safe away from the station than
the lady opposite me got out a cigarette, lighted it
with a match, and commenced to smoke the very
same as if she was a man ! Did ever you hear tell
of the likes of that ? But just you wait. She said
something to me (I was sittin' exackly opposite), in
a foreign tongue, but I didna lift her, and she went
on smoking away. Efter a whilie she took the
cigarette out of her mouth and began to whistle
"Lord, a little band and lowly." It was the
sweetest music I had heard for many a long day ;
it minded me of the bairns singing their hymns in
the Sabbath-school far across the water. The tune

melted my heart and set my tongue going. Would
you believe that the lady was a minister's widow ?
She had been away to Jerusalem helping to convert
the heretick Jews, and here she was going away home
for a holiday, and speaking about Jaffa and Jerusalem the same as Edinburgh folks speak about
Portobella and Joppa ! We had a most improvin'
conversation ; she was a fine speaker, and started on
Predestination and Freewill as soon as her cigarette
was done. Nothing dauntened her; she had chapter
and verse for everything. The other ladies was
Americans, and they joined in the conversation too.
I couldna make out what religious seck they were
members of ; but I would think they belonged to
the Atheist Church, they were that contradictious
and ignorant. But mebbe they were not *joined*
members at all. Any way they were ill-grounded in
the faith—no firm hold on the devil or original sin
at all, poor things ; but they had the gift of the gab ;
I will say that. The noise they made, all speakin'
at once, was like to deave me, and I was kind-of
glad when Florence appeared on the horizon. The
Scotch lady shook hands with me, real kind and free,
and wae was I to see the last of her cheery face : I
hadna had such a Christian conversation for many a
long day. The lady said she hoped we would meet
again, if no' in Edinburgh on the other side of
Jordan, and, says she, " I have enjoyed our chat ;
you and I have something in common," alludin' to
original sin, no doubt, for the American ladies was
free from any sic thing, by their way o't.

See and no' aye be shakin' your duster ower the
windy when posty is comin' bye the house : there's
back windies.

My old spentacles has cast up where the hieland-
man found the tongs.

My kind regairds to your mother.—Yours truly,
MARGET POW

XIV

DEAR CHRISTINA,—Mr Scott lives in a flat. We
took the parcel to him this forenoon. The house is
no' in a genteel locality, and just as well, for the
brown paper was jimp, and it opened out a good
bit and let through a white tape string. Miss
Celandine was mad, and even Miss Jean said she
would have preferred a parcel with some sense of
decency.

Florence is a fine flat town, I'll no' deny that ; but
if Edinburgh was laid out as flat, it would be bigger
nor Florence.   There are bonny hills round about,
with self-contained houses strinkled on the braes,
very like Corstorphine. We had a drive in the
afternoon in a public park they call the Casheeny.
We hired a machine by the hour—a sort of an open
cab—the chairge being much the same as we pay in
Edinburgh. The horse was much the same too,
but worse :—no' a stylish shape ; high at the head
and tail, and an awfu hollow in its back.   But I'll
warrant you never saw a horse in Scotland with
pheasant's feathers stuck in its head like a tirara,
and a red worsit tossel dangling under its chin !
Poor beastie, it took its time, and I enjoyed mysel'
fine. Miss Celandine said she didna care for funerals
as a rule, but she's aye for driving like Jehu. By
the time we got home it was one hour and forty-seven
minutes, chairged two hours. Cabmen are terrible
imposing—they are that.

The porter here—he's an oldish man—can speak
English fine through having resided in Glasgow a
good few years. He is married on a Glasgow woman ;
poor thing, it must be a waesome change for her. He
started by remarking " Good morning," or " Fine

wezzer," but foreigners are quicker at makin' friends than Scotch folk, and when the young ladies were in at the tabbledot (that's what they call pot-luck), we had a chat thegither at the front door. He aye sits there in a kind of a glass box to watch the folk come in and out, in a blue coat with brass buttons, and a white shirt.

" I haf one wife," says he.

" The usual number," says I, civil, but distant-like.

" Zee usual ? " says he.

" Number," says I, but he didna lift me, so I changed the subjeck.

" I hope your wife is very well," I says.

" Much veryweller, thankyou," says he to me.

Appearingly she had been ill, so I asked him if she was lying. Would you believe that he was black affronted ! He thought I meant was she tellin' lies ! Foreigners must be awfu slow at the uptak ; and him been in Glasgow for very near seven year. When I got him pacifeed (it took a good whilie), he made out to say "She not in bed lies," and invited me to my supper at their house next Setterday. He goes home every night late, but on Setterdays he gets away soon. It will be a fine ploy, and I'll be glad to meet with a Glasgow woman : I hope she's no' had time to take on the Italian accent.

Miss Jean has been lookin' kind-o' dwobbly the last two-three days. She reads over much; I'm a powerful reader mysel', but I dinna approve of young folk aye puttin' their eyes out over their books. I'm thinkin' mebbe she needs strengthening, and I'm going to try some stuff that I saw well recommended in an adverteezement at the end of the guide-book. It said " Absolute Specialities for stomach sufferers, and Convalescent People. Double Beefsteak, the best and most triumphing reconstituent, preferred by Stomach sufferers. To sale at the behind-coming shops." One of the shops mentionate was Danieli

Calderai. I'll warrant that's neither more nor less than Daniel Calder in plain English, so I'm just goin' away out to get some of the double beefsteak from him. Miss Jean says she's no' a stomach sufferer. But you dinna ken ; she might be if the disease wasna arrested before it began.

Never speak to me about the blue Italian sky, and the fine steady weather! Losh! it can rain in Italy just the same as it does down the west coast of Scotland : you can see that by the size of the umberellies the folks carries. Miss Celandine says they let on that thon out-sized umberellies are for the sun ! But I'm no' sae blate. What do you think I saw up in a shop-window in plain English ? No less than " Specialities in water-tight collars and cuffs." It's no' a wee shower that runs down your neck and up your sleeves, I'm thinkin'.

The Dwamo's no' a river at all, it's just anither of these great big Churches ; and, if you'll believe me, there's *more* pictures here nor what there was at Rome ! When I went with the young ladies to a place they call the Pity Palace, thinkin' I would see a grand king's house, here's one room after another full of nothing but picturs :—no beds, tables, chairs, nor nothing. It's terrible to think of the valuable time that's been putten off pentin' picturs. And there was a good few statutes that minded me of the Irishman that said he put on as little as he could avoid : I didna see how they could have avoided putten on less.

When we got through with the Pity Palace, which was no' before my corn was neither to haud nor bind, Miss Jean says, " Now we'll go to the Oofitsie." " What will that be, if you please, mem ? " says I. " Oh, Marget," says she, " you *know* it's a picture-gallery." I was like to drop, when I heard it, and glad was I when Miss Celandine said *she* wasna for any more picturs for a whilie, and away we went home to our teas. There was an American lady standin' at the door, and she started to ask me questions. She wanted to know if the young ladies had seen the Dellybellyarty. " No' that I'm aware of, mem," says I. " They must go," she says, says she, " it's one of the most elegant picture-galleries in Europe." " Mercy on us ! " says I, " how many more are there ? " She smiled kind-of pitiful like, and said there was a good few. She told me she was feeling worn-out and nervous, for she had been " drifting around trying to appreciate things " for some months. Poor lady, I was wae for her ; it didna seem to go with her heart. But I had to go and get off my boot, so I will draw this long letter to a close.—Your affectionate old friend,

MARGET POW

XV

HOTEL, FLORENCE
April 190–

DEAR CHRISTINA,—It's just much about the same, thenk-ye. Miss Celandine brought in the news yesterday that she had seen written-up in a shop near-hand " Leather Conveniences for the Feet," so away I went to see if I could get a pair of fine wide elastic-sided boots. Preserve us all ! It was footstools they were alludin' to ! However, when I was out with Miss Jean to-day, we passed a bootmaker's with " Lasts for elegant shoes for the lame, and persons suffering with their Feet," in the right-hand window, so away we went in. After a parleyvoo with the man, I came away home with a pair of soft cloth boots, buttoning up the sides with six buttons each, and I'll no' deny but what they're kind-o' comfortable. They were marked fifteen franks, but I got them for 12s. 6d. of our money : it would likely be a Spring Sale, and they would be rejuced. Handsewn, too. Miss Celandine says *she* wouldna call them exackly " elegant " ; but what with the weather turnin' warmish, and me aye on my feet lookin' at auld picturs, statutes, and edifices, I'm no' sae parteeclar about bein' elegant.

Our young ladies are greatly admired on account of their light hair and their red cheeks. I aye thought Miss Celandine's hair was red, but, says she, it's no'—it's the colour that artists love to paint. It's funny that none o' the artists she knows has pented it ; but she says it's because they're no' old masters yet. Miss Celandine has aye an answer. And the way she wins in and out of places is fair rideeclous—nothing dauntens her. There's no' a shut door but what she'll get through, if she's that way inclined. But she was very near bein' obligated to spend the night in what they call the Spanish Chapel, with her nonsense. It's a place all over with coloured picturs, opening off a great big Church, through a sma' door, and down a stair ; and she said that a person of the name of Ruskin had let on that it would take six or ten weeks to see it right :—just a haver ; but she wouldna come away when the other folks had had their fill, and so Miss Jean and me went into the Church to wait for her. What we saw there put Miss Celandine fair out of our heads. The whole Church was pitch dark, but just the end where we came in. Near the door there was a Chapel, like, all lighted up with numerous gasoleeries, with hundreds of candles in them—a fearfu' expense. They were sweein' the last one up to the roof when we got in. Then the ministers appeared, arrayed like Solomon in all his glory, with wee laddies in white silks attendin' upon them, carryin' candles. Perfeck wastry, and it as light as day already : but I'll no' deny that it was a fine sight.

When the music began, I very soon found out that

I had heard the same tune afore, and in a Scotch Church too! When once you introjuice Popish hymns, the same kind o' tunes will not be far to seek. Mind you, it's a strange thing—there's me singin' the same hymns as the Frees, and the same tunes as the Foreign Catholics, and all of us expeckin' to go to Heaven if we're spared. It appears from the Scripturs that there will be fine music there, and I hope the Psalm-tunes will no' be negleckit—it wouldna be like a Sabbath wantin' them. But you would think David would see to that, parteeclarly " Few are thy days and full of woe," that I aye hushed the bairnies to sleep with lang syne; Paraphrase No. 8.

I was tryin' to mind what tune it was, when there came a rap at the wee door we came in by. " Miss Celandine," says I to mysel', for I ken her knock fine. She didna wait a meenit till she rapped again, loud. Miss Jean looked at me, but we sat quiet, no' likin' to disturb the pious congregation. At last when the noise was attrackin' folks' attention, a stout gentleman, dressed all in black and white (Miss Jean said he was what they call a Dominicum—the minister's man, no doubt), went forrit and opened the door, and real mad he looked, as well he might. But when Miss Celandine slippet through, lookin' as mim at a May puddock, he smiled at her, quite pleased-like. Miss Celandine got a fine fright, though, and I hope it will learn her to keep aside Miss Jean and me, and no' to be so positive. She says she aye bears in mind what Shakespeare said : i.e. " Still in thy right hand carry a sixpenny-piece to silence envious tongues."

I would give twopence for a plate of porridge, and a pennysworth of sweet milk. Folks speak about Mackarrony—nesty slippery stuff. You've a work to get it lifted off the plate, and when once it's into your mouth, it's down before you've eaten it.

Miss Jean is lookin' some better, thank-you.
My kind regairds.—Yours sincerely,

MARGET POW

XVI

HOTEL, FLORENCE
April 190–

DEAR CHRISTINA,—Setterday was the day I was away to my supper at Mrs Oppenrieder's house— her that is married on the hotel-porter here. He's no' an Italian though, but just a German from Swisserland. And who do you think *she* is ? Jeanie Macgregor that was cook to the Miss Marjori- banks next door for seven year, before she went back to Glasgow ! Her and me used to be real chief. She's stouter, and no' sae red in the face. She had on deep blacks ; her good-mother died no' lang syne : the skirt was made fullish, with three folds round the foot. Black jet buttons. She looked no' bad in it.

We had our supper at the back of seven, and Jeanie asked the blessing. She started with " Oh Thou that carest for the sparrows and feedest the young ravens that call upon Thee "—I dinna mind the rest, but she brought it out fine, and didna omit to mention " the stranger at our table." That was me, and she couldna have felt more dumbfoundered to see me there nor what I was mysel'.

Mr Oppenrieder was very hearty. " Put yourself at home," says he to me, as soon as we opened our eyes, so I spread my hanky on my lap (I had on my Sabbath gown), and we started. We had a thing they call " lemm cottlet "—no' unlike mutton chops ; and freetatar, and chelly-roll mit cream. I under- stand Mr Oppenrieder's English fine, but he didna take *me* up very quick. Jeanie had to tell him what

I was saying in German more nor once. Figure her speakin' German like a lady ! It sounded fine—just the same as Glasgow but different words. We had an improvin' conversation about pancakes, &c.; there's a deal to be learnt from foreigners : and Jeanie and me had a haver about the Miss Marjoribanks and the Edinburgh folk. She has got a good down-sittin', and a kind man. He told me on the road home that his wife was a sparefu' woman, meanin' " savin' " no doubt : she was aye that.

Jeanie gave me a packet of Lux home with me to wash my flannen petticoat with, and I've been readin' the bit *Scotsman* that was wrapped round the outside. It was all about the New York Stock Market—live stock appearingly. There's been a terrible fight there between bulls and bears : I wonder they wouldna think shame ! I aye thought bull-fightin' was carried on in heathen lands like Spain, and no' in Christian countries. It said that the bears exerted pressure, and, efter the fight was over, " they were sitting on all speculative stocks." No doubt the poor beasties was glad to get a sit-down anywhere. The bulls went into a pool. There was nobody killed.

There's not a bird in Florence except the pigeons round about St Dwamo's Church : the folk has eaten all the sparows—nesty greedy things ! But mark you, there'll be a famine among their cats, and *then* they will mebbe find out that " What's in the wame's not in the testament." They will be wishin' the spruggs back again, if it's for nothing else but to remind them that the Lord careth for sparrows : many a time the chirpin' craturs has been a comfort to me.

It's a strange thing that the doos round about the Church are the very same colour as the edifice—black, and white, and yellow—it looks bonny when

they flee up. Mebbe it's a miracle, but I'm no'
sure.

So no more at present from yours etc.,

MARGET POW

P.S.—The porter gave me a fine fright yesterday.
I was asking him when the train went to a place the
young ladies wanted to see. " Zee train," says he,
reading a printed nottice on the wall, " goes at two
and forty-four ; you will be all right if you go half
an hour ago." " Preserve us all ! " says I, " and us
no' away yet ! " " Do not lament," says he, con-
cerned like, " zee train he go at two and forty-four ;
you and your ladies go at two and fourteen : it will
be a very pleasant liddle dribb." So we were time
enough, but he gave me a fright, mind you.—M. P.

XVII

HOTEL, FLORENCE
April 190–

DEAR CHRISTINA,—You will have heard folks say
" Miracles will never cease," meanin' that there's
never been any since Scriptural times, and that they
are no' very likely to happen now. Well, I am in a
poseetion to bear witness to the performance of a
miracle in this very town, having been, this very day,
to see the place where it happened.

It was in the via del Orto—a poor-like street near
the San Frediano gate. Three orphan lassies used
to bide in No. 10 (the number is on the door yet—so
folks can say what they like). They worked for their
living at sewing and knitting, and kept themselves
respectable. But bad times came : the merchants
that bought their goods failed, and they could get
nobody else to give them work. So the poor helpless
lassies began to sell their bits of things, and even the

very flower on the windy-sole, to get food. At last there came a morning (it was the 1st of May) when not a crust was left in the chest where they aye kept the bread. It was a queer place to keep it, but mebbe they had sold the crock. There was only one thing left to sell, and that was a large Crucifix hangin' on the wall. I dinna approve of them mysel'; they're ower like graven images for me; but Catholic folk are brought up different. The orphans minded that when they were wee bairns, their father used to hold them up to kiss the feet of Jesus, and they couldna think to sell the image they had worshipped many a time. So down they went upon their knees in front of it, and the eldest sister put her arms about the two younger ones, and prayed the Lord to send them bread. It wasna a printed prayer, I'll warrant, and Miss Jean says she doesna think there's one ready-made in the book; any way the lassie stated the case plain and clear.

Exackly as they rose from their knees a rap came at the door below the window: one of them looked out. (Mind you, we saw the very window!) There stood a weary dusty-foot, with a pale douce-like face, and he begged for a bit of bread.

" Alas, we have none," said the girl, " or we would gladly give it to you: our chest is empty, and we have just been praying to the good God to send us food, for we are starving."

" Look again, kind maid," pleaded the poor stranger, and just to please him, the girl went to the chest and lifted the lid. Lo and behold, it was cram-full of new bread! no' a yesterday's loaf among that batch, I'll warrant.

With a cry of joy and wonder the lassie ran to the window with a loaf in her hand for the beggar; but he was away from the door. Down the stair she ran, and lookit east the road and west the road, but nobody was to be seen. Some folk say it was an angel, and some say it was the Lord Himself; my Aunty Mary used to say " God's help is nearer than the fair e'en," and it would ill set us to believe less than foreign Italians.

The Crucifix has been well guarded, and it is exheebited to the public in a Church they call the Carmine, in this very town of Florence, every Mayday. And that's no' all, for on the same day every year, there's a Feastable held in the room where the miracle happened; and outside the house there's a nick in the wall, with a kind o' copy of the Crucifix, and of the chest that the loaves were kept in. A lamp aye burns before it night and day. Mind you, it will use a deal of oil, and Miss Jean has been tellin' me that's it the poor women round about that buys it. It's real good of them, though what call they have to think that saints and angels are parteeclarly set on lamps and candles, I'm sure I dinna ken. So, you see, you needna say that miracles will never cease after that.

Miss Jean has been readin' a book called *Roadside Songs of Tuscany*, and what do you think she has found in it ? The very hymn I used to make her and Miss Celandine say when they went to their beds, viz. :

> Now I lay me down to sleep,
> I pray the Lord my soul to keep;
> If I should die before I wake,
> I pray the Lord my soul to take.

I canna mind where I learnt it mysel', but little did I think that I was nourishing up the innocent lambs on Popish doctrines. Miss Celandine says it was a daft-like prayer to teach *her*, for she aye thought she would mebbe die in the night, and she's never done it once, nor Miss Jean either. It's as well to be on the safe side, though.

You and Merran can stick to the Psalms of David.
—Your old friend,   MARGET POW.

XVIII

HOTEL BARKEROLA, VENICE
May 190–

DEAR CHRISTINA,—We stopped at a small town on the road here. It was a place where they make sausages :—no' Cambridge, though ; that's a town in England. It began with a B, but it wasna Beef : I canna mind the name of it the now. But I'll never forget the place, for I was very near bein' left behind in a foreign land, and all through takin' chairge of a bird in a cage for an Italian lady in a red and green strippit shawl.

We had to wait twenty meenits for the train, and the young ladies went out to take a daunder on the platform, leavin' me and the traivelling-bags in the waiting-room. In came a stout lady with a bird in a cage, wrapped up in paper and string. She sat a wee whilie, and then she rose and came forrit, and set down the cage on the table, and, says she, " Will you keep the bird for me till I go and get some coffee ? " She spoke the Italian language, but I kenned fine what she wanted, for she pointed to me, and the bird, and her, and the Restorong a twa-three times. Says I, " I'll do that, mem," little thinkin' what was to befall, and away she went.

Scarcely was her back turned when in rushed one of thae fellies in blue peenies. He lifted the bags in one hand, and the cage in the other, clapped the shawls under his oxter, and " Come on," says he. " Set down that bird," says I. " Come on, wumman," says he. " The bird's no' mine," says I, " it's belongin' to a lady that's away gettin' a drink of coffee," and I gruppit the cage. He let go, and the paper screeded up the middle. " Ye're a thrawn old fool," roars he, in a temper. " Naething o' the sort," says I, stiff-like, and off he flew like the very

D

mischief, leavin' me my lane wi' a strange bird in
my hand. The poor wee cratur was frichted, and I
was cheepin' to it, when in came the porter again in
a terrible pavee, cryin' " Come on, wumman, or
ye'll loss the train ! " and with that he up with the
cage and ran, and me after him.

When I got outside the waiting-room there I sees
the train standin' on the ither side of the rails, and
Miss Jean and Miss Celandine with their heads out
at a windy, cryin' " Run, Margaret, run ! " The
gaird was clashin' the doors, and the engine was
snortin' for breath (and me too) : my certy ! I can
tell you I ran, and thankfu' was I when they hauled
me into the carriage, and the blagyard in the blue
peeny handed the bird in after me. I couldna speak,
but Miss Jean said, " No birds to-day, thank-you,"
and gave the scoundrel a doosoor.

The last I saw of the sausage-place (I've minded
it now—Bologna—I kenned it began with a B) was
the man lauchin' on the platform, and the leddy
with a crowd round her on the ither side. It was a
wee bird, gey nervous-like, but it was very near
lossin' me the train. It come over me after that
mebbe the Italian lady was takin' the bird home
for her dinner, and I wished I had hauden on to it.
But Miss Jean won't traivel with fowls of no kind,
she says, no' even parrots, so it was better to trust
the wee cratur to a higher power. " Confide ye aye
in Providence, for Providence is kind." Mebbe it's
eaten by this time.

Bologna was a dull-like town : the pavements
had stone arches all over them to keep them dry.
There was a Cathedral, and a Pictur-gallery. I didna
nottice a sausage-maker's shop ; I never was out-
bye. Venice is a celebrated locality ; I'll give you
all parteeclars in my next.

My kind remembrances to all inquirin' friends from
                                        MARGET POW

XIX

HOTEL BARKEROLA, VENICE
May 190–

DEAR CHRISTINA,—I had only been in Venice a jimp week when I felt a kind-of nesty smell in the house. I thought it was likely conneckit with cats—water-cats, mebbe—but they've been tellin' me that a queer smell is what Venice is celebrated for. I would think they might get something uncommoner to be proud of! but, mind you, I'll no' deny that it's strong. You will have heard of civic cats? It might be them. Or musk rats.

There's a good few canals, and hundreds of gong-dolies fleein' up and down them, but I've never went in them but once. That was when we came out of the train at Venice station. The land ended there, so we had to go in a boat or drown. I can tell you I was in a fine fright. I aye hated boats—nesty dangerous things. The man that rowed us had a red sash round his middle, tied at the side, and whiskers. He never sat down the whole time, keepin' a look out for danger. Every now and then he gave a most awsome howl; it curdled my very blood to hear him. Miss Jean said it was to let folks know we were comin' round the corner; as if it was any business of theirs!

Thankfu' was I when we landed at the hotel-door, and no sooner did I set my feet on Terryfurmah, as they say, than I made up my mind to *keep* them on it as long as I bide in Venice. I've no objections to a Bus, but gongdoliery boats I winna lippen to. When I go out I just take a bit daunder by the back Road to St Mark's Square; it's the biggest bit of dry ground in the place, appearingly. What for do they no' irrigate the canals, and make roads for folk to walk on?

I've seen the Dodge's Palace, and the Bridge of
Sighs ; it's poor after the Forth Bridge.

Don't ask me any more about the Churches.
How can you have a right church with no pews, an'
no foot-board, an' naething to lay down your Bible
on, and your hanky, and your glasses ? And there's
no right ministers ; just foreigners dressed up like
play-actors, and wee laddies in red gowns and white
muslin peenies carryin' candles, and lettin' fall the
waux round about them on the floor—a perfeck caper.
I'm no' sure if they have elders or no' ; but, any
way, there's a minister's man in St Mark's, and what
do you think he did ? He came round to take up
a collection when we were standin' in the place :
Miss Celandine and me gave him a copper each, and
he put them in the box he was carryin' for the purpose. But, when he saw the bit silver Miss Jean
gave him, he didna put *it* in the box—no' him ! He
said he was a gey auld man, and no' very weel ; and
it was raither much to put into the box ; and he
would just keep it to hissel' : and with that he
wrapped it in his hanky, and thank-ye kindly !

There is nothing more of importance to nottice, and
so I draw to a close.—Your affeck. old friend,

MARGET POW

XX

HOTEL BARKEROLA, VENICE
May 190–

DEAR CHRISTINA,—As I mentioned afore, the principal Estaiblished Church here is called St Mark's
It's no' a bad size, but ill-lighted. We were there
this forenoon, no' at a diet of worship, although they
say there's no fewer than three or four every day,
but just to see it, like.

When we were daunderin' about in the half-dark,
I spied a basket standing on a big tomb-stone. A

neat wee basket it was, with a high handle over the top, white net curtains drawn all round, and a wreath of flowers for a decorement. And what do you think was inside ? A bonny wee bairn, no' any more than a week old ! It minded me of Moses in the Bullrushes, poor lambie. I was lookin' about me to see where the mother was, when up there came a laddie in knicker-bockers carryin' a candle crooked, and slaisterin' the grease upon the floor as usual. It turned out to be a Christening, and no' long after we could hear the infant roarin' like a buckie. At the distance you wouldna have kent it from an Edinburgh wean, but there's no' a woman in broad Scotland that would carry her bairn in a basket like a half-dizzen of eggs, or a quarter pound of the best fresh butter, curtains or no curtains. Traivellin' opens your eyes to the defeeciencies of foreign nations.

When we come out of St Mark's we were attacked by the pigeons, and had a work to win through them. Luckily for us they spied an American lady with a bag of peas coming forrit, and we escaped when they werena lookin'. It seems that they're protected by the laws, and fine they ken that. I'm doubtin' it will no' be long afore they'll need to keep a pollis-man at the church-door to convoy folk safe through them—they will that. I like fine to hear a cushie-doo croonin' in a wood in the summer-time, but yon greedy, grumbly, pushin' things are a fair obstruction.

We visited a place called the Leedo yesterday, going by a steamer, and returning by the same means. It is an island. We walked across it (me in my new boots), in about an hour or thereaway, sittin' down on a seat by the roadside to get a bit rest. Miss Jean was awfu keen for me to go ; she said I would be standin' on the shores of the Adriatic. Me ! I would raither have been sittin' on Portobella sands, and I didna see much odds betwixt them. If I had kent that the Adriatic was just a water like any other sea, I wouldna have went. Miss Jean maintained that it was a kind of a blue *she* never saw before; and Miss Celandine thought it had a sort of a dyed look; young folk are aye for novelties. We went into a Restorong on the pier to get a piece, for it was near one o'clock. They gave us wee sandwitches with green stuff in them, like what the gentlefolks has at efternoon teas. Maist rideeclous! when you take a bite there's a long white string, with a weé green leaf on the end of it, hangin' out of your mouth, like a canary at the chickweed, and no' much nourishment in it, I'll warrant.

The weather is maist unseasonable—perfeckly warm, and it only the end of April!

Venice is real bonny in the dark, when you canna see right. I stood a whilie at the front door last night, when the young ladies was in the drawing-room, with my Shetland shawl about me, and nothing on my head but my cap. The sky was bleezin' with stars in dizens, and the gongdolies were sailin' back and forrit on the water, made visible to the naked eye by means of lights stuck abaft the stern. Miss Celandine came to take the air, too, before she went to her bed; and, after her, came two oldish ladies that we've seen many a time afore both in Rome and Florence; but they didna speak—just glowered. It's queer how often we see the same folk; they all go the same road appearingly: but, except they're Americans, they're real suspeecious-like.

I'm away to my bed, so no more at present from yours truly,

MARGET POW

XXI

HOTEL DESEERABILLY, MILAN
May 190–

DEAR CHRISTINA,—We left Venice on Tuesday, and thankfu' was I to see dry ground when we landed at Milan station.

I dinna understan' how folks can speak about traivellin' for the sake of variety. It's aye the same thing, no matter where we go! As soon as we've put past the night, then it's off to the cathedral the morn's morn as fast as we can go. When we're through with the cathedral, tombs and all, there's the pictur-gallery standin' waitin' on us. If there's any place else to see, it's the exack spot where some poor lady or gentleman has been burned to ashes in the middlin' ages, or an extry tomb : whiles it's *anither* pictur-gallery. I would like fine to see a neat pollis-office, or a Free Kirk, for a change.

We have seen the cathedral, I'm thankfu' to say— altars, picturs, relicks, pillars, floor, ceiling, statutes, windies, tombs, etcintera. But I'm bound to say we saw one thing we hadna seen afore, *i.e.* what they call a crib. When Christmas-time comes, it's all lighted up wi' candles, but we could see fine. It wasna a crib at all, but a wax-work of the Stable at Bethlehem, as like as life. The floor was covered with real straw, and there lay the new-born Babe, appearingly about two years old, with bonny, fair, curly hair, and a white silk frock all trimmed with gold spangles and a sash round the waist. The Virgin Mary was kneelin' beside Him, with a blue cloak about her. Joseph was there too, kind-of lookin' on, and the beasts was represented by an ox and an ass very near as large as life, mind you. The star of the East was shinin' up above, but it wasna' very shiny : I would have liked fine to dust it. It was an instructive sight; I aye wondered what like " swaddling clothes " was.

Before we left the Church we sat down on a seat to get a bit rest. Near by there was a decent-lookin' woman sayin' her prayers in broad daylight, with a laddie about eight year old kneelin' at her side. His eyes were wide open, though, and he soon spied a priest sittin' in a wooden box, with the name over the door. Appearingly he was a friend of he's, for off he flew, and held up a pictur he had in his hand for the priest to see : he had to stand on his tiptoes to reach high enough, poor wee chap. The priest praised the pictur, and had a parlyvoo about it, and then he leaned over the wee windy, and lifted the bairn's bonny face with both his hands, real douce-like, and kissed him as fondly as any father. I doubt Catholic priests are no' sae black as they're pented.

The pictur-gallery was filled with the very same picturs we saw at Rome and Florence. Miss Celandine says they're no' exackly the same picturs, but just the same subjecks. " It's a' yin," as Mrs M'Leerie says. There was the thin auld gentleman with a stone in his hand. And the one that's aye taken with his pet lion : the lion was smilin', puir beastie : but they would be tellin' it to look agreeable, no doubt. There was St Sebastium, too, but he's everywhere—that's the one with the arrows ; and other saints by the dizen. Also Adam and Eve, and the less said about them the better. There was the Deluge too, and a fearfu' rain it must have been. The fishes floatin' about minded the young ladies and me of kippered herrings, for no' one have we tasted since we left Auld Reekie. I was aye fond of a kipper ; but they're no very fillin' ; there's nothing in them but the taste. Speakin' of fishes, there was a neat sma' pictur of three oysters on a plate, set on a table covered with a white cloth ; the heel of a loaf; a kitchen knife; and a tallow candle burnin' away for neither end nor purpose. Miss Jean said it was called a pictur of " Still Life." Oysters are quiet craturs—no' very active.

I can understan' the foreign waiters fine now. The one here speaks very like Mr Oppenrieder, only he says " yelly-roll " instead of " chelly-roll." It's quite easy when you're habitted with it.

The next place we're goin' to is Swisserland; it's a hilly country-side, they're tellin' me. The name of the town is Lucerne, and we're to board with two Scotch ladies, the Miss Farquharsons. Do you mind of two tall ladies that used to visit next door in the winter-time? One of them used to be hurled out in a bath-chair with a Pomperanium dog sittin' on her. Well, it's no' exackly them. But *their* sister was married on a Mr Farquharson (he was a placed minister at Dremside, but they lifted him no' very long syne), and *he's* brother was Papaw to the two ladies in Swisserland. It will be a treat to meet in with somebody that can speak plain.

I'm keepin' as well as can be expeckit, thank-ye. —Yours truly,

MARGET POW

XXII

PONGSHONG EDEN, LUCERNE
May 190–

DEAR CHRISTINA,—We have landed at Swisserland safely. It was a long ride in the train from Milan, through an unjewlating country. What a space the hills takes up! And there's more of them here, and snow on the top of them yet. We came through a long tunnel called the Sang Gottar: it minded me of the Mong Snee Tunnel—you would scarcely have known the one from the other when once you were well inside.

Swisserland is the place where William Tell shot an apple off his son's head : a daft-like cantrip ; he might have flattened the laddie's nose for life.

We are boarding in the Miss Farquharson's pong-shong as per agreement, private sitting-room extry. It's a big house, and there is about twenty ladies and gentlemen in it (parteeclarly ladies), two boys, and a baby in arms, the latter being Americans, likewise their Poppa and their Momma : that's what they call their Papaw and Mamaw. It's a peety they canna learn to speak right.

The Miss Farquharsons are tall and thin, very genteel-lookin', dressed in blacks—no' *deep* blacks, just second murnings, like : it'll be for the Miss Macgillvary that used to go out in the bath-chair, poor lady. I doubt they are from the West, for the drawers in my room are papered with a *Glasgow Herald*.

There's no' exackly a Cathedral here, and I dinna hear anything about picturs, so we just glower at the loch and the hills, and cry " beautiful ! " " Change o' de'ils is lightsome."

There was a celebrated lion died here a while ago, and they've put up a bonny monument to him. It's a statute of the lion hisself when he was feelin' ill. Poor beastie : mebbe it was just as weel that he was taken away. If he was still livin' in the place, walkin' about seekin' whom he might devour, I ken fine he would have galravished me. I never can run when I'm frichted.

There's an Edinburgh faimly here that gets the *Scotsman* raiglar ; their table is next to ours, so we hear all the news. Mrs Balcarres, the Mamaw, is the first down in the mornin', and she aye opens out the paper and starts on the deaths. She's a wee lady, with brown hair and bonny red cheeks, and when she spreads out the *Scotsman* ye canna see her ahint it. But you can hear her fine, and a terrible fricht she

gave them all this very morning. " Oh, William ! "
says she, reading away to hersel' all the time, " I'm
awfully sorry—what a pity ! and I saw him just the
day before we left, at the corner of George Street ;
don't you remember ? you were with me, only
eighty-seven—' in his eighty-eighth year, after a few
days' illness——' " They were all cryin' " Who ? "
at once, but she never let on she heard them till she
had finished what she was at ; then she looked back,
and, says she, " John Smith, in his eighty-eighth
year, after a few——" " I never heard of him,"
says Mr Balcarres, disappointed-like. " He wasn't
cut off in the flower of his youth," says the son—a
tall, fair laddie, real fond of teasin' his Mamaw.
" Who's dead ? " cries the young lady ; she's aye
the last to come down, and never hears more nor
half the news. It turned out to be a gentleman that
had been in the Scottish Counties Bank about fifteen
year syne. None of them minded on him except
Mrs Balcarres ; but she's a kind-hearted lady, and
she offers me a read of the paper every day.

There's no more news of importance, so I will now
draw to a close.—Your affectionate old friend,

MARGET POW

P.S.—Some things are cheap here : we got a
pound of cherries for about 3½d. yesterday, and the
gardener kissed Miss Jean's hand and mine's for
twopence. The way o't was as follows :—Miss
Jean was admirin' a red flower in the garden, and
she was keen to learn the name of it, so, when she
saw the old gardener diggin' away near-hand, she
went to ask him. Back he came and told her all
about it, so she thanked him kindly and gave him
twopence to hissel' for his trouble. He took off his
hat (straw) and bowed down to the ground, and then
he took her hand and kissed it as if she had been
Victoria the Virtuous. Syne he looked at me and

then at Miss Jean, as much as to say, " I'll kiss her
too for the twopence if you like," and before I knew
where I was he was liftin' my hand to his lips as
respeckful as you please ! Foreigners are no' blate,
I'm thinkin'.—M.P.

XXIII

PONGSIONG EDEN, LUCERNE
June 190–

DEAR CHRISTINA,—We had a treat last Sabbath.
We went to the English Church—me and the young
ladies—at eleven o'clock, and heard a powerfu' discourse in the English language. The text was in
Joel, chapter i. verse 4, viz. : " That which the
palmerworm hath left hath the locust eaten ; and
that which the locust hath left hath the cankerworm
eaten ; and that which the cankerworm hath left
hath the caterpillar eaten." No an easy subjeck to
handle, but the minister brought it out fine. He
laid down that, firstly, the palmerworm signifeed
original sin ; secondly, the locust was the sins of
youth eatin' up the flowers of virtue ; thirdly, the
cankerworm was the sins of middle age, eatin' up the
locusts' leavins ; and fourthly, the caterpillar signifeed the sins of old age, devourin' the wee bit good
fruits the cankerworm hadna notticed. " Finally,"
was a fearsome pictur of the total galravishment of
the sinner ; and " To Conclude," reminded us that
we were all worms of one kind or another. It was a
maist solemn warning, and the collection was to buy
new windy-blinds.

Miss Celandine's on the nonsense the day. She
says she dreamt the whole night that there was
palmerworms in her bed (just a wee bit horsehair
stickin' through the mattress) ; and she aye calls
the Miss Farquharsons " the caterpillars " now, for

she says they get nothing but the leavins, decent
ladies. But the sermon made an impression on her,
mind you. Miss Jean told me that when they were
sittin' at the dinner on Sabbath night, Miss Celandine
looked round about her, and hove a deep sigh.
When her sister asked her what ailed her, she said,
" The cankerworms have started on the ice." Miss
Celandine was aye fond of ice, but even in the midst
of feastin' and revelry, the minister's words was
soundin' in her ears : well might she cry with David,
the Psalmist,

> My heart unto thy testimonies
> And not to greed incline.
>
> Psalm 119, verse 36.

The furniture here has been bought at an unction ;
there's 43 written in white chalk on the back of my
lookin'-glass.

The house is cram-full of folk now. The fame of
the Miss Farquharson's estaiblishment has flown far
and wide, and many a beautiful testimony to their
Cleanliness, Comfort, and Cooking is written clear in
the Visitors' Book, and no' a single complaint from
beginnin' to end ! Miss Celandine says there will be
one after *she* leaves, for she's perfeckly determined
to tell on the cat. She aye calls him " Sir Having
Greedy," but he gets " Catsy " in the kitchen, and
Miss Farquharson says his real name is " Munch,"
for he's all black and white like a Dominicum monk.
He gets into our sittin'-room by the windy, and
yowls for the cream when the young ladies are at
their teas. Miss Celandine brought in three cream-
cakes one day, at twopence each, and I put them on
a plate for the tea. Losh ! when Miss Jean came
downstairs they were licked empy, and Munch was
sittin' on the sofy in the sun, singin' with joy and
fulness.

Miss Jean fair spoils him, and so does Mrs Bal-

carres and her faimly. She got a fright on Monday
night, though. They were all sittin' quite calm-like
at the table, when, all of a sudden, Mrs Balcarres put
her hand in her pocket, and rummeled in it a wee
whilie. Then her face flew up scarlet, and says she
in horror, " Oh, William, I've lost my purse ! and
all my money is in it—and my ticket, and the little
gold chain you gave me ! " " It may be upstairs,"
says her husband. " Feel again," says the young
lady. " Please don't disturb yourselves," says the
young gentleman, no' the least putten about, " My
Mother loses her purse regularly twice a week."
Well, she felt again in her pocket, and she looked
under the table ; syne she tried the front of her
gown, but it wasna there. She was very near
desperate, when finally she gave a sigh of relief and
rose up. " I remember now," says she ; " I always
turn my *under* pocket round to the *back* when I put
on my evening dress " ; and sure enough it was
there all the time. " Not lost but gone behind,"
says the young gentleman, and they all went on with
their denners the same as if nothing had happened.
But Mrs Balcarres got a fright, mind you. I like
her fine ; she's just the same as me about nesty
smells—she canna abide them—and many a pleasant
conversation we've had on the subjeck, although
Swisserland is far behind Venice that way ; there's
no the same variety, by no means.

We're " gathering as we gang." Miss Celandine
was for buying a wee dog, but Miss Jean and me put
her off it owing to the bark, and she's got a musical
chair instead. They're one of the producks of
Swisserland, the same as cuckoo-clocks, musical-
boxes, etc. etc. It's a neat wee chair, and she'll no
tell what she paid for it. The back is carved to
represent a cubit with wings, sittin' cross-legged,
playin' on a mandarin. The seat is just plain wood,
gey an' hard, but the meenit you sit down there's a

click and a gurr, and away goes the tune. It's an easy instrument to play, and a bonny tune, but I doubt Miss Celandine will soon tire of it; she never could sit long. She says she likes the tickly feeling the music makes inside her, and she's always going to carry the chair about with her for Miss Jean to get a sit-down at the stations: I doubt we'll soon have a crowd round about us.

I'm real glad to think that we are kind-of on the road home at last; folks dinna ken what home is till once they traivel from it.—Your affeckate old friend,

MARGET POW

P.S.—I add these few lines to let you know that we have just got a letter from Lady Lindesay to say that Sir Ian has been ordered to go to a place they call Grenoble, on some kind of business. She is going with him, and the three bairns, and the two nurses, and she wishes the young ladies and me to join them there for a whilie to learn them to speak the French better. Michty me! if they could learn Miss Celandine to hold her tongue it would be far wiser-like; there's no' a language that'll halt her. I thought Miss Jean would have been vexed, for she doesna do with hot weather, but she seems glad; mebbe she is wearying to see her wee Namesake. Miss Celandine is mad; she says she can speak the French fine, and she wants home for the gooseberries. I canna deny that I'm sorely disappointed; we'll no' be home or Nevermas at this rate; but "things mun aye be some way, even if they're crookit."—M. P.

XXIV

Dear Christina,—We came away from Lucerne
yesterday, at eight o'clock in the mornin' in a
terrible pavee, and very near lost the train : Miss
Jean had to say good-bye to the cat at the last
meenit, and the poor beastie stuck his claws that
firm into her dress-sleeve that we had a work to get
him unhooked. Miss Celandine said she was tired
waitin' on us, and she would just sit down on her
chair till we were ready. Off went the tune fit to
deave a body, and thankfu' was I when the omnibus
came forrit, and she had to rise. The tune stopped
as usual ; I shut down the back, and shut up the
legs, and tied a good strong cord round it, and away
went the chair on the top of the omnibus—but just
you wait : let me not precipitate, as the story-
books say.

When we landed at the station Miss Celandine was
for taking her chair in the carriage beside her, but
we had that many things, that Miss Jean and me
said it would just need to traivel in the van with the
luggage ; we were feared it would fall down on our
heads and brain us. But mind you, Miss Celandine
wasna pleased, and she and Miss Jean were very near
castin' out about it. Little did we suspeck what was
to befall. For a good whilie *nothing* befell. Miss
Celandine, appearingly, was asleep, and Miss Jean
was dovering when the guaird came in to look at the
tickets. He took his time, us havin' pages of tickets
of every hue. He was readin' mine's when suddenly
Miss Celandine opens her eyes, and, says she, " He's
singing my tune ; he has been sitting on my chair ;
I *know* it ! " The felly never let on he heard her ;
he just hummed away to hisself and tore bits off

the tickets. " Tell him, Jean," says Miss Celandine,
real mad, "Tell him he's not to sit on my chair—
a great heavy thing like that ; he'll break it." Miss
Jean did her best to make the maitter plain, but the
guaird just laughed and said the song he was singin'
was poplar, but there was nothing about a chair in it.
Miss Celandine wasna easy pacifeed, however, and,
the meenit we landed in this hotel, she untied the
chair, and down she sat. Mercy on me ! it just
gave a fuff and a tick, and stopped ! Up got Miss
Celandine without one word and sat down again hard
and firm (she's a light weight, though) : no' a sound
of any sort seceded. Poor lassie ; I was vexed for
her. " I'll never hear my tune again," says she, very
like to greet ; " I *told* you not to put it in the van."
Then Miss Jean, *she* began to laugh. She said it
minded her of the lady that lost the chord when she
was sittin' at the organ ill at ease (it's no' a comfortable
chair to sit on, I will say that), and she told Miss
Celandine that she would likely hear her tune again
in Heaven. Perfeck nonsense : and it no' a psalm
tune or anything like it. I don't think Miss Jean
was carin' very much about the accident, but Miss
Celandine was real hurt at it, and thankfu' was I to
get them both away to their beds. Another thing
that upset Miss Celandine afore ever we left Lucerne
was that Miss Jean dared her to tell the truth in
the Miss Farquharsons' Visitors' Book. She said we
were all Annanniasses and Suffiras, and that we were
making her the same, and she would be eighteen in
August, and then she would do what she liked. But
all she put in the book was her name, and " I never
met a more religious cat."

Mind you, it's a fickley thing to tell the truth and
no' hurt folk's feelings. These Visitors' Books are
a fair torment. Miss Jean says she believes they are
a remnant of the Spanish Disposition ; I wouldna
wonder.

E

And who do you think is bidin' in the same hotel as us ? You'll never guess, and I've no time to tell you about it the now : Miss Celandine's wantin' me in a hurry.—Your affeckate old friend,

MARGET POW

XXV

DEAR CHRISTINA,—I daursay no' ! How could Phemie win to Geneva ? *She's* no' a lady's-maid ; she's just a housemaid " where only one is kept," as the adverteezements say. No, no ; it's Mrs Macrorie, her that's been maid to the Honourable Miss Menzies for ten year and more. And to think that I was in the same house for two days and never kent her ! I saw a shilpit bit cratur glowerin' at me whiles, and once I met her in the lobby, and she gave me an awfu stiff-like smile, poor thing—but just you wait till you hear.

Yestreen Miss Jean says to me, " Miss Menzies tells me that you know her maid." " 'Deed ay, mem," says I, " I've kent Maggie Macrorie ever since she was a bairn at the school in a peeny." So, hearin' she was in room 103, top flat, away I went to give her a cry in. She opened the door and I kent her fine. " Weel, Maggie," says I, " I've seen you goin' about this very house mebbe a dizen times, and I never kent ye ; figure that ! " She snecked the door, and she says sadly, says she, " It's the teeth." With that she took a cup off the mantel-piece, and there sure enough, were thirty-two teeth in two rows, very neat and reglar-like, and as white as snow. So she told me the whole history of them, viz. what with crumpin' peppermint-balls in the Free Kirk when she was a bairn, and what with

maskticating tough meat in gentlefolk's houses, she
had no more than five teeth left when she took
service with Miss Menzies.   Latterally the old lady
began to cast up that a servant with £25 a year and
all found should have more than that to show for
it, and advised her to gather up and buy thirty-
two new ones.   Poor silly cratur, so she did ; they
pulled out the fixed ones, and gave her the imitation
ones home with her in a pasteboard box.   They
wanted to leave them in her mouth, but she was
feared she would loss them.   The dentist told her
she would be crumpin' toast with them in a wee
whilie ; the rascal ! it's all she can do to take a bit
butter and bread.   They've made an awfu odds
upon her : when they're out she looks like a canary-
bird, and when they're in she minds me of a shark,
so she does.   She aye keeps them in a cupfu' of
water on the mantelpiece ; they're no' much use,
but they're bonny wee teeth.   All further news in
my next.—Yours truthfully,

MARGET POW

XXVI

DEAR CHRISTINA,—The young ladies settled on this
hotel on account of a pictur of it that met the eye
at very near every station we've passed for miles
around.   It was a bonny pictur, I'll no' deny that.
In the foreground (as the artists say) was the hotel
itself, neat and clean-lookin', with green grass all
about it ; beds of geraniums full out ; and fine big
trees here and there.   Away to the right you saw
a blue water, with wee bridges over it, and a lady
and gentleman in evenin' dress, fishin' for minnows.
On the left side, a machine with a pair of brown

horses, and luggage on the top, was gallopin' up to
the front door ; and a gentleman on horseback was
going the other way, with a dog runnin' after him.
In the hindground was a row of hills, blue below,
with red and white peaks on the top—gey theatrical-
lookin'.

Miss Jean wrote about the rooms, and the letter
they wrote back had a lot of printin' on it. It said
" *Vaste Parc*," meanin' vast park in English, and
the young ladies thought that would be fine for the
bairns from Cavendish Square to play about in.
Also it mentioned " Central Heating," but we'll
mebbe no' need that, the South of France being
counted mild in the summer-time. There was a
Garage too, which was a mercy, seein' that Sir Ian
is purposing to come all the way from Lyons in a
nottymobeel—one of these daft-like machines that
go by smell. " Rates of best convenience " was
mentioned, but the thing that decided Miss Celandine
was what the letter said about Lobsters :—it was in
English, as follows, *i.e.* " Speciality of Lobsters' Tails
with Crumbs. Creation of the Hotel." Miss Celandine said that a hotel that could create lobsters' tails
must be clean and thoroughly well-conducted ; and
Miss Jean said that if there was crumbs there would
mebbe be loaves, and no' these everlasting pettee
pangs. I'm wearying for a slice off of a half-loaf,
yesterday's baking, mysel', so I am.

Miss Celandine was up at the skreigh of day, and
away out to the park to look about her. In less
than a quarter of an hour, here she was back again !
It seems that she had just walked a wee bittie yont
the house when she came to a wire fence, no' very
high nor notticeable, but she couldna' step over it.
Then she tried the walk away to the water, and she
found she couldna' get that road either ; so away
she went round by the back of the house, but the
fence went that way too ! There was a man washin'

lettuces outside the back-door, and he told Miss
Celandine that the "*vaste parc*" belongs to an old
gentleman, and he'll no' let anybody walk in it but
hisself and his grandchildren ! The bit grass in front
of the house is belonging to the hotel, and four green
wooden tubs with pink flowers growin' in them, and
the graivel walk at the back. Miss Celandine says
the Garage is a henhouse ; anyway, there's hens in
it the now. They'll get a fright if Sir Ian catches
them in his machine.

The heat is no' confined to the centre of the hotel
—it's in every room, and there's nesty insecks they
call moskeeties fleein' about and bizzin'.

Miss Celandine is pestering me to take her to the
town, so I'll need to conclude.—Your affectionate
friend,

MARGET POW

XXVII

GRENOBLE, *July* 190–

DEAR CHRISTINA,—Yes ; he was Miss Jean's jo, and
she was engaged to him for more than two year
before he died ; that was three year ago come the
winter. Lady Lindesay took me to the cementery
on Sabbath afternoon to see his grave. We were at
the Church in the forenoon. They say it was a
Protestant Church, but the language spoken was
French—just a perfeck haver. We went in the
knottymobeel. Master Johneen was fain to bide at
home. "It's not my Sunday out," says he, when
Anne caught him in the garden, "and I don't want
to go to the bovering Church anyhow," did ever you
hear the like ! But when once he was in the Church
he behaved fine, and slept like a lamb the most part
of the time. The heat was rideeclous. Grenoble is
a hot place, and the moskeeties have been very bad ;

but the weather has been blowy the last week and the wind has shifted a good few of them.

Mr Erskine was one of those gentlemen that traivel far and wide to discover countries that have probably been there ever since the earth was made without bein' notticed, the folk that live in them no' sayin' much about it, for fear of being discovered, and annecksated for the good of their souls. He was a great friend of Colonel Murray's, and far too old for Miss Jean, so he had to wait for her. Whiles he lived in Edinburgh and whiles in London, but he never could settle right, and wandered about from the East Pole to the West. Finally, what between " Greenland's icy mountains and India's coral strand," he came home from Africa with a cold, and never totally got rid of it. He was at Grenoble on his way home from a districk they ca' the Reeviarea, when he died. " A winter day, and a wintry way is the life of man," as the proverb says. He might have kenned that folk that leave their own homes when they are ill often end their days somewhere else. I've seen it mysel' many a time, and well I mind of the man at Inchmakenneth that sold coals and hired out wagonettes, sendin' round a nottice to the visitors in the month of August to say that " in order to meet a long-felt want, he would now keep a hearse."

We went to the cementery by means of an open cab ; it was a long hurl, right through the town and out at a gate called the " *Porte des adieux.*" It was a bonny place when we got there, and the gate was standin' wide open. We hadna gone far when we came to a plain white stone under the blue shade of the cedars with " Arnold Erskine " on it, and not another word but just "Waiting" down below. No Text. Lady Lindesay says that was the orders he left. Miss Jean's blue-bells were lying withered on the ground. My heart was wae for her. They

grow round the roots of the trees in the avenue
where the hotel is, and, strange to say, you wouldna
know them from the blue-bells of Scotland. Lady
Lindesay says that Mr Erskine is in Paradise; I
wouldna wonder. When I was young there was
only heaven and hell, but he never could settle, poor
gentleman.

Miss Celandine is for takin' home a bird with her.
I minded her that the canary she had when she was
a bairn died of starvation, and that the bullfinch
she got after died of what they ca' completion, but
she says this one'll no' kill easy. She's seen it in a
shop; it's black and it speaks. I'll warrant it's
neither more nor less than a dyed parrot.

The baby is a bonny, good-tempered wee lamb,
blue eyes, and no' a hair on her head: Miss Jean's
real content. Master Johneen makes an awfu work
with the bairn, and he'll no' allow that any other
wean could be like it. There's an American lady
in the hotel has a baby with her, and she said at
lunch to-day, says she, " My baby is as bald as a
plate." Master Johneen took her up in a meenit,
and says he, haughty-like, " _Our_ baby is balder than
a plate." He was very near greetin' yesterday
because a French nurse showed him a baby with
four teeth. Lady Lindesay has ordered a wee blue
suit for him from a tailor in the town; the tailor's
name is Mulligan; I doubt he canna be pure French,
but he'll have the French style mebbe.

Miss C. L. is growin' like her Auntie Celandine;
she'll speak a foreign language rather as hold her
tongue, and she's aye playin' about with the little
Madmozelles, me and the buns (as they ca' their
nurses) lookin' on: it's a fair pantomine, and the
shortness of the French bairns' petticoats you
wouldna believe without you saw it.

It's all very fine for the people at home to be
singin' " Peace perfeck peace with loved ones far

away," and no doubt you and Merran are having a grand quiet time, but it's a weary wait we'll have if we bide here till Sir Ian wins away ! So I will draw to a close.—Yours sincerely,

MARGET POW

XXVIII

GRENOBLE, *August* 190–

DEAR CHRISTINA,—As regairds news nothing parteeclar has come to pass. The town is well enough if it was better arranged. There's a Cathedral and a Pictur-gallery. It's the blowiest airt I ever was in, the wind risin' every day at twenty-five meenits past twelve exack, and the inhabitants wearin' white waddin' in their ears to break the draught. One of the principal inhabitants in ancient times was a gentleman called Bayard, and there's picturs and statutes of him on every side. Another of the nobeelity they've put up a monument to was him that invented kid gloves—his name began with a J or an X, I dinna mind which, " Johnston " mebbe, but I'm no' sure. He is represented standin' firm on a stone, holdin' a glove-cuttin' machine in his hand, life-size. Very naitral-like. When you refleck that we've only seen four kids in the town and two on a hill-side, you would wonder to see the thousands of kid-gloves in the shop-windows. But there's a good few cuddies down by the river, and sheep are prolific on the mountains.

There's a Catholic priest livin' in the hotel, and he's grand at the music. Last Sabbath night he sat down to the piany and played and sang, us sittin' on the verandah outside the windy listenin' to him. It was a slow reverential tune, and he sang it real solemnly in a base voice, but I couldna make head nor tail of the words, them bein' French, as usual in this country. Would you believe Miss Jean was tellin' me this mornin' that it was all about a daft-like King called Daggo Baird, who put on his breeks wrong-side out, and never notticed till a saint came and told him! And me thinkin' it was mebbe a new version of one of the Psalms of David, what they ca' " another of the same " in the book. Strange to say when we went to a Pictur-gallery yesterday, here was no less than five picturs picturifying the principal events in the career of the same Daggo Baird, and the same saint; the latter's name was L. Waw. The one I liked best was when the King lost his breath on account of bein' chased by a rabbit. The rabbit was in the front of the pictur, brown, as like as life, wi' a kind o' smilin' face, and a bonny wee tail; the King was away on a hill-side, fleein' afore the face of the rabbit. Saint L. Waw was just comin' forrit to see what kind of a pliskie the King was in now; *he* was aye to the fore. Lady Lindesay's tellin' me that there's the remains of a Chapel ereckit in honour of St L. Waw in St Giles's Cathedral in the High Street of Edinburgh: it would likely be the Baird family that would put it up: or a descendant of Mr L. Waw.

We've been to see the oldest Church in France; it's a low flat—what they ca' a cripp—and they say it's been there, off and on, for thirteen hundred year. When we got to the bottom of the area-stair, who should we see but Mrs Balcarres and her son, speakin' to an American lady with a pinch-neb in her hand. I dinna mind her name, but she was real taken-up with the aged Edifice, and St Laurent, and the tombs. Says she, " It is a sweet and solemn thought that the saints are lying all around us, so near and yet so far." " I don't think they can be very near," says the young gentleman, " or my mother would smell them." " So I do," says she, and away she went up the stair and me after her, thankfu' to get

the young ladies away into the fresh air afore the
germs could settle on them.

On the way home we met a man in the street with
sixteen goats and four kids. He was playing a waesome tune on an instrument they ca' " pan-pipes "
—a wee whistlin' concern, no' like bag-pipes at all :
well enough to amuse the goats with, mebbe, but
useless on a hill-side ; no skirl. The folk in the
houses heard it, though, and out they came with a
bowl in one hand and a songteem in the other, to
get the milk from the fountain-head, like. If they
would bring the cows to the doors in Edinburgh the
same way, it would mebbe cure the dairy folk of
puttin' in these nesty tewberkewlosies.

Lady Lindesay has been in to tell me that she's
taken the rue, and she thinks now that it is rideeclous to keep the young ladies here in the heat of the
summer waitin' on Sir Ian. Miss Celandine is that
annoyed with the muskeeties and one thing and
another that " a' thing angers her and the cat breaks
her heart," as the Scotch folk say. She's had a fine
walk in the *Vaste Parc* to-day, though ; I knew fine
that she would win through, sune or syne. Sir Ian
was mad. He looked out at the back-windy, and
here he sees Miss Celandine daunderin' along as cool
as ye like, wi' an auld gentleman at her side, and
two young ones ahint her. She said she was lookin'
over the fence, and she gave a bit sigh, like, she was
that hot ; the old gentleman came forrit, and said
would she like to enter, and in she went. Sir Ian
said he would thank her no' to sigh over other folks'
fences when she was in his chairge, so she came
upstairs in a tirrivee and told Miss Jean and me
that appearingly she couldna call her breath her own,
and naething would pacifee her till she heard we
were to get away home next week. We are to be
a wee while in London to rest Miss Jean, but no
in Cavendish Square—it's all shut up. We're to go

to a seleck boarding-house that Lady Lindesay knows
about.

My kind regairds to all inquirin' friends,

MARGET POW

XXIX

DEAR CHRISTINA,—Little did I think when I left
Edinburgh that ever I would be callin' London near
home, but thankfu' am I to say that it feels like it.
The language is no' that different, although, this
very day, there was an omnibus conductor made me
get out at a place they ca' " Blahtch," and me on
my road to the Marble Arch, ong root for Palace
Court, as the French say.

We left Grenoble at five in the morning to catch
the train to Paris, and a fine bustle we were in.
Maist mercifully the only thing we forgot was Miss
Celandine's soap. I very near broke my leg gettin'
into the cab : I had my bonnet-box in my hand,
and a bag, and a holdall, and my umbrella, and
waddin' in my ears, and the wind very near took me
off my feet ; but I landed in Miss Jean's lap, mair
by good luck than good guidin'. No sooner were
we safe in the train, than Miss Celandine minded
that she had forgotten to buy the bird ; sad's her
fate ! But it didna daunten her ; she talked even
on nearly the whole road to Paris. I dinna like
these quick trains, although I'm no' what you would
call nervish when I'm in a bus. My grandmother
was a terrible nervish woman ; she was aye feared it
was goin' to rain—I doubt it cast a kind o' a gloom
over her life. She would have been one hundred
and ten come the 27th of next month, if she had
been spared.

This boarding-house is cram-full of ladies and gentlemen from every part of the known world, and texts. There's no' a room wantin' *them*, framed and glazed. Mine's has two, and a haver about puttin' on your clothes wrong-side out in cloudy weather to show the linin'; but it's no' easy to read, bein' high up and grand printin'. As you go down the stair there's a bit about gettin' up every day with a smile on your face; a perfeck waste in a single-bedded room. Miss Celandine is mad because hers is " Silence is golden," and I will say that it's no' in the Bible : she says there'll be a text in the Visitors' Book after she leaves, so we'll need to try and no' let her get time to put in any of her nonsense.

Miss Jean sent Miss Celandine and me to see the Tower of London this forenoon. Miss Celandine wasna for goin'; she said it was a nesty place—just a mass o' murders. But Miss Jean said it was a disgrace that none of the two of us had seen it. So away we went in a machine they ca' a Tacksie cab, the price bein' written up in a round thing like a clock, and risin' 2d. if you look at it. Would you believe that before ever we were out of the Square it was up to a shilling !

The Tower's a big place takin' it by and large. Some of the buildings are towery, like the Edinburgh Jail, and some of them are just like self-contained houses. There's notties up tellin' what the different places are—very handy. One high-up part was ticketted " The King's House," and I must say I was surprised to see a washin' hangin' out (it was a fine day for dryin') : I would have thought His Majesty's flannens would have been done more private-like; and they were no' very well done either—far too much pulled to the length. Merino. We trailed through the place where they keep the armour, but the sight I liked best was the Coronating Robes. There they were, full-length under a glass case, the very way that the King and Queen had them on : purple silk-velvet, embroidered with gold and various colours, and edged all round with fur— white, with wee black tails strinkled all over it : I'll warrant that even Solomon in all his glory had nothing suitabler for keepin' the backs of the legs warm. Miss Celandine says that the weather was hot, but you never can tell ; it might have turned cold at night. We notticed that the Queen's fur was a good bittie narrier than the King's, to indentify her, like : there would be a difference of two shillings and sixpence in the yaird, mebbe.

When we had seen the edifices, etc., we were glad to get a sit-down out-bye, on a gairden-seat under the trees. It was real bonny, the sun shinin' bright, and the wind rustlin' in the green leaves. Some sojers near by were doin' steps very neatly, though how they could understan' the bawlin' fellow that was teachin' them nobody could say.

Suddenly Miss Celandine says, " It's a pity we are too late for the execution ; I see it took place on this very spot." " Mercy on us," says I, " What execution ? " " Mrs Anne Bullen," she says, as cool as you like. " When was she hung ? " says I, all of a tremmle to think I had been so near seein' sic a gruesome sight. " 1536," says Miss Celandine. When I counted it up, it was more than 350 years syne ! She was a Queen, young and beautiful. I wonder was the sun shinin', and the trees wavin', and the bairns playin' down by the water-side when she laid her head on the block for the last time, poor young lady ! It's a nesty place, the Tower ; I was thankfu' to get away back to my denner.

You'll get all further news when we meet.—Yours faithfully,

MARGET POW

XXX

DEAR CHRISTINA,—Seein' that we've now been very near all over Europe, with the exception of Asia Minor, Corsica, and Sardinia, etc., you will no doubt be expeckin' me to give you my opeenion of foreign parts; you'll be askin' me as soon as I'm back, " What did you like best ? " All things in this subloonary world bein' far from perfeck, " No' that bad " is the most that mortal man can venture to say while here below. But this I will say :—there's no' a street that ever I saw in France, Europe, Grenoble, or Italy, half as bonny as Princes Street, Edinburgh ; so you can just bide at home and be doin'. Where could you expeck to see a grander row of shops with strippit blinds stickin' out when the sun shines hot in the summer-time ? And it's no' every town that has a castle standin' up on high in the very middle, and a gun goin' off exackly at one o'clock, rain or fair. Mebbe there's higher hills than Arthur's Seat in Swisserland—I'm no' denying that there *may* be—but they're dreich and cauld-lookin'. And the Firth of Forth is a bonny water lyin' like silver between the green shores of Fife and Midlothian. Many a time have I crossed it in the Burntisland steamer, and gotten a good heeze on the way, no' a few of the passengers bein' sea-sick, and the blind fiddler playin' " By the Banks of Allan Water " to soothe their anguish. I mind him fine : I doubt the Forth Bridge will have spoiled his perfession.

It's a grand thing to live in a land where a' the folks speak plain Scotch. They say Italian is a beautiful language ; so it may be to them that understands it. But a'body likes the tongue best that their Minnie used to sing hush-a-bye to them when they were weans, and it's the language they would be fain to hear when they close their eyes in the sleep that needs no rockin'.

The young ladies have got new hats, and they've given me a new bonnet. London's a grand place for bonnets—mine's sets me fine. Black. It's mebbe ower high; I'm feared I'll look like a Mintocraig Lion in it—but we'll see.

If I'm spared, and it's fair, I'll be sittin' (come Sabbath) in Mr M'Duigald's Church, with a book-board before me, and a stool to my feet. Thankfu' am I that I dinna worship in one o' thae Romish Basilisk Churches where there's nothing to sit on. When I'm a winged angel I'll mebbe no' be carin' about sittin', partly on account of squeezin' the feathers; but as long as I'm just auld Marget Pow, gey done in the legs, I aye like to get a sit-down on the Sabbath.

When I consider, like Paul the Apostle, the perils that we've won through—earthquakes, draughts, and damp sheets; perils by railways, perils by lifts, perils by folks givin' ye bad money, perils by queer smells; brigands in blue cotton peenies at every station, no' to mention chamber-maids aye dustin' on their knees outside the bedroom-door when you're leavin', and you like to fall over them—when I re-fleck on these things I see that we've been maist wonderfully and mercifully preserved, and it behoves us to show our gratitude by stoppin' at hame for the rest of our days, and takin' good care of ourselves. So no more foreign letters from

MISTRESS MARGET POW

MARGET POW COMES HOME

I

I'M real thankfu' that I'm safe home. "Hame's hamely," as the de'il said when he fand hissel' in the Court of Session.

Christina and Merran are tellin' me that I'm lookin' fine efter my traivels. I was glad to hear it, for Miss Celandine said she had notticed symptoms of curvature of the stomach the night I put on my new gown. That was the last night we were at the Seleck Boarding Establishment in London, and glad was I that it *was* the last night, for what between tongs and texts I was fair sick of other folk's houses. What for can they no' get tongs that'll grup? It was the very same way wherever we went, *i.e.* the two shanks was that loose that they folded over yin anither perfeckly tired-out like; or else naething on earth would make them open more nor a crack till you gave them an awfu' jerk, and then out they flew as wide as the coal-bunker, let alone the coals. Coals is wee in England by ours.

The texts was anither provoke. They minded me of the hints the minister aye reads out in the English Church when the poke is handed round; I dinna like yon. There was one house I mind where the texts was by-ordinar. The very windy-curtain had one pinned to it, namely, "Lean hard." My certy! And me leant quite naitral-like on a chair when I

F   81 was tidying up the room, and the back of it come away in my hand !

Miss Jean used aye to tell me that " Old women's window-plants have guardian angels," when she was admirin' the pots on the windy-sole in the kitchen. But that was when I was at home to look efter them mysel' ; naebody would ken them now. Miss Celandine says that mebbe I'm under the statutory age for gettin' a flower-angel. I'm no' sure, but there's been negleck some way. Mrs M'Curd gave me a maidenhair fern at the back-end of the year, and the leaves is that wee now that you wouldna ken what it was meant for, and my castor-oil bush is dwinin' terrible. I bought it at the door from a man that just needed ninepence to secure a grand poseetion as head-gardener to a lady in a self-contained house in Morningside. Castor-oil's a thing I never could enjoy, some way, but the plant was bonny when it was new. No smell. Miss Jean said she thought there must be a worm in the pot, and she told me to water it with mustard and water. So I did, and, if you'll believe me, it wasna more than two meenits before up came the worm lookin' annoyed-like. Poor wee beastie, it would mebbe no' like the mustard. Miss Celandine took it out to the back-green on a sheet of paper ; she said it would do fine to kill the weeds. But the queer thing is that my castor-oil bush is no' a bit better ! It's awfu' yelly-lookin'. Miss Celandine says it's a judgment on me for accusing an innocent fellow-worm unjustly—a perfeck haver.

There's an awfu' odds on the neighbourhood since we've been away ! The folk next door has had their washin'-house windy-pane mended, and the back-door is pented green—no' a bright green—a kind-o' solemn shade ; it'll wear fine, I would jalouse.

There's a ticket with " To Let, furnished or unfurnished " on No. 19, so the faimly will be thinkin' on flittin', but they're no' goin' to let on if they'll take the furniture with them or no'.

But the Bank beats a' ! It's done up inside and out as good as new, and they've got all the latest improvements and addeetions, includin' an iron umberelly-stand inside, and one of thae daft-like whirligig things at the door. I canna bide them. Miss Celandine says that I'll mebbe get snecked in some day, owin' to me bein' inclined to ombongpong, and she's feared I'll stop the machinery, and they'll no' be able to eckstricate me from my unpleasant poseetion for hours ; dear peety me ! But she went in with me hersel' the day, in the same compartment, and the door whirled round fine, and let us out inside. But I was that nervish for fear we would stick, that I couldna mind if I had put my pocket ablow the skirt of my gown or under my strippit petticoat. And Miss Celandine cast up that she had requested me to keep my purse nearer the surface when I was goin' to the Bank with *her*. And what with one thing and another, I was that putten-about that when the gentleman behind the counter told me to sind my name, I stuck my pen into the wet-sponge dish, and I wunnered when it wouldna write black; I was fair affrontit. But I ken fine they put the damp-dish in the place the ink should be on purpose, so they do.

I got my book at long and at last, by means of standing at a hole with " P " painted over it, and Miss Celandine and me got safely home. It's a chancy thing goin' to a Bank, though, mind you, and I'm aye glad when the term-day's bye.

II

THE young ladies has had one of thae telephone machines putten into the house. Miss Jean said it would be handy for sendin' for cabs on a wet day,

the cabstand bein' round the corner, and no' visible
to the naked eye. They've set it up on the lobby-
table. Mind you, yon's a queer thing! I doubt it's
no' canny. There's naebody can hear but the person
with the trumpet to their ear, an' us! It's funny
to hear Miss Jean parly-vooin' away, and naebody
speakin' back. But you can aye guess the subjeck
of the conversation easy. It's for sending messages
private-like. I got an awfu' fright the first time I
had to answer the bell. The young ladies were out
at an efternoon-tea, and Christina and Merran were
at the top of the house, when, lo and behold, there
came a fearfu' jowl! I was petrifeed at first, and
didna ken which way to run; and then I was for
fleein' to get Kirsty, but they wouldna give me time.
So I put the trumpet to my ear, and I hears a gentleman cryin', " Are you there ? " " No, sir," says I,
" I'm here." He didna lift me appearinly, for he
bawled again, " Are you there ? Who is speaking ? "
I wasna goin' to tell him till I knew what he wanted,
and him a perfeck stranger, so I kept quiet, and I
heard him kind-o' wonderin'. Then he let fly
anither deefenin' roar, and says he, " Can you hear
me ? " " Fine that, sir," says I, dry-like. " Then
who is speakin' ? " says he. " There's naebody
speakin' but yersel, sir," I says, says I. He took a
thought, and then he said something very calm-like
that I couldna hear right. " Beg pardon, sir," says
I. " What ? " says he. " Beg pardon, sir." " Are
you number One hundred and seven ? " " I daursay no'," says I. " It'll be the prison you're seekin'."
And with that, never anither word! It was most
peculiar. And when Kirsty came down she said she
was certain it was a burglar. That's the way they
do; they ring the bell, and if the folk are no' in, they
take their chance to burgle the house. Did ever you
hear the like ? And mebbe No. 107 was an accom-
plish. But they've no' made an attemp on the

house yet. It was a mercy I never let on who I was, but Miss Celandine was wild ; she said it was likely a young gentleman that was thinkin' on makin' her a proposal of marriage, and he would be put off it. I dinna believe it ; he'll call again if that's all he wants.

Miss Celandine has been neither to haud nor to bind since she " came of age " as she ca's it. She was eighteen on her last birthday, and she gets her income now the same as Miss Jean. But she aye ca's it her " salary," the same as if she was workin' for it, and if I check her she casts up that she waters the bushes on the balcony very near every day ; and fine the folk in the street below kens that ! But it's best to let Miss Celandine alone. " Dinna meddle with the de'il and the laird's bairns," as my mither used to say. Miss Jean can manage her fine, but she doesna like ither folk to find fau't with her ; she canna see the light of day to Miss Celandine.

But anyway, now the young ladies is both grown up, the house down the water is to be opened up again for them to go to in the summer-time, and we've been adverteezin' for a gardener, old Andra bein' dead and buried seven year syne. We had a work to compose the advertizment, it no' bein' an easy maitter to write for the public press (as they ca' it) and no' exceed the sixpence, nor the fourteen words, parteeclarly with Miss Celandine findin' fau't with everything me and Miss Jean tried. We kind-o' copied a nottice we saw in " Seetiations Wanted," and we started with " Gardener inside and out, single-handed," meanin' that he would need to attend to the bit hot-house forbye the gairden, as onybody with a thinkin' mind could comprehend. But Miss Celandine she up and says it was liable to misconstruckshon, and that it was a waste of words valued at very near a halfpenny each, for if the man was a gardener *inside* he would likely be a gardener *outside*; and if he was a gardener outside she wasna' carin' what he was inside; just a blether. And then she yokit on "single-handed," and said we might as well have a whole gardener when we were about it. We saw a "Bright Christian Couple" in the *Church Times* (an English paper Miss Jean takes a read of nows and thens), but I once neeboured one of thae Bright Christian folk, and she was a fair provoke. Finally, we made out a neat, plain statement ending with "Wages Moderate"; but, when we counted it up, it was only thirteen words, and Miss Celandine was disappointed-like, so we put "please" at the end to get the good of the sixpence, and it'll be in the paper come Setterday, if we're spared.

III

Mrs M'Curd's maidenhair fern is stone deid, and she's given me a palm she brought up hersel' instead, I've no' had it for a fortnight yet, but I'm wearied of it already, she makes such a work aboot it. It's naething but a source of anxiety. She never comes to see me but what she asks how it's gettin' on, and if I sponge it every day, and when I watered it; or she says the place is ower hot for it; or it's no' warm enough; or there's a draught! I doubt it's ower parteeclar for a kitchen. It's a long shankie-lookin' srub with sharp leaves—no' very bonny. I tried it on the middle of the dining-room table one day, but Miss Celandine said it would cast a gloom over the the most cheerful meal, and she soon brought it ben again; she said it was ower like Mrs M'Curd for her. Merran canna abide it either, it jags her eyes when she goes forret to the windy; mebbe it'll cure her of wastin' her time lookin' efter Postie.

Mrs M'Curd and me very near had words about it.

She says to me last Sabbath, says she, "Why are the ends of the leaves yelly?" Well, ye see, Tatty the cat whiles eats the leaves—she's the only person in the house that really *likes* the palm, but I wasna goin' to let on to Mrs M'Curd that I kenned that, so I just said, "Yelly?" "Aye," says she, "yelly; it's ower damp; the roots'll rot; and the gas is no' good for it; and the windy near it should be keepit snecked; and the——" "Aweel," says I, "if I'm to be obligated to light, heat, and venterlate the whole kitchen to suit yon palm, it's mair nor I can undertake." So with that she gave a sniff, offended-like, and said she heard the church bells.

I was tellin' Miss Jean, and she said she never heard a sniff like mine's for variety and richness of meanin'; but mind you, Mrs M'Curd can sniff too. Yon meant something.

Tatty's the mother of twenty-nine now, decent beastie, but there's only thirteen of them survived bein' drowned in infancy. The one we've kept this time is a genteel-lookin' kitling—white with a black end to its tail. Miss Celandine ca's it Twopenny.

I mind when Tatty was young we took her to the country with us in a basket, the time we went to a Rectory in Aberdeenshire for the month of August. It was attached to a church they ca'ed Auld Saints, and the house was fornent the churchyard.

One Sabbath day when the laddies with white peenies that sings in the choir were walkin' in two by two, here I sees Tatty walkin' ahint the minister! She had a broad blue ribbon round her throat, and her tail in the air, and she was keepin' step with the procession as neat as you like. I never let on I saw her. Efter a wee whilie she came down the steps and disappeared, and I was hopin' she was away home, when Miss Jean gives me a kind of a meanin' look. Would you believe that Tatty was tryin' to climb a stone pillar the same as if it was a tree, and gettin' on no' that bad ! She's a meek cat now by what she was sinsyne.

IV

Our advertizment for a gardener looked fine in the papers, and we were kind of surprised not to get any applications for the seetiation; we didn't put an address, though—it would mebbe be that. Anyway, when we had it in on the Wednesday, with all parteeclars, you would have thought half the orra men in the land had turned gardeners.

There was one that wrott, " With regards to your Adv. for a gardener, I have had two years' experence in the Bar and Cellar department of Messrs Campbell's Restaurant ! "—figure that ! And he ended by tellin' us that he was tired of the job, and that he would like fine to be a gardener : " Hoping for a sootable reply, etc." I dinna mind his name. There was a retired sweep too, and a good few married men with wives that milked cows, and large families, and understood hens. But, taking them bye and large, there wasna one exackly sooted to the poseetion, so Miss Celandine said we would need to try the *Church Times*, and she would invent the nottice herself, and not leave out the address like us. Miss Jean told her to put " unmarried," but Miss Celandine said you couldna say that in the *Church Times*, it would need to be " Celibate." Miss Jean dared her to say anything of the sort; she said " no children " would do fine. So Miss Celandine said she would stroke it out. But, when she copied out the nottice, if she didna forget, and here we sees in the public print, " Wanted, gardener, single-handed ; celibate ; no children ; inside and out. Tot. abs." Miss Jean and me were fair annoyed, but Miss Celandine said anyway she had put the address ; it was the only bit that was right.

The two young ladies and me went in to see the picturs in what they ca' the Royal Scottish Academy, chairge one shilling each. It's no' a school—just a place for sellin' picturs wholesale, like. There's a good few, but not near so many as what there was in the Pity Palace in Florence; they're fine and clean though, with bonny gold frames. Miss Jean bought a book for tellin' the names, and we soon fand out that it was needed. The very first pictur that attrackit our nottice was a young lady leanin' against a tree with her hand to her face, lookin' real miserable. "The Toothache," says I to mysel'. No such a thing; it was "The Millar's Daughter"; but Miss Jean said a millar's lassie might be subjeck to the toothache like other folk, and no wonder, standin' on the damp grass, at the edge of a water, and no' even a shawl about her, all in pure whites; she was bound to catch the cold.

I never saw as many picturs of animals in an exhibeetion afore. There was one lilac and brown beast, with sma' spots of red, and blue, and green strinkled over it—it was called "The Cow"; there would only be one the same, likely. Nearhand there was an awfu' starved-lookin' dog, sittin' on a seashore, eatin' a lobster; the gentleman that pented it called it a "Lioness Feeding." I dinna believe it—no' me. Then there was a flat, wee cratur hunkerin' on a stone its lee-lane, called "Frog"; and a cuddy doverin' with sleep; and horses, and Hieland stotts, hens, pigeons, etc.; it minded me of a Cattle Show. But, if you'll believe me, there wasna a single saint, except two ministers, and a young lady they ca'ed Saint Bride! Mind you, that's an awfu' drap-doun on the Italian pictur-galleries. Appearingly saints grow easier in Italy nor they do here. Saint Bride was bein' carried by two angels over the sea-waves— no' very chancy-lookin'. I doubt she was feared they would let her fa', she was that pale in the face.

It's a funny thing that folk are aye like to yawn in a pictur-gallery! Miss Celandine was the first to begin; she said she was needin' her tea. So away we went to the Restorong, passin' through the Sculpterers' exhibeetion ong root. There we saw a sma' statute ca'ed "Loin du monde." I jaloused that it would be something conneckit with a flesher's shop, but Miss Jean said it meant, "Far from the World." A catalogue's a handy thing.

We got our teas right enough, but what a price they chairge! It's naething but daylight robbery.

Miss Celandine was for going away home without any more picturs, she said she was needin' a rest efter her tea; but Miss Jean said we would need to go through with it now we were there, so we went away ben, and took a sit-down. We landed right opposeed a bonny pictur of a young lady very dark in the skin (she would likely be a native of somewhere), sittin' hand-idle, with her elby on a cushion, and a red rose in her hair.

The last thing we saw was another lady; she was tryin' to get the hooks out of the body of her dress, and lookin' very much putten-about. It was ca'ed "Sorrow" in the catalogue, but it would have been mair sorryful if her gown had hooked up the back, so it would. I've seen folk fair mad when they couldna hook theirsels up.

We took a caxitab home.

We've got a gardener. "Mr S. Tosh," he calls hissel' in the letter, and he comes from the same village as me. I mind his faither fine; we used aye to call him "Snabbie" for a bye-name when we were bairns at the school. *He's* name was Samuel Tosh too; he'll be an old man now, though.

V

WOULD you believe that the man that sold me the castor-oil plant was back the day to get me to take another ? And him let on, the last time he called, that ninepence would get him into a grand seetiation ! He said that it was a kind of a conspiracy that kept him out of it, and, if I would take anither plant he would rejooce it to eightpence as he saw that I was a real leddy—the auld haveral ! So I pinted out to him that there was a worm in the pot. " Aweel," says he, " there was a serpent in the gairden o' Eden, so what could ye expeck ? And how do ye ken that there was a worm in the pot ? " says he.

So I told him that we brought it out with a drink of mustard and water, and the young lady carried it to the back-green.

With that he flew into a tirrivee, and he said that the worm was *he's* property, and it should have been returned to him, and he threped down my throat that it was a pet worm that he had kept for years, and that it knew him fine, and aye gave him a bit smile when he came home in the gloamin'—did ever ye hear sic a leear ? But he'll no' get me to buy any more castor-oil plants from *him*—no likely ! We'll soon have a grand gairden of our own down the water. Miss Jean has been orderin' the roses, and the lilies, and all the like of that, and Miss Celandine brought the catalogue ben to me to settle about the vegetables needed for the faimly ! My word ! I never saw as many picturs of vegetables in my life afore. What cauliflowers for size—three in a row ! Very near all flower and no cauly. Miss Celandine was disappointed because I didna recognise the tatties either by the portraits or the names, so we settled to take the sort they ca'ed " Beauty of

Hebron," because the book said it was a " heavy cropper." No sooner was it written down than Miss Celandine discovers anither kind ca'ed " magnificent cropper," so she thought it would be more economical-like to get them. Would you believe that when we turned over the page to see about the peas, here *anither* kind of a tatty that they said was a " phenomenally heavy cropper ! " Miss Celandine was mad ; she said she didna believe a word of it, so she tore up the paper and put down the names she liked best, namely, " Great Scot," and " Beauty of Bute," and " Jeanie Deans." They're bonny names, anyway.

There was a pictur of the peas, life size—mebbe more. One pod was burst open to show that there was no deception. There was ten peas in it, very near the size of bools, lyin' side by side, and the middle ones heids and thraws, to make more room. Fine big peas, I will say that. And the queer thing was that they were ca'ed " dwarf peas "; I dinna ken what like the giants would be.

There was no such a thing as sybies mentioned from beginnin' to end of the book—rideeclous ! But we set down onions, neeps, cabbages, etc., etc. There was a neat pictur of a pansy, three inches square, ca'ed " Masterpiece " ; we're to get a packet of them. I doubt they'll take up the ground, though.

Miss Celandine said she was sure the Eccremocarpusses would be bonny wee flowers by the name, and we put down Dimorphotheca because the catalogue said they were of a " neat, bushy habit." But I dinna mind all the things in the list ; it will be a weel-stocked gairden, if we're spared.

Near the end there was a bit about " Retarded Bulbs and Roots." They needna fash theirsels. The weather down the West Coast will retard them fine, I'll warrant.

There's one thing I've fand out—you can get a whole packet of castor-oil seeds for sixpence—figure that! and me paid ninepence for one bush at the door! Yon man is a fair extortioner.

It seems that we'll need gairden implements, and horticultural manures, and tallies and spiral carnation stakes, and a Alpha spraying machine, and I dinna ken all what. I'm sure Mr Samuel Tosh, senior, never had mair nor a spade, and a rake, and an old watering-pot that let out at the handle, and *he's* gairden looked fine. And " Insecticides " is a needcessity appearinly. Miss C. says she'll require a Mealy Bug Destroyer (in jars, 1s.), for if she was meetin' a bug walkin' in the gairden—anyway a mealy one—she would likely take a fit. No' her; she's no' that kind. The Slugicide's in a box, price 1s. 6d.; and we're to get a 42-oz. bottle of Beetle-destroyer; and there's antidotes for Red spiders, Mildew, Thrips, Grubs, and Parasites highly recommended. I see fine the gairden's goin' to be an awfu' fight; but I'm thankfu' to say they've got a wasp destroyer—" thoroughly effectual, and very simple in application, per bottle 1s. 6d." It doesna say how we're to apply it, though. We'll need to wait till the wasp sits down, I would think, and then pour a wee droppie of the stuff on it; unconsciousness will likely sooperveen shortly. I hope it'll no' slaister the windy-sole; but there's aye a something.

Tatty's an awfu' cat for flies; we dinna need a flydecide wi' her in the house. Many a time have I seen her eatin' a bluebottle in full song; they go buzzin' down her throat, so they do, poor wee craturs, no' half chewed. I would think they would promote the indigesting; but, when I check Tatty for it, she just glowers into the fire and never lets on she hears me.

There was a man used to sell an antiflier in London, yon time we were in the boardin'-house, on the road home from Rome. I mind fine what a fright I got the first time he came round the Square roarin' like murder, " Ketch 'em aloive; troublesome floies; ketch 'em aloive, all aloive ! " It was fearsome; my very blood ran cold.

VI

MRS M'CURD and me has had a grand ploy—we went to see Edinburgh Castle.

It was a Thursday efternoon, blowy, but no' a bad day. We walked up the Mound. Mrs M'Curd wasna pleased at the buildin' bein' seetiated high up; she said it would have been far handier down about Princes Street, or, mebbe, Comely Bank (she lives in Raeburn Place hersel'), and genteeler too; we were pechin' when we got to the top of the brae. The first objeck of interest was the Explanade, broad and flat, bounded by a row of monuments on the right, and a row of cabs on the left.[1] They've let the walls get into a terrible state of disrepair—holes round and round—and when we came nearer we saw there was guns keekin' through. I dinna like yon; you never can be sure of guns no' goin' off without word or wittens, whether they're loaded or no' — nesty dangerous things; many a one has been shot dead by them afore ever they notticed.

When we got to the top it was awfu' blowy, and we was glad to get inside a door with " To The Regalia " on it. Mrs M'Curd thought it would likely be a Restorong. No' it; it was just jools of one sort and anither, under a glass shade, with the Crown of Scotland in the middle. We bought a pictur post card, price 2d., tellin' the whole story. It seems that Sir Walter Scott found the regalia where the hielanman found the tongs, in the box where it was packed. It had been lost for more than a hundred year—what careless ! You would have

[1] The Castle is right afore ye—any way if you're goin' that way.

thought they might have notticed it sooner nor that
—it was a big box. It would be the Railway Co.
that would loss it, likely. Mary Queen of Scots
was the last to wear the crown. Poor young lady,
she was maist unfortnit in her husbands (three), and
the wee-ness of the room where James the Sixth was
born you wouldna believe. Mine's is twice the size.

The next place we viewed was the Banqueting
Hall. It's ill-lighted. I got a fright when we were
comin' away. I saw a round, shiny, black thing
lyin' in a corner, exactly like a bomm, and I was
thinkin' I would be expeckit to plump it into a pail
of water, when it turned out to be a wee black pussy-
cat. Mrs M'Curd is awfu' feared of cats; she says
they whiles go mad, and she would raither have a
bomm in the house—the kind that doesna go off.
No' me; I dinna like explosions of no sort. I
mind once, though, when we were goin' to the seaside, and Tatty was packed in her basket all ready,
Miss Celandine put Gowk on the lid just to torment
her, like, and she exploded wi' rage like a ginger-
beer bottle—it was awesome to hear her. But she
never could abide Gowk, although he was her eldest
son, and born on the 1st of April, poor beastie; we
used to leave him at home to attend to the mice.

When we had seen the sights *inside* the Castle, we
saw some folk keekin' over the wall out-bye, so we
looked over too, and there we saw a sma' cementery,
seetiated, so to say, on the rock. There was a
bonny row of flowers, and about twenty graves,
with different names on every one. The tombstones werena life-sized, and we jaloused that they
had been putten-up for bairns—sojer's bairns. We
could read the names fine—Pat, and Chips, and Flora,
and Yum-Yum (that would be the Chinese language,
Mrs M'Curd said), and Little Tim, and Canteen Pet
(that would be Chinese too), and Billy. We was
refleckin' on the prevalence of infant morality, as

they ca' it, when a sojer sittin' on the edge of the
wall fit to turn you dizzy, explained that they were
dogs' sepulcurs—regimental dogs—maist o' them
well stricken in years. Mrs M'Curd was hurt at it ;
she said it was a perfeck intake, and she was needin'
her tea. So we came away down the brae, and
home in the car, but not without accident, as you'll
hear. The way of it was as follows :—

We took transfers, *i.e.* green tickets that let you
get a bit ride on two different cars, if you're goin'
that way, for the same penny. When we landed at
the foot of the Mound, here did I no' fling away my
ticket as if it had been a wee bit waste paper ! And
I never minded that I should have keepit it till I
was sittin' in the Murrayfield car liable to prosecu-
tion for traivellin' without a ticket ! It was maist
affrontin', and thankfu' was I to pay anither penny
for a ticket to hold in my hand for decency's sake.
But it was a dear ride to me, mind you, and many
a time I thought on my ticket lyin' in the mud and
nobody gettin' the use of it. Miss Celandine was
interested to hear about the dogs' graves, and she's
makin' up an epitaff to put on Tatty's tomb if we're
spared to bury her. It's to be—

TATTY

FIFTH AND ONLY SURVIVING WIFE

OF THE LATE

CHAMPION HOWLER.

It looks fine. She was wantin' to put below,
" Her children rise up and call her blessed," but
Miss Jean wouldna let her. If all Tatty's bairns was
speakin' at once, it would be a fearsome noise.

Miss Celandine says there was folk that objeckit
to me tellin' that the pussies we saw in a church in
Rome was principally young married ladies ; they

said it wasna respeckable. Mercy on us! I would like to ken if it would have been mair respeckable if they *hadna* been married? But some folks is never pleased.

VII

MISS CELANDINE is that set on gardening the now that she canna wait till she gets to the West Coast, and she's begun to make a rockery in the back-green here. She's bought a magazine tellin' how to do it, and she aye comes in and reads me the bit, and then she gets me to go out and help her, and me that stiff in the legs! "According to the materials on hand let the rockery be fashioned." That's the way the book began—gey pompish-like. "Aweel," says I, "we've no rocks on hand that *I'm* aware of, so we'll just need to wait till we get to Kilmorag; two or three rocks offa the shore there will never be notticed."

But when once Miss Celandine's mind is set on a thing, nothing will daunten her, so she never let on she heard me. Away she went out-bye, and she worked away till she found some bricks and four great big stones that had been left behind when the wall was sorted; and then back she came with her hands as black as soot, and the book open at the place. "Now, Marget, listen," says she; "the book says we are to 'Put the rockery up in such a way as if nature had had a hand in the construction.'" "So it will," says I, "ill-natur, if *I'm* to help wi' it anyway;" and 'deed I was very near lossin' my temper when Miss Celandine told me that it was not natur that was wanted, but grace.

"Hoots, lassie," says I, "you would think it was a kirk we was goin' to build!" But I soon fand out that there's mair grace needed to ereck a rockery

G

nor a kirk ; when once a kirk is built it stays up a
whilie, but the rockery was aye fallin' down, and I
was feared for my corns.

The next thing was to get flowers to grow on it,
and the book said, " Near the ground-line may be
planted saxifrages, sedums, and ajuga ; further up
polystichums, chionodoxa, lucella, and other pretty
Alpine plants." Did ever you hear the like ! Miss
Celandine said she would just be doin' with ferns and
ivy till she could find out, causually-like, how to
prenounce Alpine plants. But she's never got that
length. When she was stickin' in a fern she took
out of the box at the drawing-room windy, I heard
her give a squeal, and when I went to the door to
see what was the maitter, here she is fleein' to the
house for refuge. One of the stones had couped
when she meddled with it, and out flew thousands
of clipshears, centipedes, etc., etc. Miss Celandine
never could abide wild insecks, and she said there
was about 5000 of them, and they were a' running
efter her. It was a peety we had no insecticides
handy, but I've notticed that Miss Celandine has no'
been near so set on the rockery sinsyne.

But she's awfu' set on me gettin' my caird taken,
and so is Miss Jean. It seems that Lady Lindesay
has been askin' for it, and Kirsty and Merran are aye
at me to get my photygraph done. Miss Celandine
says it will be needed, for she is intendin' to be
a great poet, and a'body conneckit with her will be
famous. She's been tellin' me that " The Funeral of
' Powsie-Wowsie ' " will be in all the papers, anyway
if I'm spared no' to get over my last illness, and
there'll be a photygraph needed for the *Evenin'*
News. A perfeck haver ! She's begun her poetry-
book though, and it's dictated to me. First, there's
my name with " To " at the top, and then it pro-
ceeds as follows, namely :—

My second-cousin ! My first aunt !

(Miss Celandine used aye to ca' me " Aunty " when she was a bairn.)

> Who fostered me—a tender plant.

She never had a thing the maitter with her ; but she says now that many's the pain she had in her wee inside, and nobly concealed for fear of Gregory's mixture—I dinna believe a word of it.

> Who ran to catch me when I fell,
> And very wisely let me yell.

I've heard something like that afore, but Miss Celandine says that all great minds are liable to say the same thing twice. I've notticed mysel' that Mrs M'Curd and me is apt to say " It's warm the day," at the very same meenit ; it's queer.

> Who grew in beauty by my side, [that's me]
> Not so much high as passing wide ;
> Who taught me to unfasten strings,
> And many other useful things ;
> And pointed me the way to heaven,
> And put me to my bed at seven.

There's to be more.

When it was settled that I was to be done, there arose a deeficulty about dressin' mysel'. I was for puttin' on my Paris bonnet that I bought in Brussels, but Miss Celandine said I minded her of a defiant washer-wife in it (it's the way the feather cocks up and wags), and Miss Jean says I'm " just sweet " in my kep ; so I put on the black silk gown the young ladies gave me, and the real lace collar that belonged to Mrs Murray, and my hair brooch, and my waterproof, and Miss Jean carried my dress kep—the one with the lilac ribbon bows—and a clean hanky, in a sma' band-box, for I had to hold up my skirt—it was a dirty day.

The gentleman was ready for us, and I put off my bonnet in a wee room furnished with a looking-glass and a comb. Miss Jean sorted my hair ; she

aye tells me that I've got "quaint straight curls,
like horns." (It's out of a poetry-book, you may
be sure; how can curls be straight?) The gentleman then proceeded to let down the scenery. There
was a kind of a seashore, and a water, and a high
hill with a grand castle on it, at my back; and me
sittin' on a chair in the very middle, with my right
foot stuck up on a footstool and my elby restin' on
a wee round table. I was vexed that I had kind o'
overlooked my feet, and here had I no' put on the
boots I got soled and heeled for coarse weather; I
could have carried my Florence boots with me, and
changed my feet in the wee room, so I could. But
Miss Jean said she didna think they would be much
notticed. I was glowerin' frae me like a wull-cat,
and the gentleman had stuck his head under the
clout for the last time, when in came Miss Celandine!
She was to meet us efter I was taken, but there she
was too soon, and naitrally she begude to find fau't.
She said my hanky on my lap gave me an awfu'
hungry-like look—as if I was waitin' for my tea,
and no' likely to get it—and she didna care for the
fixed gloom of my expression. I was tellin' her to
hold her tongue, when the gentleman said, "Close
the lips, please" (to *me*!) and when I shut my
mouth he says, "Not too firmly," so I opened it a
wee bittie. "A little more," says he. I did my
best, and I was fair provoked to hear Miss Jean
murmuring, "'The little more, and how much it
is!'" and Miss Celandine said loud out that I was
dreadfully sharky-lookin'. The gentleman took out
his head, vexed-like, and asked could I no' look
more cheerful? Miss Celandine whispered, "*Fais la
risette à monsieur*," and I couldna help smilin', for
that's what the French nurses aye said to the babies
at Grenoble, meanin', "Smile to the gentleman,"—
and afore I knew how I was lookin' the photographer
shut the lid with a snap, and lo and behold it was

done ! And the last time I got my caird taken (it was at Portobella, on the Queen's Birthday), I had to glower at a fixed spot for mebbe two meenits, and no' wink once. I doubt it was ower quick this time to be well done ; but we'll see.

Miss Celandine was for buyin' me a silver frame on the road home if Miss Jean would advance her the money ; but Miss Jean said she would do nothing of the sort, and Miss Celandine settled to wait till Christmas.

VIII

THE young ladies has been away at Kilmorag to see about the pentin' of the house, and Miss Jean left word that me and Mrs M'Curd was to go and see the Pictur-house while they were away ; it was to be a treat from her, and we were to sit in the best seats, so as to see a'thing that was to be seen. There's no set time for the show to begin appearin'ly ; go when you like there's aye picturs jumpin' off and on the black-board, and a gentleman playin' tunes on the pianny. It's what they ca' a Cinema. I never saw one afore, although many's the time I've etten cinamon drops ; they're fine. The best seats was up the stair, and when we got to the top and inside a door, here's the whole place like mirk midnight ! How I got creepit down the inside stair without breakin' my neck I'm sure I'll never ken. I was just sittin' down on an auld gentleman in the dark, when up he rose in an awfu' fright, and dunched down a seat for me next him. I was thankfu' to sit down anywhere, and I laid my bag on the empy place next me to keep it for Mrs M'Curd. But it was empier than I thought, and my bag fell right through to the floor wi' a fearfu' clash, the seat no' bein' there at the time—a daft-like arrangement. There was no' a sign of Mrs M'Curd, and I couldna

seek her, for the gentleman had snecked my skirt in
that firm, and I didna like to bother him to let me
out, so I just sat still and looked afore me. A pictur
was fleein' awa', and I didna see right what the subjeck was, but no sooner had it disappeared than I
was dumbfoundered to see written up in green letters
wi' a red stroke round them, " Where is she ? "
" That's just what I would like to ken," says I.
" Beg pardon ? " says the gentleman. " I'm wonderin' where Mrs M'Curd is," I says. He thought a
wee, and then he says very polite-like, " May I ask
how you know her name ? " " Hoots ! " says I,
" Mrs M'Curd and me has sat in the same pew in the
kirk for very near twenty year." That settled him,
and he held his tongue for a whilie. " Where is
she ? " flew out, and in dashed a pictur of a young
lady and gentleman fleein' along a country road all
in a trem'le. I hadna time to see right what she
had on, when away they flichtered, and two gentlemen in a motor-car appeared. The car was rushin'
along at a fine rate without gettin' much forarder,
when it flew away a'thegither, and here's the young
lady and gentleman back again. This time they
were appearin'ly baith afflicted with St Vitus's dance
—awfu' jerky. He had his arm round her waist, and
she was talkin' away to him real affectionate-like ;
by the way she opened her mouth I would jalouse
that the gentleman was very near stone-deaf—poor
felly. The next pictur was a nottice to say " Were
they married ? " " What for are they aye givin'
guesses ? " says I. " Beg pardon," says the gentleman. Afore I got time to say anither word in they
come again, bigger nor they were afore, laughin' and
carryin' on rideeclous. But that was the end of the
story, and up went the gas, and the whole place was
as light as day in a jiffy. And if you'll believe me,
here was me and one old gentleman sittin' our lee-
lane in the front row of the best seats, cheek by jowl,

and no' anither person in the same compartment but
Mrs M'Curd sittin' on a step half-way down the
stair! I wagged to her to come forret, and the
gentleman tried to rise to let her by, but *he's* coat
was snecked in too, and we baith had to stand up
afore we could get our clothes eckstrickated. Up
rose the seats too, and naething but sittin' firm on
them would keep them flat for a second; yon's a
maist annoyin' invention.

Efter that we saw dizens of pictures with bits of
writin' in between. Some of them was ca'd "Interest," and we saw bum-bees buzzin' about and
makin' honey. No wonder it's dear; yon's an awfu'
work! It minded me of the verse Miss Celandine
used to say when she was a bairn—

> How doth the little busy bee
> Delight to bark and bite,
> To gather honey all the day,
> And eat it up at night.

I liked the "Travel" pictures best, though. Would
you believe that we saw the hotel the young ladies
and me was in in Paris, and I was enabled to pint
out to Mrs M'Curd the very windy the wee pussy fell
out of! Many a time I've told her the story; it was
a fair trogedy. The kitling was pure white, and it
belonged to a young lady that was livin' high up in
the hotel. One fine day it went outside the windy
to smell the fresh air. Unfortnitly it set its paws
on the edge of a wee box that was standin' on the
windy-sole, and away went the box, and the pussy,
an' a'! The first we heard of the accident was by
means of the head-waiter burstin' into the room,
cryin' out something about the Shah. Away went Miss
Celandine down the stair, fleein' like an antilope, and
me efter her. It was a solemn percession that I met
comin' up the stair—Miss Celandine was first carryin'
the corpse as flat as a pancake; efter her was the
young lady, immersed in tears; the waiter was hind-

most dichtin' his een on a table-napkin. The young
lady flung hersel' on a sofy, and gave way to her
grief; "Tootott, ma feel," says she in the French
language (she spoke it fine, bein' French hersel'),
meanin', "Tootott, my daughter"; a perfeck pro-
fanity. Then Miss Jean came to the fore, and *she*
rang for milk and brandy, and Miss Celandine and
her and me combined got it down the cat's throat.
Efter a wee whilie it gave a kind of hiccup, and then
a wink and a sneeze ; finally it sat up and began to
lick its jaws and clean its bit face. You'll mebbe no'
believe me when I tell you that, no more nor a week
efter, it played the very same trick again, alightin'
exackly in the middle of a gentleman's hat ! He was
hurt at it, and up he came in a tirrivee, with the
pussy scamperin' behind him, and his hat in his hand ;
it was that way bashed that it minded me of a con-
certeeny, so it did, and the hair was rugged off it with
the cat's claws, but no doubt it would break the fa'.
Mrs M'Curd and me saw the very windy, mind you,
and it all came back to me as clear as day. Anither
interestin' place we saw was no' exackly the seleck
boardin'-house we bode in when we stopped in
London, but it was a church that you could see the
crown of—what they ca' the " dome "—if you stuck
your head out of the back windy ; it was ca'ed St
Paul's, if I'm right. But anyway, it minded me of
the boardin'-house, and the work Miss Jean had to
keep Miss Celandine from puttin' an affrontin' nottice
in the visitors' book. And did we no' find out syne
that she did it efter a' ! Miss Celandine never can
hold her tongue long when she's done a mischeef, and
it was in the train on the road home that she let out
that she had got a haud of the book at the last
meenit. At first she wouldna say more than just
that she had put " a few well-chosen words " (allow
her !). But efterwards she said it was a piece from
a well-known gentleman, that was a poet to his trade,

ca'ed Danty, namely, "Abandon hope all ye who enter here." We'll no' need to try *that* boardin'-house again in a hurry, and us recommended by Lady Lindesay !

To reshume. We walked home and enjoyed our teas fine—finnan haddies and scones.

I notticed that there was a marked cessation of Samson efter we sat down to our teas : he never once asked in or out for mebbe half an hour.

You'll never guess what was keepin' him quiet, though—he was chewin' the ends off of Mrs M'Curd's bonnet-strings ! She laid her bonnet on the wee table in the kitchen to save goin' up the stair, but the strings was danglin' down, and that's a thing Samson canna abide. So here, when I went to lift the bonnet, if the strings wasna etten half-way up ! Mrs M'Curd was real nice about it—I will say that —she said the strings was mebbe ower long ; and they were pretty well through anyway, and short strings was worn. So Kirsty cut off the wet ends, and tied up the wee bits that was left, tidy-like, but poor Mrs M'Curd had a docket look, and I was vexed for her ; it cast a gloom over the evenin'.

IX

TWOPENNY'S got a place. It's the grocer that has taken him, and he looks fine sittin' on a high chair in the front shop with a tartan ribbon round his throat. The last time I was in a message there was a lady awfu' taken up with him. " Oh, you *Sweet* ! " says she ; she was sortin' his bow for him, maist atten-tive. He likes fine for the customers to make a work with him. But appearin'ly his purrin'-works is difeecient ; it takes me all my time to hear them goin'. I kind-of miss the cratur ; but we've no' been left a'thegither destitute, for Tatty's had four

mair kitlings, and we've kept a bonny wee yelly one.
It has got the longest claws that ever you saw—
perfeck talents, so Miss Celandine called it Santa
Claws at first.   But when the poor wee thing was a
fortnight old it took a tremlin' in the head, and she
thought St Vitus would be a mair sootable name.
And now, if you please, it's to be Delilah, and what
for, do you think ?   Just because Miss Celandine has
got a dog by the name of Samson !   Miss Jean gave
it to her to make up for the one we wouldna let her
bring away from Lucerne.   It's a Dandy Dinmont—
no' very bonny.   It has got a big head, and a long
body, and a poor-lookin' tail, and it's bandy in the
legs.   Miss Celandine says it *ought* to be bandy-
legged—it's a sign of high breedin'—but I told her it
didna need to be hen-taed into the bargain ; it's ower
much to pay for genteelity, I would think.   But he
does for Delilah to play with, and he'll no' meddle
Tatty, he's feared for her ; if she just gives him a
look he shivers, so he does.

Now that Miss Celandine has got a dog, she's
terrible taken up wi' wild beasts, and no sooner was
the new Sological Park opened in Edinburgh, than
she pestered me to go with her to see it.   I knew fine
I would have to go with her some day, so I says to
mysel', " As weel sune as syne," and away we started
on a Setterday efternoon when the lunch was by.
We took a cab, and the cab took its time, but it's a
good length of a hurl.   When we landed at the gate
Miss Celandine cast up to the driver that his horse
was fearfu' slow, and he explained that it was that
fresh and spirity that he didna dare to let it away,
and he had had a job the whole road to haud it in.
Miss Celandine said that he had succeeded pairfeckly,
and she gave him sixpence to hissel' for his trouble ;
a nice, respeckful young man, and clean-lookin'.   We
paid sixpence each to get in, and the first sight we
saw was a bit pond with ducks and ither fowls takin'

a bit swim in the water. They looked as if they were expeckin' us to feed them ; fowls is naitrally greedy, never done eatin'—they're just the same in private life. I never could open the back-door at Carldoddie without all the hens drawin' theirsels up in a row, with their necks stretched and their heads gee'd, and them had a good meal no' ten meenits syne ; a fair disgust. Further up the hill we came to a post with a white ticket on the top. The readin' on it was " Proposed site for Sea-lions' Pool." They will likely wait till the pool is made afore they set out for the lion-fishin'. I was askin' Miss Celandine what like sea-lions was, and she said the very same as ither lions, wet through ; but I dinna believe she's ever seen them.

The next thing we saw was sheep of various sorts. The first kind we came to wasna there, but we saw where they were goin' to live. Every couple has a wee green to theirsels with a fence round about it, and their name on the gate handy for visitors.

I was forgettin' to enumerate the poler bears ; there was three o' them, but they've no' got a pole yet, so they just splash about in the water, and fish for the bread, nuts, etc., that the folk throw to them ; it's an idle life.

But the thing I was set to see was the Lion's Den, for many a time have I pictured Dan'el at the bottom of *he's*. It was away up the hill, and when we got there here we sees anither nottice with " Site of Lions' Den " *on* it, and no' a single lion *in* it, so appearin'ly there's as many sites as sights in the place. Miss Celandine says that's a pun. I'm sure I dinna ken ; I was meanin' it for a sort of a joke, but they say Scotch folk canna see jokes. Anyway we saw the Den plain enough. It looks fine and dry, but it's no' furnished yet.

Along a bittie we saw wolves, lionesses, zebras, leopards, and very near the whole Noah's ark collection, sittin' in cages, or takin' a turn back and forret behind the railins. It must be a fearfu' change from rampin' about in desert lands, seekin' whom they may devour, and enjoyin' their denners in peace and quiet withoot folk that has paid sixpence each to get in glowerin' at them, and passin' remarks. The one I liked best was the very moral of a domestic cat, but out-size, like. I took a good look at the Zebra, for I minded the verse in the *Book of Beasts for Young Persons* that I was learned at the school :—

> The Zebra from African clime,
> A beautiful quadruped kind ;
> Smooth hair, is most pleasingly striped,
> If we view him before or behind.

He was lyin' on his side, though ; so we just had to view him flat.

Miss Celandine and me started to yawn at the very same meenit (these excitin' amusements is gey wearisome, some way), and she said she couldna be bothered with any more beasts of any sort whatever ; so I says to mysel', " Laziness is muckle worth when it's weel guided," and I started to daunder down the hill, hopin' to see a ticket with " Proposed Site for Exit Out " on it ; but it wasna needed, for most of the folk was goin' the same way, and we fand the gate easy. We saw a pair of Golden Eagles on the road ; they opened their bonny brown eyes and gave us a sorryful, despairin' look; my heart was wae for them. I doubt a Sological Park costs more nor money.

X

MISS CELANDINE has been left alone for a week-end, and she's had me away to the Theeter—a place I've no' been in since my Aunty Bell took me to see the

Pantomine when I was a lassie. I was sweir to go, but she said it was a fine piece ca'ed *Hamlet,* and it would learn me no' to marry my diseased husband's brother—and me never been married on onybody's brother ! However, she took seats in the back row of the dressed circle ; but, deed, some of the ladies looked as if they had come away afore they had put all their clothes on ; they must have been ditherin' wi' cold.

We landed at the Theeter in good time, and I was thankfu' to get settled afore they screwed down the gas.

Up went the curtain, and the first thing we saw was a black darkness—it minded me of the Cinema. Efter a wee whilie we made out that there was two or three men somewhere speakin' high English. They let on that they saw a ghost—a perfeck haver. I saw it fine mysel' ; it was just a gentleman takin' the air. They said it went away when the cock crew, but I never heard a cock ; no' me.

The next thing we saw was a king and a queen and a lot of ither folk (queer-lookin' tickets they were !) sittin' in a room with a stone floor, and long blue curtains hangin' at the back. They were an awfu' length ; it will be a job to get them shaken at the cleanin'-time ; I doubt they'll be obleeged to send them out. Maist of the company was dressed in light clothes ; the king was in red, and the queen had on lilac and green ; but there was one young gentleman all in deep blacks. We found out that *he* was Hamlet, although the king didna seem very sure whether he was his cousin or his son ; mind you, that was peculiar, if *he* didna ken, who would ? Anyway, he was lookin' very poorly ; he was terrible thin in the legs, and pale in the face, and he was aye holdin' his hand to his chest, uneasy-like ; I doubt it would be the indigestin'. Miss Celandine said that a soda-mint tabloid would afford immediate relief, but mebbe he would get a mouthfu' of spirits behind the scenes. Anyway, when his friends recommended him to come away out and see the ghost, to brighten him up, like, he said he would go, although I didna think he was very keen about it, and the night-air was no' the thing for him at a'. Luckily it was grand weather—the sky was just bleezin' wi' stars. I was glad to see he had put a cloak about him, for the ghost wasna' forret when first they arrived. He came in a wee whilie, though, and wagged on Hamlet to come away with him, for he wanted to speak a meenit. Away they went thegither, Hamlet keepin' at a respeckful distance, and then they reappeared on the very same spot as they were afore. But the ither two gentlemen had played the kip ; they were gey nervish-like. Hamlet wasna' long of findin' out that the ghost was his poor papaw, dressed as usual in his everyday suit ; he had died, appearin'ly, no' very long syne. He minded me of the United Free Minister at Carldoddie ; *he's* an awfu' slow speaker, but yon ghost was worse. What for can they no' come away wi' it ? He gave us a long discourse about him bein' murdered when he was doverin' in the gairden—just a make-up. It was terrible wearisome, and fine I knew that when he said " Brief let me be," he would be anither ten meenits. That's aye the way. " A few words in conclusion " is a fair deception.

They've a way in the English Church of sayin' " And now " when the sermon's done, to let the congregation know that it's time to rise to their feet. But it is liable to cause disappintment, as the young ladies and me fand out when we were in London. We went to a church ca'ed St Gengulphusses, where there was a grand preacher. But he was away for a change of air, and the minister that preached was nothing by-ordinar except for length. At last we hears " And now," and more nor half of the congregation flew to their feet without waitin' for the rest of the sentence, which was far from bein' what they had hoped, for it was just, " to pass to the practical part of our text." The folk sat down again, disjaskit-like, tryin' to look as if they had been gettin' up anyway, and the ones that was only half-way up was thankfu'. The next time the minister said " And now," they were feared to trust their ears. It would learn them no' to be in such a hurry, mebbe.

To return to the subjeck.

There was a young lady in the piece, and her papaw ; *he* was aye to the fore, givin' good advice. But mebbe folk didna take it, for there was naething but a stramash from beginnin' to end. I didna like the Hamlets—no' as a faimly. First the son turned queer—no' exackly mad, but just no' a' there, so to say. He was gey daft the first time we saw him, and " A Gowk at Yule will no' be bright at Beltane." Then the young lady but to follow suit ; her poor papaw's death, through bein' accidentally murdered, turned her brain. But, to tell you the truth, I couldna understan' half the story. What for could they no' speak plain and sensible like ither folk ? They aye began at the tail-end of the maitter—a fair provoke. But that's the way wi' grand language. I've notticed it whiles in the Psalms of David set to metre—see Psalm Forty-two : " His loving-kindness yet the Lord command will in the day." It'll be poetry.

I was beginnin' to yawn long afore the story was ended. I never heard folk speak as even on in my life afore ; it was wearisome to hear them.

The last scene was a sma' private massacre, like. When it was feenished there was three lyin' dead, and one sittin' ditto, namely, the queen upon the throne. Hamlet was the last to suggnumb, he was makin' remarks as usual when the curtain came down.

We were all standin' up to get out when in came the whole troop hand in hand, with a gentleman in private clothes in chairge of them ; the folk clapped their hands, and Hamlet and his papaw and mamaw bowed and smiled (the best of friends appearin'ly), and the drowned young lady came forret too, and then away they went, and away *we* went, thankfu' to get away home to our beds, and it past eleven o'clock at night.

XI

Shuttin' up a house is a fearfu' work, and it's worse when there's domestic animals to colleck. Delilah stayed out till the last meenit, and I had a' the shutters on the low flat shut, and Tatty safe in the basket, afore the wee pussy came yowling to the kitchen-windy. I opened the shutters a bittie, and put up the windy to let her in. She was just comin' when something drew her attention, and down she sat as cool as you like to scratch the back of her ear with her hind-leg—I was fair mad—and the cab standin' at the door ! I got a hold of her, though, and pulled her through the bars endways ; but she didna like bein' interrupted, and she gave me a fine scratch on the road, the wee vixen ! I stuffed her in beside her mamaw, and Merran shut the shutters. When I lifted the basket to carry it up the area-stairs, I was surprised to feel how light it was—if Tatty hadna leapt out when I put Delilah in, and me never notticed it in the dark ! And here she was sittin' at the head of the stairs lookin' nine ways for Friday. I made short work of *her*, and the cabman put the basket on the dicky. When I come to the high door I was dumbfoundered to hear Miss Celandine cryin', " Samson, Samson," at the top of the house, for the poor beastie had been a' ready,

and dressed in his best collar since mebbe eight
o'clock, sittin' aside the boxes in the lobby. Then
Miss Jean appeared on the doorstep, and she looked
east the road and west the road, and syne she cried
" Idiot ! " (She says it's the name Samson answers
to quickest ; it's the novelty attracks his attention),
but no' a sign of the dog. Down flew Miss Celandine
bawlin' " Samson " louder and louder, till the very
cabman turned round. " Is it a dog you're lookin'
for, mem ? " says he. "He's been sittin' in the cab
waitin' on ye for very near ten meenits." Yon dog's
a fair provoke ; there's no' a vehicle that's safe
from him, he's aye the first to mount, and nothing
will take him out when once he's in.

But we started at last, and thankfu' was I that I
had ordered the cab half an hour sooner nor Miss
Jean told me. I ken fine what a time it takes to
leave an empy house, what with turnin' the water
off at the metre, and the gas at the main ; and no'
leavin' a spark of drippin' or anything to attrack
mice ; and a' the snibbs in, and the back-door locked ;
and a ticket in the windy with " Letters and Parcels "
on it ; and the kitchen fire black out.

Tatty yowled a' the way to the station ; she was
hurt at her bein' in a basket outside the cab, and
Samson loose inside ; she kent fine.

Mrs M'Curd was at the station to see us off, and
to let Miss Celandine see the new bonnet-strings
she gave her, on ; they looked handsome—watered
ribbon, down to her waist. Samson took a good
look at them, I notticed.

The platform was crowded ; I would jalouse that
there was three people to see away every one that
was in the train, all standin' about the doors of the
carriages, tryin' to think on something approbious
to say, and wearyin' of the job. But they cheered
up when the ticket-collector came and banged the
doors, and, when the train started, they were wavin'

H

their hands, and cryin' "Good-bye," and smilin' with joy and gladness.

We had two hours to wait in Glasgow before we could get the train that catches the Kilmorag boat, so Miss Jean said we would go either to the pictur-gallery or the cathedral, to put past the time, efter we had had a bit piece. Miss Celandine said "no' her," for she would need to hold Samson's hand a' the time (he's an awfu' nervish beastie), and she would raither sit in the waitin'-room with the maids and the cats, and read her book. Miss Celandine is no' near so keen on picturs and cathedrals as Miss Jean. I was hopin' mysel' that they were mainly confined to Italy, and ither continental localities, and little did I think I would be trailed to a cathe-dral in Glasgow! It's no' needed. We went in a cab, and Miss Jean walked round and round the place, and saw the cripp and a' thing, and I got a sit-down. I was opposeed a great big windy with picturs on it, red and fearsome-lookin'. I had a work to make out the subjeck. I was thinkin' it was Jezebel, or the Scarlet Woman, or mebbe the Seven Deadly Sins, when, lo and behold, I read up, "Now Hannah feared the Lord!" Allow *them*! You wouldna have thought it by the pictur. It's no' fair; I dinna think ony of her folk would like to see a respeckable married woman handed down to prosperity like yon, wi' her hair hangin' down her back, and no' dressed like her station in life at a'. I canna understan' what for they dinna employ these ladies that breaks windies reglar to try their hand on some of the kirk windies. If their talents was well direckit there's many a congregation would rise up and call them blessed.

When it came to gettin' on to the steamer Samson very near committed suicide; but at long and at last we were all safe landed at Kilmorag pier in a downpour o' rain. The tide was out, and there was

a cruel smell of the sea. The young ladies likes it—
they ca' it " eau zone " ; French, nae doot.

Bertram's cab was waitin' on us, wi' Stephen, the
long-nebbit white horse in it, that took us to the
pier seven year ago come November. He never was
exackly a racehorse, but he's awfu' slow now, poor
beastie ; he seemed to be thinkin' on sittin' down
every wee while. I doubt he's mair sootable for a
hearse. But you daurna say a word to Bertram ;
he aye says, " Stephen's awfu' wullunt, so he is—
he's *awfu*' wullunt." Anyway, he's no' dangerous—
he would raither stand still as risk an accident, and
he took us all safe to the old house in course of time.

XII

THE cat's oot o' the pock—it's the *auld* Samuel Tosh
that's the new gairdner ! He's a weedier, and he says
he's younger nor me, for he was aye in a lower class
at the school ; but, as I pinted out to him, it was no'
so much age as abeelity that settled that. He's a
healthy-lookin' body, though—thin and brown—he
minds me of a kippered herrin'. He says he's a good
gairdner, and he'll do fine for the place ; he's no'
blate.

The flowers is lookin' fine. The eccremocarpusses
are ten feet high already, and they need things to hold
them up straight. Mr Tosh says that we've got the
taties all late kinds, and we'll need to buy them at
the shop till ours are forret ; it's a peety.

Would you believe that the house is no' right
feenished yet ? There's workmen daunderin' in and
out ; painters is awfu' gradual. Miss Jean is dis-
appinted with the doors ; it said in the estimate,
" treated mahogany," but they've turned out treated
red. The foresman says, mahogany is kind o' red ;
but it's no magenty. " There's blue and better blue,"

as the sayin' is. And the paint is sticky yet. Miss
Celandine leaned out at the windy to smell the fresh
air, and she come away with a red stripe across the
front of her, poor lassie; she was fair mad. The
gentleman from Glasgow that undertook the work
said that it would be a " class job," but you'll obsairve that he didna say *what* class; trust him!

There's a pipe lettin' out near the back-door, and
when I asked the man that was bangin' at the kitchen
range to take a look at it, he says, " It's no' my
work," says he, " Ah'm a smuth," and away he flees
at the first stroke of twelve o'clock, leavin' us to sink
or swim the best way we could. It was very near three
in the efternoon, and the water was in the house,
afore a Weary Wullie came wanderin' in, wi' his neck
round and round with pipes, and asked where the
leak was. " Leak ! " says I ; " it's a catarack." I
soon showed him where it was, and he thought a
whilie, and scratched his head, and looked at the
water rinnin' about his feet, and then he said the best
way would be to turn the water off at the main,
because when there was no water comin' *in*, there
would be no water comin' *out*, and you would never
nottice that there was a hole, and he would come
back the morn's morn, or mebbe the day efter, and
see if the water was keepin' fine and dry, and bring
red lead with him; and with that he screwed off
the water and put the pipes round his neck again,
and away he went. Workmen are a provoke, but
necessary whiles.

The furniture looks gey auld-fashioned, and Miss
Celandine says that she'll need a new bed. When I
asked her how she had slept, she said, " My rest a
stone," and when I put her in mind that she was lyin'
on a feather bed—a thing she hadna got in Edinbury
—she said, " Well, I wish they hadn't left the hens
on the feathers." But it's no' a thing they would
seek to do; hens are fine for eatin'; but feather-

beds get lumpy if they're no' well shaken—I'll admit
that. And she's grumblin' at the name of the house.
It's put down as Kilmorag House in the Directory,
but the folk round about just aye call it " The Auld
Hoose," and Miss Celandine says she never hears it
without gettin' a tune in her head that lasts her off
and on for weeks ; she's real ill at it. Miss Jean's
been askin' her what name she would like better, and
she said she would like " *Tranquille* " efter a French
Shahtoe she once visited in, but she's feared the folk
in the village would call it " Trankwilly," and she
couldna abide that ; she's gey an' fikie. Miss Jean
said she could call it " The Firs," for there's a wee
wood at the back, but Miss Celandine wouldna hear
of it ; she said it minded her of a villa in a London
suburb, with two wee Christmas-trees in the front
gairden, and she would raither call it " The Twigs "
and be done with it ! She's for a motty over the
front-door, too : " Poor, but scrupuliously clean,"
(they're nice words). She says folks ought aye to
have a house-motty, if no' a text ; just a haver.
There's a text on the sun-dial, namely, " Think that
to-day will never dawn again," and she never reads
it. She says you might just as well say, " Consider
that yesterday will never be the day after to-morrow."
It's no' the same thing at a', but Miss Celandine is
thrawn whiles—she minds me of her poor papaw.
Sun-dials is all the fashion the now ; the new house
on the other side of the pier has got a great big one
with, " It is later than you think," on it. How do
they ken ? It a' depends on the folk. Here did I
no' get up at five-and-twenty meenits to three this
very day, thinkin' it was a quarter past seeven ! I
thought I had slept in.

There's no' much change in the village. The shop
has been enlarged and moderndized, and there's a
new windy at the side—but it's a wee windy ; there
was nothing in it but a good-sized stone hot-water

bottle, and it filled it from head to foot.   Someway it minded me of a shop-windy we looked in at in a narry crooked street in Grenoble.   It had a neat sma' meat-safe in it, with two waterin'-pots on the top, standin' face to face, and a printed bill sayin', " *Articles de chasse.*"   Miss Jean said that meant, " Things for going hunting with," but they didna seem sootable for the purpose.

We're goin' to have a visitor next week.   It's Mrs Prendergast's wee boy from Tasmania.   She's a cousin of the young ladies that married on an Englishman, and went away with him over the seas. He is comin' home on business, but no' her ; she has a baby three month old, and a bairn of two to look efter.   The laddie's name is Paul, but they call him Barnabas for a bye-name.   Many a time we've heard about him in letters ; his mother whiles calls him " Barney," and whiles, " My angel boy," and she says he's an awfu' Consolation, so we ken what to expeck.   I wouldna lippen to any angel boy I ever saw ; it's no' naitral.

XIII

The gairden is lookin' real bonny—I dinna mind of as bonny a gairden any place I've been in.   It wanders away up the brae to the wee wood on the top, and when you keek over the wall there's the hill, and the heather, and the ky, as the poet says—

> In simmer when the gress is green,
>   An' grossets crumpin' sour,
> The cows is in the meadow seen
>   Wi' mony anither flower.

The grossets are no' forward yet, although Miss Celandine says she's seen them in the shop-windy with " Ripe " on them ; just a lee.   They grow on

the flat ground, no' far from the house, and there's
sweet-peas and forget-me-nots round about them,
but I dinna see the Masterpiece Pansies; they'll no'
be out yet. The kitchen-gairden is far up the hill-
side and so is the clothes-green, and there's naething
to be seen round about but green hills, and blue hills,
and the loch lapperin' down below. The vegetables
were gettin' on fine till a vegetarium lady came for
a week-end and gave them a fright; but they're
gettin' the better o' it now.

The wee gairdens the young ladies had when they
were bairns is still there; I showed Mr Tosh Miss
Celandine's. It has a fine healthy leek in it, and a
tatie in full bloom, and a good few pinks. He lookit
at it, and says he, " It's like the Gairden o' Eden—
there's gey little intull't."

I asked him what way he made out that there
wasna muckle in the Gairden o' Eden? " Weel,"
says he, " there's nae mention o' taties intull't; and
there's nae mention o' ing'ns; and there's nae
mention o' cabbage: na, na; it couldna ha' been
ony great shakes o' a gairden—no' for a faimly. It
micht hae dune weel eneugh for a new mairret couple,
like, but no' for the folks doun at the hoose." He's
well-learned in the Scriptures, Mr Tosh. Him speakin'
about the Gairden o' Eden minded me of a pictur we
saw of it in Rome. I think it was pented by a man
they ca' Dominie Keeno—he would likely be a school-
maister. There was the gairden, as like as life, and
Eve sittin' on a grassy bank on the left-hand side
lookin' real disjaskit. Adam was up a tree, and down
below on the green gress, amongst the bonny flowers,
there was a row of animals and birds mixed, sittin'
lookin' on, sad-like. Poor wee craturs, they felt that
something had gone wrong in the peacefu' place where
they got their names; it was a waefu' pictur.
It put me in mind of the Sological Park. Sam'el
said it would never succeed with all the wild beasts

perowlin' about, and eatin' the flowers. I told him they were a' shut up in cages. He said it was a daft-like thing to keep wild animals in cages; and I said it would be a dafter-like thing to let them out once they were in; so, for fear he would conter me again, and I would loss my temper, I asked him where was the dwarf peas? "Thonder," says he, lookin' at the sky—poor body, he was vexed-like—they were wavin' far ower his head! They will have sent the wrong kind, mebbe. The taties with the stylish names Miss Celandine and me seleckit are comin' on fine. I was askin' which was the best kind, and Sam'el Tosh says they might just as well have ca'ed the three of them the same name for a' the odds there is betwixt them. Catalugs is deceivin'.

Miss Celandine told me this very day that she doesn't believe Snabbie (she *will* call him "Snabbie" behind his back), kens anything about insecticides; she thinks she heard a mealy bug singin' in the night-time—she said it put her in mind of the frogs at Grenoble—and I must say that I met a good few slugs takin' a daunder round about the place yestreen; but the weather has been gey an' saft. I said to Sam'el, "There's a box of slugicide on the shelf in the tool-house"; but he just said, "Is there?" He's dour whiles. He's been usin' the wasp-destroyer, though, and he says they like it fine —they're back and forret to it a' day; it appears to ack as a tonic. It's no' what was intended, but "All ills are gude untried." I hope Snabbie will no' try it on hissel', though, or it will be a case of Sam'el-cide, I doubt. He's awfu' contemptious about the "Corpses," as he calls them, meanin' the eccremo-carpusses; they're dwobbly-lookin'.

Miss Celandine is gettin' on fine wi' her poetry-book —it's to be ca'ed "Little Lays and Big Lies." I never mind of seein' her sittin' as steady at anything afore, so Miss Jean and me encourages her for peace sake.

It's all to be written in broad Scotch—" Dialeck,"
she ca's it—and many a time she comes ben to me
for a word she's seekin'. The last piece she's done
is founded on fack—but let me not antissipate.
There's a bit of readin' out of an old *Scotsman* at the
top, as follows :—" Scotland's share of legislation
during a certain session was a measure for the pro-
tection of the wren in St Kilda. . . . Almost the
sole fruit of the numerous discussions in the course
of the session now closing will be an Act for the purpose of regulating the capture of the whale in Shetland
waters."

Then there's the poetry—

> It's a grand thing legislation !
>   But mebbe ye'll no ken,
> The M.P.s up in London
>   Ha' been sittin' on the wren ?
>
> An' syne they've got that settled,
>   They've yokit on the whale ;
> An' there's word that, come next session,
>   They'll mak' up on the snail.
>
> They keep their eye on a' thing
>   That roves the sky or sea ;
> It's a maist exackin' business
>   To be a Scotch M.P.
>
> For, troth, there's naething great or sma'
>   But what they'll put it richt ;
> They'll sort the hale creation
>   If they sit up half the nicht !

XIV

MASTER PRENDERGAST arrived last week. He's not
four years old yet, but he's dressed in breeks already
—white flannen, short and tight, and a wee white
pinny over them. The first I saw of him he was
rum'lin' in his pocket, breathin' hard, and gettin'

gey red in the face. Miss Celandine knelt down aside him and she says, "What is the matter, Barney?" "Can't get the damned things out of my pocket," says the bairn, in the sweetest voice you ever heard, like a pet lamb! There was a quietness in the room as if a bomm had exploded, and then Miss Celandine bursted out a-laughin', and she laughed and laughed, and the infant joined in, and he laughed too, although he little kent what she was laughin' at. Then he come over to me, and he says, very polite-like. "Please, will *you* take the damned things out of my pocket?" "I will that, my dearie," says I, "but you'll no' need to say words like yon." "What is 'words like yon'?" says he, tryin' to keek into his pocket. I got him out a sma' tin box, and efter a whilie he come ben to me in the store-room, and I felt his wee sticky fingers creepin' into my hand, and says he, "See! you can have a lolly if you like!" That's what they ca' sweeties at the ends of the earth appearin'ly. He's a kindly cratur, and well-mainnered, but his language would make your blood curdle. Where he got it naebody kens; it would mebbe be from the sailors on the road home. And he's that meek-lookin' on the outside—as fair as a lily, with solemn eyes, and yellow hair. Miss Jean is tryin' to learn him to say "dear me" when he's annoyed instead of "damme," and he's quick at the uptak. One day when Miss Celandine was goin' to take him down to the shore, she cried on the dog to come too. "Come on, Sammy-dammy," says she. Would you believe that Master Paul picked her up in a meenit, and he roared and laughed and pointed at Miss Celandine, and we heard him cryin', "The funny one said 'damme'; the funny one said 'damme'!" all the way down to the shore. He aye calls Miss Celandine "The funny one," and Miss Jean "The lady with the nice face," and me, "The lady with the old hair." I dinna believe that he's ever seen grey hair in his life afore, poor wee man.

Of course Miss Celandine took her chance to change Samson's name. She said she could not allow a mere dog to be a stumbling-block in the way of a youthful Christian brother, and she's settled on " Granville Barker." It's no' a bad name, I will say that; Samson can bark with the best of them. He answers to it fine already; he never comes when he's called anyway.

But one thing leads to another, and here's Delilah had to be altered too! She is to be " Dumbpet," if you please. It's a daft-like name that was invented by a Mr Browning, Miss Jean says; he was something in the poetry-line, I understan'. But I never can mind it right, and the pussy gets " Delilah " yet from me. Miss Celandine doesna aye remember hersel'—she called her " Delumpet " this very day. She's a terrible cat for catchin' birds, and mice, and even rabbits; and her that young! Samson Barker canna abide it; when he sees her at it and hears the poor wee mouse squeakin', he goes to his bed, so he does, decent cratur. But Delilah takes it off her mamaw. Tatty was a reglar Rimnod of a hunter when she was young, and many a sparrow did she catch in the back-green at the Terrace, and bring in for me to see. She had a way of daunderin' along the front balconies the whole length of the Terrace, and I was aye feared she would bring in a canary-bird, belongin' one of the neighbours, some fine day. But little did I think she would catch a coakatoo! I was fair dumbfoundered when she appeared at my room door one efternoon haulin' a great muckle fowl a' the colours of the rainbow, efter her. She laid it down at my feet as proud as you like, and I lifted it up all in a trem'le, to see if there was any hope of resussitatin' the corpse. But life must have been extinck, for it was a stuffed bird wi' glass eyes and

an awfu' sharp beak. It was weeks afore we eluci-
dated, by means of the grocer's laddie, where it came
from, and Miss Jean sent it back with an abjeck
apology. I'm thankfu' to say Tatty has never done
the likes of yon again. But she's no' near as respeckable a cat at the seaside as what she was in
the town—comin' in late, and rollin' on her back
in the road, she's fair uplifted wi' the change of
air.

Master Prendergast's language has created a painful impression in the neighbourhood, I doubt. We
met Mrs Sibbald Smith from The Palms (the new
house on the other side of the pier), when I had him
along to the village one day, and she said to me, says
she, " I really cannot repeat what that child said to
me on Sunday, Mrs Pow ; it was *shocking*. I could
not tell my own sister ! " It was vexin' for her,
poor lady ; it was easy seen she was keen to tell
somebody. The very bairn saw it, and he said,
" *I'll* tell her what I said," and I had to hold my
hand over his mouth and haul him away afore he
got it out. And there's a rumour that the minister
tells a story about Master Barney objeckin' to his
sermons because they were " devilish long," and I
doubt there'll mebbe be some foundation for it.

Miss Jean gave me a read of a wee book ca'ed *Pet
Marjorie*, to let me see that Master Paul is no' the
first bairn that's been celebrated for strong language.
I was glad to see that *she* put in her Diary, " The
most Devilish thing is 8 times 8 and 7 times 7," and
she wrott a poem dictated to Mrs H. Crawford, as
follows :—

> Three turkeys fair their last have breathed,
> And now this world for ever leaved ;
> Their father and their mother too,
> They sigh and weep as well as you ;
> Indeed, the rats their bones have crunched,
> Into eternity theire laanched.

A direful death indeed they had,
As wad put any parent mad ;
But she was more than usual calm,
She did not give a single dam.

Appearin'ly folks was no' near so parteeclar in those days. But I hope we'll get Master Prendergast cured long afore he can write ; the bairn's no' four year old yet !

XV

THE principal event of the year took place in the Schoolroom on 2nd August, at 7 p.m., in a perfeck downpour of rain. A gentleman came all the way from Glasgow to deliver a lectur on fire-engines, and he brought a wee model engine with him to let the folk see what like they are, and how they ack. There's no demand for them here, though, and it's just as weel, for Greenock's the nearest place they keep them, and it would be a work to get them across the water under night.

We had fine seats near the front, among the gentry, and we got a good view of the platform, and all there was to be seen : First, a Table, with a Jug of Cold Water and a Tumbler on it ; secondly, the model Fire-engine on the right-hand side of the Water ; thirdly, a Chair for onybody that liked to sit on it ; fourthly, a Pianny, and a Pianny-stool.

The first piece on the programme was a song called, " How beautiful is Night ! " It took two ladies and two gentlemen in dress-clothes to sing it, and they were a' needed, for the rain pelted that way on the skylight that we could scarcely hear them ; it was a heavy shower.

When they were done a young lady played a tune on the pianny. She was in a fearfu' hurry ; her fingers flew up and down like lightning ; what for

could she no' take time ? I said to Miss Jean that
it must be difficult to play as quick as yon, and she
said I minded her of something she read in a French
book about a gentleman that was listenin' to a lady
playin' on the pianny, loud and fast. His neebour
asked him if he liked it, and he said, " No' me."
" You must remember that it is very difficult," says
his friend. " I wish it had been impossible ! "
says he.

When the pianny-piece was past, on came a great
tall felly and sang something about—

> It's awfu' nice to ken
> That you're bonny, wee hen.

He would be what they ca' a bird-fancier. Efter
him there was a recitation. It was unexpected, and
I got a sort of a fright, for the young lady that said
the poetry didna come forret like the rest of the
company ; she just rose to her feet suddenly and
bawled out—

> Billy's dead and gone to glory,
> So is Billy's sister, Nell.

" Measles likely, and no' right nursed," I says to
mysel' ; but it wasna infection, it was mair like
starvation, poor wee tots, and I doubt it was an
ower-true tale ; our hearts were wae within us when
it was told, and I hope it would be a lesson to all
the negleckfu' parents in the place.

The next item was a painfu' contrast, it was a
song—and no' a genteel song at a'. Miss Celandine
has been singin' the o'ercome even on ever since ; it
was a bonny lilt. The words were as follows—

> Durnum doo-y doo-y day,
> Durnum doo-y daddy, oh !
> Durnum doo-y doo-y day,
> The fisherman hinged the puggy, oh !

It was a nesty, cruel-like thing to do, and it was no
excuse that he thought it was a sma'-sized foreign

gentleman that he was murderin'. I wonder folk
would laugh at the like of yon, but the laddies at the
back enjoyed it fine, and naething would serve them
but an angcore—that's the way Miss Celandine learnt
the words, and the tune too ; a' the message-laddies
in the place are whustlin' it, and Master Barney
tries to do the same, the darlin'.

The next song was solemn and slow, and I kind-of
dovered (the place was closs) ; but the feenish of it
woke me up, it was that loud and triumphant—

Having kicked the woman, and left her dead.

Allow *them* ! It was naething less than manslaughter.
But afore ever I could ask Miss Jean the meanin' o't,
here was the Glasgow gentleman sittin' on the chair
aside the wee fire-engine, ready to start the lectur.
It was a good long parleyvoo, and the gentleman
had a soothin' voice. Wee Jamie Forbes fell sound
asleep on his faither's knee, and never woke up till
Mr Forbes needed his hanky, and roused the bairn
wi' rumblin' in his pocket for it. " I'll gie ye a
wee len' o' mine's, faither," says he, loud out, and a'
the folk round about laughed hearty ; he's a nice
bairn, and there was his new hanky stickin' out of
his pocket sure enough—white, with red and blue
picturs on it.

It was unfortnit that, while the lecturer was
lecturin', the water in the wee fire-engine was drib-
blin' out little by little, and when the time came to
show how it worked, here it was bone-dry, and a
perfeck burn of water rinnin' ower the floor ! The
gentleman was fair provoked, and no wonder ; it
cast a kind of damp over the audience, and we never
saw how fires was put out efter a'. But he told us
how they were started. He said that buildings were
usually ignited by coming into contack with fire ;
I've notticed that mysel'—it's nearly always the
way. It was a maist instructive lectur.

Efter the lectur there was anither recitation—

> Break, break, break,
> On thy cold grey stones, O Sea !

but 'deed the water was break-breakin' that way
on the shore, without any advice o' *he's*, that the
gentleman could scarcely hear hissel' speak. The
concluding piece was a song by one of the bairns at
the school, namely—

> Did you ever put a penny
> In the Missionary-boax,
> Instead of spending it on sweets
> Like other little folks ?

She sang it no' bad, poor wee lassie, and the laddies
liked it fine. I heard them bawlin' to one another
when they came out, " Did you ever put a penny in
the Missionary-boax ? " But I doubt there's no'
very many o' them that'll take a lesson.

When the gentleman from Glasgow and the rest
of the company had been thankit, and all was at an
end, the folk rose up to go away home ; and when
they spied old Bertram at the door, they jaloused
that his cab would be there too, and they fair sur-
rounded him, implorin' him to take them home dry.
But he wouldna listen to one of them—" Ah'm trysted
wi' an auld leddy," says he (it was me that gave him
the order to come back), and naebody else would he
take, except the Precentor the length of the pier-
head. " Stephen's awfu' wullunt," says he, " but
he'll no' go out of his road for orra folk ; ' an inch
is as good as an ell to a blind horse.' " I've been
suspeckin' for a whilie that Stephen was blind, by
the way he took nottice of things with his nose, but
I never heard Bertram let on afore that he was any
way difeecient. If they could get him dyed black
he would do fine for funerals, though. I dinna like
the way folks are hurried to the tomb nowadays ;

it's no' respeckfu'. Last week when I had Master
Barney out for a walk along the Inchmakenneth road,
here I sees a funeral comin' full trot. There was a
hairse and two coaches, and I bade the bairn take off
his hat. Here didna he think it was just folk out takin'
a ride for the sake of the air, and he kissed his hand,
and waved it to the murners, and bowed and smiled,
the same as if it had been the laird or any of the
neebours ! I doubt the faimly of the corp would be
scandulised ; but 'deed it served them right for goin'
the pace the way they were doin' ; a disgrace to the
districk.

XVI

At the back-end of August I got a post-card from
Mrs M'Curd askin' me to spend " a long day " with
her at Blairbonny, where she aye goes for a fortnight
in the summer time. Miss Celandine said she didn't
need to say a " long " day, for the shortest day in
the year would *feel* long if you were spendin' it with
other folk on purpose. It's mebbe bein' hand-idle
for hours thegither, but I've felt that way mysel'.

Blairbonny is no' a handy place to get at ; you've
to take the boat to Greenock, and the train the
rest of the way ; it's an awfu' length of a journey
for one day. The steamer calls at Kilmorag at a
quarter to nine, but whiles it's afore the appinted
time, and whiles it's late, so I set out early. It was
showery-like, and no' very warm, so I put on my
twilted petticoat, and carried my waterproof cloak
over my arm, and my best umberelly in my hand.
I had my kep in a riddicle, and a bag with my hanky,
and my spectacles, and my purse, and a box of
Helensburgh Toffee for Mrs M'Curd, and a wee poke
of strong peppermints for fear of the indisgestin' ;
folks is very apt to eat mair nor they're habbited

I

with when they're spendin' the day—it's mebbe just
for something to do.

Kirsty went with me to the pier to see me safe
off, and Samson came daunderin' efter her. We
were in fine time—five-and-twenty meenits to wait
—so we got a sit-down at the end of the pier,
and Samson enjoyed hissel' barkin' at the sea-gulls.
The steamer hove in sight a wee thing late ; they
hurled the gangway forret in a terrible hurry, and
afore ever the folk got off, here's Samson on !
There's no' a machine of any sort but what he'll
get into it, right or wrong. Kirsty cried, " Barker,"
and I cried, " Samson," and the man that was
holdin' the hen's-ladder steady cried, " Come on,
wumman, if you're comin' ! " Away I went stoiterin'
across the gangway, and I very near stuck half-
roads through the handle of my umberelly catchin' a
haud of the railin'. Samson was waitin' on me with
his tongue hangin' out, but, afore ever he could say
a word, a young naval gentleman in brass buttons
hauled him off his feet, and flung him on to the pier
that sudden that he landed wi' all his four legs
pintin' in different directions and his tail in the air.
Poor felly ! the last I saw of him he was lookin'
efter the steamer quite disjaskit, and Kirsty was
wavin' her hand to the crew. Some of them would
be her cousins ; her mother has six brothers all
married on different women, and every one of them
has large faimlies of one sort or another, so Kirsty's
cousins are just a bye-word on the coast.

I never can mind what " abaft the funnel " means,
and I'm aye feared of sittin' down in the first-class
department of the steamer by mistake, so I asked
one of the gentlemen that manned the boat where
to go, and he gave me a seat in a sheltered locality
near the funnel. The voyage was what they ca'
" uneventful," and we landed at Greenock on the
back of ten o'clock. The train was waitin' on us,

and I arrived at the end of my journey afore eleven o'clock. It's fearfu' the rate folk traivels at now.

Mrs M'Curd was meetin' me. She had on the bonnet she saw us off in, lookin' as good as new. We had a bit piece—cookies, and scones, and ginger wine—and then we went over the house. It's a tidy wee place—three rooms and a kitchen—and clean, I will say that. Efter that we took a turn in the gairden, and saw the cabbages, leeks, parsley, curly-greens, etc., growin' fine. The folk the cottage belongs to keep cocks and hens, and there they were, keekin', and croakin', and grumblin' for food, but we never let on we saw them; fowls is seldom satisfied. When we had seen the house and the gairden we took a turn through the village, and Mrs M'Curd pinted out the principal edifices, *i.e.* the kirk, and the manse, and the pollis-office. There was a shower comin' on, so we went back to the house. I thought it would be denner-time, but, losh! it was only twenty meenits past twelve! So I sat in the room till Mrs M'Curd got the denner forret. The time passed quickly; Mrs M'Curd said I was sleepin' when she brought ben the tray, and mebbe my een were shut, but I heard her fine. We had a handsome two-course denner—a beefsteak pie covered at the baker's, and taties out of the gairden, and a shape and goose-berry jam; I enjoyed it fine. When it was by, an open cab came to the door to take us for an hour's drive about the districk. It was real mindfu' of Mrs M'Curd, and it must have been a heavy expense, but she's no' the kind of a woman to do things half. It was cloudy-lookin' when we set out, and half-roads it came on a heavy pelt, but the driver got down and shut up the machine, and closed the windies, so we had a grand hurl without gettin' damp. The horse was slow—no' near as wullunt as Stephen —and when we were goin' up a brae Mrs M'Curd put out her head and she cries to the coachman,

" Can your horse no' go any faster nor that ? "   At
first he didna heed her ; then he stopped the machine
and came down to hear what she was wantin'.
" Faster ! " says he.   " My certy, wumman !   Div
ye no' ken this is the first time he's been in onything
but a hairse ? "

Mind you that was queer, for the poor beastie was
no' a pure black—just a kind of a second-murnin'
shade, but he had a fine steady walk, so he had.
We were back at the house five meenits afore the
hour was up, but the man said it was because Mrs
M'Curd made him drive like Jehu at the end ; so she
gave him 2d. to hissel', and all was peace and goodwill.   It was very near a quarter to four by the time
we got our things off, and our keps on, so we took
our teas as soon as the water was boilin'.   Mrs
M'Curd said we could take a daunder efter, if it
cleared up, but it was damp-lookin', so we bode
where we were by the kitchen fireside, and looked
at the awlbum, and the poetry-books that was lyin'
on the room-table, and the time passed wonderful.
Out came the sun, exackly when it was time to go
to the station.   Mrs M'Curd wouldna let me away
without a biscuit and half a glass of ginger wine to
keep out the damp, and I was very near lossin' the
train at the hinder-end.   It arrived at Blairbonny at
seven exack, and I had just time to say " thenk-ye "
for my fine ploy, afore it was off again.   The steamer
was fuffin' away at Greenock, and soon the anchor
was heaved, and the sails furled, and away we went.
It was a fine warm night efter the rain, and I sat
up on the deck to admire the sunset.   Afore we had
gone far there was a slight accident, but no' nothing
of importance.   A young woman that was leanin' on
the railins enjoyin' the prospeck, got out a twopenny
mutton-pie to eat on the voyage, but the very first
bite she took of it, did it no' a' fall to pieces in her
hand, and afore you could say Jack Robison, here a

dog flew forward and devoured it up, and licked the gravy that clean that, in less than a meenit, there was nothing left to tell the tale but the wee bit outside paste in her fingers! What a provoke! I was real vexed for her. She sat down aside me, and told me what fine these pies were, and where you could get them, and the dog came and sat in front of her, and never lifted his eyes off of her the whole voyage. I gave her a peppermint, and it lifted her up a bittie, so I put some more in a wee bit paper for her, and she thanked me kindly and landed at Cove.

Kirsty was waitin' on me with her eyes glued to the man at the wheel; she never saw me come off the boat; she said it was the crowd—me, and anither auld man! The walk along the shore was peacefu' and pleasant, with the gloamin'-star shinin' in the West, and the loch lapperin' among the seaweed; but I was glad when I saw the lights of the Auld Hoose twinklin' among the trees. It's funny what wearied folks are efter a day's pleasure!

XVII

WE'VE fallen in with Mrs Balcarres again—the Scotch lady that we became acquent with when we were traivellin' on the Continent—the one that used to give me a read of the *Scotsman*. We fand her by means of an advertizement. It was in the windy of the post-office: "Lost—a Purse, containing a small sum of money, between Staneriggs and the pier. Reward. Apply to Mrs Balcarres." We minded that she was celebrate for lossin' her purse, and the very day I read the nottice, here I meets her comin' down the road in a hurry to tell the folk at the shop her purse was found, so they could take down the intimation; she says she's aye lucky

about gettin' things back. She knew me perfeckly,
she said, and she asked me how I liked my own
country efter bein' abroad; she's a real unosten-
taneous lady. She told me there was a nice letter
in the paper about the smells of Edinburgh, so
when Kirsty brought ben the *Scottish Oracle*, I read
it. It's an interestin' subjeck, and I'm fair sick of
readin' about birds day efter day for weeks thegither.
I'm sure if they've asked once, "Do Woodcock
carry their Young ? " they've asked it a dozen
times. And they hadna got it settled afore a
Bohemian Waxwing come fleein' forret, and they
argle-bargled about *it* till they were fair bumbazed.
Then they wrott about Lloyd George as a stormy
petrol—just a haver—but they couldna get their
minds offa birds appearin'ly. "Corncrake carrying Young" was anither set-away, and "Blackbird
attacks Mouse." What for can they no' write
something usfu' ? The letter about the smells of
Edinburgh minded me that I had notticed a wild
smell of the dog lately, so I showed Miss Celandine
an advertizement about "Dry-clean your Dog." I
didna ken what it meant mysel', but *she* said she
knew fine—she had had her hair washed that way
once in London—and she said she would try it on
Granville Barker immedently, parteeclarly as there
was some folks comin' to their teas in the efternoon,
and he would be an affront the way he was. So she
first showered him all over with oatmeal, thick ; and
then she set to work to brush it out. You never saw
such a slaister ! Kirsty had to lay a dust-sheet on
the kitchen-floor, and here's Samson lyin' wrong side
up, as white as snow, and Miss Celandine brushin'
away as hard as she was able, and Master Barney
helpin' her with an old tooth-brush, and baith of
them like dusty millars ! And then in comes Delilah
to see what's goin' on ; and she licked a' the bits of
Samson she could get at, and made a perfeck porridge

of the poor cratur. At the hinder end Kirsty had to come to the rescue with black soap and hot water, and she says there'll be no more dry-cleaned dogs in *this* house if she's to bide in it. Such a work she had to get the beast his naitral colour again! But he was awfu' proud to be so clean and smooth, and the company said he was a lovely dog, and petted him, and gave him wee bits of cake; he was daft with conceit the whole day efter.

Miss Jean wasna very sure at first about lettin' Master Barney into the drawing-room when the folks were there; but his language has been that genteel lately, and he was lookin' that meek, that she decided to let him get his tea with the rest, and hand round the cake; he's fond of handin' the cake, and real dentily he does it. Miss Jean has given him a wee linen tunic, with a green sash round his middle, and green stockin's, and he looks exackly like a nimf. He nearly always minds to say " Dear me," when he's annoyed, and it's funny the way he says it; and he puts his wee finger to his lips the way Miss Jean does to remind him no' to use language; but one word is as good as another to him, the genty wee innocent! Efter the party was over and the company away, Miss Jean come ben to tell me that she's suspeckin' that Master Barney is a reglar matchmaker, and him no' four year old yet! Figure that! It seems that when Sir Simon Bradstreet and Miss Somerville were talkin' to one another, sittin' in the big windy-seat, up comes Master Barney and stands gazin' at the lady, fu' of admiration—he likes big folk. When he got his chance he laid his bit handie on Miss Somerville's knee, to draw attraction, like, so she says, " Well, Barney, what is it?" " Miss Somerville," says he, lookin' up in her face very solemn, " are you a mother?" " No," she says, laughin' in a kind-of nervous way. Miss Jean couldna help hearin' every word, sittin' makin'

out the tea with her back to the three of them.
Master Barney thought a meenit, and then he says,
" But you could *be* a mother, couldn't you ? Our
cat—— " Goodness knows what he was goin' to
tell about the cat, but Miss Somerville stopped him
by lifting him up on her lap and sayin', " Will you
give me a kiss ? " Now there's nothin' that bairn
hates like kissin', and he wriggled off her knee like
lightning, and says he to Sir Simon, stiff-like, " Will
you kiss her for me, please ? " and away he marched
black-affronted. In his hurry he caught his foot in a
rug, and very near fell on his nose. " Dear me ! "
was all he said, but unfortnitly a lady heard him,
and she remarked to her neighbour that it was
quaint the way the child said " dear me." " I
can say ' damme ' just as quaint," says he, and the
poor lady fair gasped ; but we're hoping she'll no'
let it go any further.

XVIII

THERE'S been a wave of releegious excitement (as
they ca' it) at the Church the young ladies worships
in at Inchmakenneth, and a minister belongin' the
English Church has been preachin' in season and out
of season, Wednesdays and Fridays inclusive. He's
visitin' the laird, and I'll no' deny that he's a
fine preacher—Irish—they've got the gift of the gab.
It's what they ca' The Patronal Feastable at the
Church, something ado with St Ninian ; it started
with an evenin' service they ca' " Feastable Even-
on " on the Setterday night, and they've been at
it ever since ; it's a mercy that " Meat and Mass
never hindered work." Last Sabbath the minister
announced that there would be a sermon to Women
only, come Wednesday. Miss Jean said, when she
was tellin' me, that if he hadna *said* " Women only "

there would likely no' have been a man there, for
many and many a time there's naething but ladies
on week-days, or else nobody. But sure enough,
when we got there at five meenits to seven, here a
man in the very front row; and, afore the service
began, two or three more fellies drifted in, mair by
good luck than good guidin'. The hymn afore the
sermon was a warnin' to sleepers—" Christian, seek
not yet repose," and many's the time I've heard it
sung, but I dinna think that ever I saw a Christian
seek, and find, repose efter it as quick as that
felly in the front row! The text was hardly out
of the minister's mouth afore he settled hissel' and
went to sleep; maist affrontin'. He missed a grand
sermon anyway; he never woke up till the end when
the minister said, " Finally, I would ask all you
women, and especially those among you that are
men, to think seriously on the solemn questions which
I have laid before you." I dinna believe the sleepy
gentleman knew what the subjeck of the discourse
was—no' him—and it was just as weel sooted for
men as for women, for when you come to original
sin they're just six and sax. There was no collection
—no' even a plate at the door. Miss Celandine said
it was little short o' a miracle, and I must say I
dinna mind of ever bein' in an Episcopal Church
afore without a gentleman comin' round for the
pennies; it would mebbe just be a forget.

Miss S. is away. (Miss Celandine said I was just
to say " S " and then naebody would ken who I
mean.) It was a lady from London, her that was
governess to the young ladies when they were
bairns; she aye pays them a visit in the summer-
time. Miss Celandine and her never was very chief,
and now she's eighteen Miss Celandine doesna like
bein' guided, and Miss S. canna forget that she's no'
the governess yet; so Miss Jean and me are aye
thankfu' when they get through the visit without a

rippat. Miss Celandine says that this is a bit of the book that I'm no' fit for; the departure of " Miss Elizabeth S." is a subjeck that's beyond me, and *she'll* undertake it! She's an awfu' lassie, and she aye gets her own way, but I'm no' responsible for *her* havers—mind you that.

" Elisabeth S. is gone, and my heart is dancing with joy. She went this morning by the quarter to nine boat, to catch the London express. To be sure I can see no reason why she might not have gone a week ago; but, on the other hand, there was nothing to show that she did not intend to stay for another fortnight. But Elisabeth is gone, and all nature rejoices with me.

" Strange and touching it is to trace this unconscious sympathy. The tender lettuces lift their heads and rejoice in the autumnal sunshine (Elisabeth was mercilessly fond of salads). The daisies tilt the dew from their shining eyes, and spread their cheery faces out to dry. The turnips—the turnips— well, strange as it may appear, the turnips look much as usual. They may not have realised yet that Elisabeth really *is* gone; she spoke of going days before she went.

" Meditating on the joy of speeding a parting guest—one of the purest, loftiest pleasures of our fallen human nature—I wander towards the arbour. How cool, how calm, how damp a thing is an arbour! The light filters greenly through the eccremocarpusses arched above the rustic seat; the merry earwig trickles between the pebbles on the walk with a fluency of motion that even a fish might envy; and I seat myself carefully, so as not to disturb the quiet and estimable avocations of the industrious spider.

" The sound of wheels! an early visitor? I reluctantly rise and take the path towards the house. The nasturtiums look gayer than ever; the daisies 'wink their golden eyes' almost as if they meant something, bless them! How delicious the warm sun is: how deli—— Bertram's cab at the door; boxes on the cab; 'E.S.' on the boxes; E-lisabeth on the step! In an instant the truth flashes across my mind—'10 a.m. *d* (Saturdays only).' And this is Tuesday!"

And it was a Friday, as sure as I'm here! And the train goin' every day from Glasgow to London, rain or fair, and no wee "*d*" conneckit with it; but I doubt these wee "*d's*" has given rise to many a big one; they're awfu' annoyin' whiles.

XIX

KILMORAG is quiet-like the now. The folk that had furnished houses in the village are away back to Glasgow, and there's no' a sound to be heard but the wind, and the water, and the birds. When I was standin' at the back-door, I thought I heard a motor-car down by the loch-side, but it was just a bumbee tryin' to get into a red flower that was ower jimp for it; it was a fearfu' size of a bee, though.

The gairden is very near a' etten up, what between the faimly and the birds, and the snails, and the caterpillars, and the visitors, and other insecks. I was away up to the top last week to see if I could get a few peas to brighten up a stew, but there was naething but bare sticks, and empy pods, and withered shanks, and Sam'el Tosh meditatin' among the tombs, so to say. I was askin' him where he had put the Masterpiece Pansies that Miss Celandine and me ordered, for I've never set eyes on them yet; he said he kent naething about them, and mebbe they were the retarded sort, and gairdens was awfu' disappintin', and the weather on the west coast was a' thegither terrible, and the soil was no' near as

rich as the Fife soil, and the insecks was that free
and impident, and the folks was no' like the Fife
folks, and the wasps wouldna kill, and if he was
stayin' another simmer he would need a laddie under
him for the rough work—a laddie fra Fife, for the
west coast laddies was no' like the Fifeshire laddies.
Did ever you hear the like ? a perfeck Jeremiah.

And there's scarcely a thing left in the shop ; and
the price they chairge ! I went to the village to try
to get a cauliflower, for ours is that delicate-lookin'
it would be murder to eat them. I saw three in the
windy of the post-office, so I went in and I says to
the lassie ahint the counter, " How much are your
penny cauliflowers ? " " Thruppence each," says
she ; and them very near as wee as our own !

So we've been away up to Glasgow for a day to
get in supplies ; it's a long traivel to take for tea,
coffee, bacon, cheese, etc., but Miss Celandine was
needin' boots, and Miss Jean wanted a book, and she
said it would be a nice bit change for me, as it was a
good whilie since I had had a day out. It was a
bonny mornin', and we were off by the quarter to
nine boat, and landed at Greenock in good time for
the train. In the railway-carriage between Greenock
and Glasgow there was two nice-lookin', well-put-on
young gentlemen, sittin' opposeed to the young
ladies and me. When we were comin' near Paisley,
they had a long consultation thegither in whispers,
and they aye lookit at me, and juffled a bundle of
papers. And what do you think the upshot of it
was ? They gave me a Track ! *Me* : I aye thought
I was ower respeckable-lookin' for that. " Where
are your dead ? " was the name of it. I was bumbazed, and I just had time to say " Thenk-ye kindly,
sir," when they got out at Paisley Station. They
would be what they ca' revivialists, mebbe. But it
gave me a kind of a turn, mind you, and me settin'
out on a day's shoppin', and no' thinkin' about

graves or any such thing. My faither and my mother
are lyin' side by side in Carldoddie kirkyard, and
there's room for me aside them, and here have I
been payin' 1s. 6d. a year for cuttin' the grass on
the grave for fifteen year and me derivin' no benefit
from it whatever ! it's a heavy expense. But it's a
bonny cementery, and the new bit they've added to
it has been a great success ; it's very near half-full
already—maist encouragin'.

When we got to Glasgow it was rainin', so we took
a tacksie. We hadna been five meenits in it afore
the clock was standin' at 1s. 2d. ! No sooner were
we habitted with seein' 1s. 2d. starin' us in the face,
than away goes the 2, and in jumps a 4, for all the
world like a magic-lantern at a Swaree. " Preserve
us a'," says I to mysel', " there's something wrong
with the machinery, that clock's feverish." I said
nothing to alarm the young ladies, but I keepit my
eye on the face of it, and in bangs 6, 8, 10, and no
grocer's in sight. It went on that way the whole
time we were in the machine, and little did I see of
the scenery of Glasgow for watchin' yon clock : it's
anxious work ; I would raither take a plain cab,
and risk the fare.

We had a look-in at the shop-windies.

There was a Rob-Roy tartan mantle with " Chaste "
on it that Miss Celandine said would set me fine ;
but I aye think I'm best in blacks, and so does Miss
Jean. We took our lunches in a big restorong with
a band playin' tunes to distrack attention, and came
away home in the efternoon train. We'll no' be in
Glasgow again till we're on the road back to Edinbury, with the summer-time, and the sea, and the
hills left ahint us like a dream when it's day. But
the country pales upon you when you get ower much
of it ; " A Yule feast may be done at Pasche," and
the weather is gettin' gey cold.

Kirsty and Merran had put in an awfu' day with

Master Barney, by their way o't: he's no' habitted
to do wantin' Miss Jean. First, he brought up a crab
from the shore, and he was playin' with it in the hall,
when his mind was distrackit with something he
notticed in the gairden. Out he flew, but afore he went
he says, "Klistina" (he canna say's r's right yet),
"please watch my clab." She seized her chance to
put the poor cratur into the loch again, and when she
come back Master Barney was crawlin' under the
furniture in the hall seekin' his crab. When she told
him where it was he flew into a tirrivee and stamped,
and roared, and grat, and said she had drowned his
"clab." She had an awfu' job to make him believe
that it wouldna drown: she had to take him down
to the wee pier and show him a crab in the water
afore he would leave off lamentin'. Efter dinner
Merran met him trailin' Tatty round the gairden
with his airms clasped that tight about her waist
that she was fair gaspin', and all her legs hangin' down
to the ground. She took the pussy from him, and
told him he must be carefu' with her, because she
wasna very weel. In a whilie he appeared with a
stone ginger-beer bottle, and asked Merran to fill it
with hot water. She thought he was playin' at a
house, so she put a droppie in, and corked it, and
away he went quite content. When tea-time came
they began to wonder where the bairn was—the
house was that still—and find him they couldna!
They were gettin' cold wi' fright afore they thought
of lookin' in Miss Jean's room. When they opened
the door here he was sittin' aside his own wee bed as
quiet as a mouse, with the windy-blind drawn half-
way down. When Kirsty pulled it up here's Tatty
lyin' on the eider-down quilt with the ginger-beer
bottle at her feet, and Master Barney's neckerchief
folded over her shoulders. He put his wee finger to
his lips, and says he, "She's sleeping; she'll soon
be better." He's a queer bairn yon! I dinna

wonder that his mother ca's him a consolation *whiles*; I hope he's no doomed to an airly death. Merran was that relieved to find him that she kissed him accidentally, and he up with his wee foot and kicked her as hard as he was able. She carried him down the stair kickin' a' the way, and gave him cake to his tea, but he wasna' his right sel' till Miss Jean got home : then he told her the whole story, and gave Merran a kiss, and went to his bed like a lamb. Poor we mannie, we'll miss him sorely when his faither sets sail.

XX

POOR old Maggie's away. She's been in the cottage at the gate ever since I can mind the Auld House, and that's forty-five year come the elevent of November! She was here when I got my first place with the Mrs Murray that was the young ladies' grandmamaw. Maggie was old by me, though; she would be over eighty, I would say : but she never kent her age; poor folk doesna take the same nottice of birthdays as the gentry, and they look old sooner; it's the hard work that does it. But the Insurance has lifted them up a good bittie; it's wonderfu' what young-like septy-genariums looks now! it'll be the relief to their minds. And there's no' a few that didna ken their ages afore, that exclaims now with the Psalmist,

> Three-score and ten years do sum up,
> Our days and years, we see.

Maggie was real pleased to see the young ladies in their old home again, and many's the time they've been in and out this summer, and Master Barney and Samson efter them. Miss Jean allowed her a jug of sweet milk every day, and her Sabbath dinner was aye carried to her from the house.

Last week she was washin' on the Tuesday, but on
the Thursday she took to her bed, and when I went
in to make her a drop arrowroot, she was done-like.
Efter she took it I sat aside her and she seemed to
dover. Suddenly, just when the sun set, and a cold
greyness came over the room, she opened her eyes—
they were bright and bonny—and she says, anxiously,
" Is the henhouse door shut, Marget ? " I'll never
forget the words ; little did I think they would be
her last ! but Maggie never spoke again. She
slippit awa' without a sign when the dawn was
creepin' white ower the water and the mist was
liftin' from the land. I wished efter that she had
said a text to feenish with, for the neebours a' asked
me to tell them her dyin' words, and they didna
seem content. But Maggie was thinkin' on doin'
her plain duty to the last day of her life, and she
never was one to make grand speeches, dead or
alive.

The chestin' was on the Setterday evenin'. Maggie
had nobody belongin' her, but we invited a few
old friends to the tea—Mr Tosh was there, he was
aye attentive in the way of taties, leeks, etc.—and
the elder came and laid her head in the coffin
with his own hands, while the minister was readin'
" The Lord is my shepherd ; I shall not want,"
and then they prayed time about. A queer thing
happened just before the minister feenished his
prayer. The door opened slowly, slowly, and a
wee dirty lassie keeked in. I kent her fine ; she
comes from the Gipsies' camp at the point, and she
was carryin' a cast-off Teddy Bear of Master Barney's
that Miss Jean had given her. She stood a wee,
doutsum, and then she said, " Where's Baggie."
(She's aye a cold in her head, poor bairn.) Nobody
spoke, and she came forret and looked into the
coffin. " She'll catch the cauld," says she, speakin'
to hersel' like ; and then she stroked the bear's

back-hair, and screwed round his head, and gave
him a kiss, and laid him in the coffin aside
Maggie, with one of his legs kickin' in the air.
"He'll be comp'ny for her," says she, and away
she went to the table to see if she could get a bit
piece.

The funeral day was bonny—blinks o' sun, and
saft showers—and Maggie would have been proud
if she could have seen the cortage, as they ca' it.
Miss Jean knew fine that if the poor old body had a
wish left for anything on this side of the grave, it
was for a handsome funeral, and she took care that
she had it. The hairse came from Inchmakenneth
—it was the one the cab-hirer stocked "to meet
a long-felt want," as he said in the circular—and a
very nice one it is, with a vawse on the top and four
tappiloories at the corners. Then came no less than
three murnin' coaches, with very near every man in
the village in them, all in deep blacks and lum hats.
The young ladies laid a beautiful white wreath on
the coffin, and Lady Lindesay sent a cross of purple
pansies a' the way from London, with a card hangin'
on to it, with a message in her own hand of write.
Maggie didna exackly make a will, but she left
the milk she got every day to the lassie Bruce
that's been lyin' since June, and she said that the
ham Lady Lindesay aye sent her at Christmastime
was to go to Betsy Syme; it was real mindfu'
of her.

It's very near five mile to the old kirkyard, so
the company gathered airly in the efternoon. And
who do you think was in the first coach aside the
chief murners ? Samson. The young ladies, and
Kirsty and me were in the cottage at the service, and
Merran was walkin' to Miss Somerville's with Master
Barney and the dog—as *she* thought. But he took
advantage of a slight shower to turn back half-roads
(he canna abide gettin' hissel' wet), and when he

K

saw a carriage standin' at his own gate, in he got and
took a seat to be ready. The chief murners, includin'
the minister and the elder, thought he was Maggie's
pet dog, and they said what beautiful it was to see
such faithful affection in a poor dumb animal ;
Sam'el Tosh heard efterwards, from Peter M'Nab
the carpenter, that they spoke about nothing else
the whole road to the kirkyard ; and they pinted out
the tears in his pathetic eyes to one anither and said
he would likely lie on the grave till he died of a
broken heart. Catch him ! *He's* no' a Grayfriar's
Bobby. They were surprised that he didna folly to
the grave : little did they ken that he was feared of
lossin' the hurl back. But when the minister got
out at the manse on the road home, Samson took
the rue, and *he* got out too, and away home as fast
as his legs would carry him. Sam'el Tosh saw
him. He appeared, quite joco, about tea-time. The
story's all over the place. Folk keekin' out below
their blinds at the funeral saw the dog in the first
coach, and maist o' them said it was a touchin'
sight ; but them that kent him (like auld Bertram)
said it was just like his impidence. Well, it's all
over now, and if Maggie never had much in her lifetime, she's been putten awa' very genteel.

Would you believe that the American lady that's
bidin' at the hotel at Inchmakenneth, mentioned the
subjeck to me this very day ? She came and sat
down beside me on the seat near the water, and gave
me a long screed about the remarkable faithfulness
and saggasity of Dandie Dinmont dogs, a' founded
on fack ; and she said it was an elegant funeral : I
wished poor Maggie had heard her. Then she put
up her pinchneb and she glowered at the yachts in
the water, and efter she had considered the thing
for a while, she said, " I think the people that go
in these boats must be very dependent upon knowing
how to manage the sails." I never heard a truer

word ; she'll likely be conneckit with the Admirality,
or mebbe the Navy.

The place is no' the same wantin' Maggie. Miss
Jean put a beautiful nottice of her in the papers :—
" For fifty years a faithful friend and servant et
cintera." Ever since I was a bit servant-lassie I've
thought I would like to see these very words on my
tombstone, but Miss Celandine's prophesyin' that I
never will, for she's sure I'll live to be a centenorium,
and it'll need to be " seventy years " at least. But
it'll no' seem long anyway : "Tout ce qui finit est si
court." Miss Jean made me put that bit in ; it's
French, and it means " All that finishes is so short."
Miss Celandine says it's no' true, for she never knew
a long sermon that was short, even when it was done ;
but there's times when she would pick a quarrel wi'
a stein wa' ; and she has an awfu' ill-will at long
sermons.

XXI

Miss Celandine has been tormentin' me to tell her
where I was born, and what my faither's name was,
and I dinna ken a' what, for she says that now I'm a
celebrated author I'll be put in *Who's Who ?* (the red
book that ladies keep to look up ither folk's ages in),
and she's been gettin' the nottice ready. She's been
ben to let me hear it—" Marget Pow, daughter of
Weelum and Jane Ann Pow, born at Carldoddie,
Fife ; relick of Mr Pow (still-born)." Preserve us
a' ! that's daft ! But she says she canna explain me
bein' Mrs Pow, and him no' bein' either dead or alive,
any other way. Then there's " Writings : chiefly
post-cards ; published *Marget Pow in Foreign Parts*
in 1912. Favourite amusement : Tango Teas." I'll
no' deny that I enjoy my cup of tea, but I dinna hold
with thae foreign teas—just a plain household tea, at
2s. a lb., with a drop cream in it, and a bit hot toast,

or a scone and butter, does me fine; I've never tried
the Tango Tea. I've been readin' about wonderfu'
cures in the papers and the way to get thin, and the
way to get fat; and how to produce a luxurious crop
of hair, no maitter if you're perfectly bald. There's
an advertizement of a medicine that begins " Tell
Everyone I Suffered Two Years with Stomach Indigestion " ! Allow *her* ! I hope I've more to do than
advertize ither folk's indigestion for them ! Then
there's a bit that says, " A distinct growth of hair
you can actually see, or your money back." I would
think so : it's no' likely folk would be content with
hair they couldna see. But the stuff seems to give
satisfaction. " A Mother " writes to say, " My little
boy became completely bald through collecting tramway tickets." That was queer ; you wouldna have
thought he would have picked them up with his pow.
But collectin's an awfu' work—parteeclarly money
However, efter one bottle of the " Hairyleenia," the
laddie's head was covered with a luxurious crop of
chestnut curls : it would be a great offset to him,
poor wee felly ; I was glad to hear it ; and I hope
his mother will have the sense to keep him away from
tramway lines for the rest of his life. Miss Celandine
has been readin' the paper too, and she's real taken-
up with a pictur of two gentlemen—a sma' one ca'ed
" Before," and a tall one ca'ed " After "—with
" Height increased three inches in three months "
written above them. She's advisin' me to try the
system ; she says it would improve my appearance.
No' very likely ; it's just a fleein' in the face of the
Scripturs, and a' my skirts would need to be let
down. I'll be needin' a new black gown for the
Sabbath, but I'll wait till we go back to Edinbury
to buy it. We'll soon be away now ; " The evenin'
brings a' hame " ; and the year's at the gloamin',
and the nights are drawin' in, and lamps are poor
efter the electric light, and the weather's saft, and

Master Barney's wee breeks is that short and tight!
But he's goin' home a reformed character, and the
feenishin' touch was done by means of a doll. Miss
Somerville brought a wee French bairn that was
visitin' her to her tea one efternoon—Mamselle Marjo-
laine, they ca'ed her. She was very near two year
old, but she could scarcely speak a word, either French
or English. She could kiss your hand though, and
" make a reverence," if you please! It turned out
to be a kind of a curtsey, but she was that fat and
short that when she tried it she very near couped.
She was carryin' the loveliest doll that ever you saw,
and Master Barney couldna take his eyes off of it.
At last Miss Somerville told Mamselle to let him hold
it in his arms. I never saw a sweeter sight than that
bairn's face when he got it. He never spoke a word;
he just heezed the doll up and down very gently to
see it openin' and shuttin' its eyes, and every now
and then he looked up at the folk round about him
with a heavenly smile, as much as to say, " Did ever
you see the like of that? " I never saw a mother
look at her first bairn mair reverent and sublime than
Master Barney looked at that doll. We thought
there would be an explosion when he had to give it
up, but no' a bit; he let it go without a word. Miss
Jean took her chance and promised him a doll like
it, with een that would open and shut, if she never
heard another word she doesna like out of his mouth.
And he's that carefu'! He's aye askin' if what he's
goin' to say is a bad word; and he canna understan'
that naebody can tell him without he'll let us hear
what it is, and he'll no' risk it; I nottice he's never
very sure about " ham." Miss Celandine says we're
makin' a perfeck prig of the bairn, and she much
preferred his past strong language to his present
Glesca accent; but she's contrairy whiles: she's
been practisin' what she ca's " strong nervous
English " hersel' lately; it's fearsome.

I'm busy : what with shuttin' up the house, and catchin' the cats and keepin' them handy for packin', and one thing and another, there's a terrible lot to do.   But I'm thankfu' to say we'll soon be safe back in Auld Reekie.

To him that farthest went away,
The sweetest music was " come home."

MARGET POW LOOKS BACK

I

MISS CELANDINE's been tellin' me that it's high time I was gettin' on with writin' my reminisiencies, or mebbe I'll be dead and buried afore ever I'll can get them feenished.

She says the way to begin is as follows, namely, " The subjeck of this interesting memoir was born at Carldoddie, in the Kingdom of Fife, in the year Anno Domini——" and then I'm to put the exack year. No' me ! I'm no' near auld enough yet to be proud o' my age—no' *near* ; so the folk that reads this book will just need to content theirsels with the news that Marget Pow was born in the same year as the ither auld bodies of the same age—or thereabout. And Mrs M'Curd is older nor me.

Then I'm to tell the names and ages of my grand-faither and my grandmither. I dinna mind them. They both died afore I was born—some serious trouble, likely.

Miss Celandine's annoyed—she says a'body has four grandparents each, and where was mine's ? They never let on where they were—no' them.

But I mind my mother fine ; and the first time ever I tasted sausages (it was at a funeral-tea) ; and a hat I had when I was ten year auld—pink rosebuds in the front, and long ends hangin' down my back ; and the Sunday-school trip when we went to Pit-bladdo, and me and all the lassies in the first cart

(we traivelled by cart) were set to sing a hymn to
put past the time. The teachers seleckit, " We are
pilgrims in the narry way to Heaven "—tune, " John
Brown's body lies buried in the ground," and the
laddies in the second cart were to sing the second
verse. Mebbe they didna take the thing up right,
but here did they no' commence wi' " John Brown's
cuddy has a Stuart-tairtan kult ! "

And when the teachers got out of the cart and
quarrelled them, they said they would do it different
the next time, but a' the differ they made, when
their turn came, was, " John Brown's cuddy has a
Dolly Vairden hat." The teachers were real ill at
it, but laddies are a fair provoke.

If I was tellin' ye a' the important events I mind
or ever I went to sairvice, my book would be as long
as the one Miss Jean's readin' the now. It's ca'ed
Collections and Recollections. I dinna mind the name
of the gentleman that wrott it ; but if he's putten in
a' the collections he's given to, nae wonder it's long !
What with collections *inside* the kirk, and a plate at
the door comin' out, ca'ed a " retirin' collection "—
and it's queer to see how retirin' the folks are when
they see the dish, castin' their e'en down to the
ground, and gettin' ahint yin anither in their hurry
to get safe past without puttin' in ; and collections
from house to house ; and special collections, and
Sustentation Funds, and Jews, and Foreign Mission
Skeems, and leddies leavin' books at the door, and
they'll call in a few days—it's a regular profession,
so it is.

Every time we come back from Kilmorag, when
we open up the house, here a perfeck pile of collectin'-
books waitin' on us. I aye take a look at them ;
they're instructive, mind you. Whiles they put the
folk that gives the most at the top o' the list, and
the " Anons," and " Widdy's Mites," and " A Friend,
1s.," away at the very end, modest-like, poor things ;

I dinna like that style. Miss Jean's aye keen to give quick. She says, "He gives twice who gives quickly." It's perfeckly true. Many's the time I've notticed it mysel'. If ye give at the very beginning of a collection, they'll be at ye again afore they've got as muckle as they need, so they will : it's maist discouragin' to quick folk like Miss Jean and me. But I'm no' gettin' on with my Recollections ; it was collections put them oot o' my heid. No' but what I can mind many a peculiar thing—deaths and marriages and us lossin' the cat, and it yowlin' at the door when a' hope seemed past, and the cloud-burst in the glen when the burn rose that high that there was a trout under the bed. It was the only one ever I catched, although many's the hour I've spent danglin' a string with a crooked pin at the end o't in the watter, catchin' the cauld, and no' anither thing. What burstit the cloud was never exackly fand oot, but that day is spoken about in the Glen yet, and our Trout is aye mentioned ; it formed a kind o' silver linin' to the cloud.

I was annoyed, though, to find oot, the very last time I was in Carldoddie, that the folk in the farm lower down the glen let on that *they* caught *three* trouts in a tin basin on the same momentious occasion. I dinna believe it. Miss Jean says that fishers' stories about what they catch is just " competitive mythology." I'm no' sure what it means, but it sounds very like the thing, so it does.

II

I WAS sixteen or ever I got my first place in a gentleman's faimly, namely, Mrs Scott at the Bield. She was a widdy woman at the time, and ended a long and useful career as grandmother to our young leddies, her only daughter bein' mairret on Captain

Murray. Weel do I mind the day of the marriage, for it was the first time ever I tasted wedding-cake and shampane wine. I liked them fine.

When first I went to the Bield my wages was twelve pound, and find your own tea and sugar. There was nae word of minimium wages then; minimium wages was the reglar thing, and what for they make such an argle-bargle about them now, dear knows! But I'm no' denyin' it's a fine thing when you're given a rise, and I was gettin' twenty-two pound and all found when I left the Bield; and many's the lad cast his eyes on me seein' I was an illegible partee, as they ca' it. But I never lippened to ony of them—jist an off-put of time. A sairvant's life in a country-house fifty year ago was no' the same thing at a' as it is the now. There was no' near as much time for crochet, and visitors, and rinnin' aboot on bycicles, and pairties, and carryin' on. There was aye plenty work to do, and what between washin'-days, and bakin'-days, and turnin'-out days, and gatherin' the berries, and makin' the jam, and days out (there was a minimium of *them*), and Sabbath days—the usual number—there was nae time to weary, and the years jist flew.

It was no' till I was very near leavin' to go to Mrs Murray, when her first bairn was born, that I heard of the trodegy that had cast a gloom over the life of Mrs Macrorie, the housekeeper, since ever she was a lassie. She was a cheery-lookin' wee body, fat, wi' rosy cheeks, and little did I think she was the skeleton in the cupboard, so to say. But it was many a year since the startlin' event to which I elude took place. Mrs Macrorie told me a' about it hersel'; she said it would be a lesson to me no' to throw stones—a thing I've maist particularly avoided syne.

The way o't was this. When Maggie Mushet—that's Mrs Macrorie—was a lassie goin' on twelve, she was engaged to help the kitchen-maid at the Bield at six pound in the year. At that time Mrs Scott's mother—auld Leddy Bethune—bode in the house, and she keepit a pet pig. No' a very nice pet for a titled leddy. I dinna like they snotterin' wee dogs leddies carries about wi' them nowadays, but pigs are no' very handy either. Anyway, Mrs Scott's cook couldna abide Sir Topaz—that was the pig's name the auld leddy gave him, on account of him havin' " a seemly nose," she said. I never could abide pigs' noses mysel', and Mrs Macrorie said Sir Topaz was jist like ony ither pig ; but the auld leddy had a fancy for him some way. Well, one wet day, the pig came huntin' into the kitchen, makin' dirty marks all over the clean floor, and the cook shooed him out. A wee whilie efter, Maggie—the wee kitchen-maid—went out into the backyaird to get some firewood. Here she meets the pig makin' for the kitchen-door again. She chased him away with a stick, but, when she lookit round, here he's efter her again. So she took up a stone offa the ground, and flung it at him. Imagine the poor lassie's horror when the pig fell down as deid as a door-nail ! The stone must have struck a vital part. Mrs Macrorie said she thought it was the first time that ever she had hit the thing she was aimin' at. I've notticed that mysel' when I've been playin' at the ba' with the bairns ; it's awfu' apt to go the ither way. But, anyway, the pig was deid, and the poor lassie felt like a perfeck murderer. She had heard of folk bein' hung for stealin' sheep, and she jaloused that killin' pigs was worse, and her very blood ran cold.

But the cook cried to her, and in she went to help with the denner, with a hert like lead, and a face like a clout. The gloamin' was comin' on, but every now and then she keeked out, hopin' the pig was only in a dwalm. Once, when she got a chance, she poured a wee drop water on his face, but life was extinck, and he never rose to his feet again. Poor Mrs Macrorie! who would have suspeckit that her smooth exterior (she aye wore black saitan when she rose to be house-keeper) concealed such a gruesome memory. She told me that it was a queer thing that, the meenit Sir Topaz was deid, she loved him, and all that fearfu' night she grat like to break her hert.

She expeckit to be taken up the next day, and was aye watchin' for the pollis to come and haul her awa' to the jail; and when she saw the detectives measuring the marks of her feet in the graivel, she felt the rope round her neck, so she did. But detectives are gleg, mind you, and they fitted the marks exack to the feet of a gangrel they had notticed near Cupar no' lang syne; and they pinted out the way he had gotten in an' oot, and Leddy Bethune was real pleased, and gave them one shillin' each; but they never caught the man, and little wonder!

Mrs Macrorie never could mind whether Sir Topaz was buried, or eaten, or what, but many a night she lay awake tryin' to make up her mind to tell on hersel'. Then old Leddy Bethune died, and it was ower late. For a whilie efter that, she forgot, but when the time came for her to jine the Church she was hopin' the minister would ask her, "Did you ever kill anything?" and her mind was made up to say, "Yes, Sir, one pig." But Mr Macmillan never would think that ony of his Bible-class had onything parteeclar on their consciences, so he just let alone.

But murder will out, and when Mrs Scott sent for Mrs Macrorie, long years after, and complimented her on the way she had served the faimly, and said they could never do wantin' her, and would she accept the place of housekeeper, she burstit into tears, and assured her mistress that she had been nourishing a sairpent in her bosom. Mrs Scott lookit ; and Mrs Macrorie says, " Do you mind on Leddy Bethune's pet pig, mum ? "

" Yes, I do," says Mrs Scott. " A nasty, interfering, guzzling beast."

" Well, it was me that killed him, mum," says Mrs Macrorie, dichtin' her een, and she tellt me that the meenit she spoke she felt as if a pound of lead had risen off her bosom. Mrs Scott seemed kind-of stunned at first, and just glowered at the housekeeper as if she had never seen her afore, while she listened to her story ; and then she took to the laughin', and she laughed and laughed till the tears ran down her cheeks, and she keekit out behind her hanky, and says she in a trembly voice, " You look so unlike it ! " And finally she blew her nose and remarked causually-like, " Well, he would have been killed anyhow," and dismissed the subjeck.

And if I hadna been throwin' stones into the burn, to see if the ice would break, I would never have heard the story ; no' me.

III

IT was efter I had been twenty year at the Bield that I went to be nurse to Mrs Murray's baby. And here I will introjuce the first letter of general interest ever I got. It was in the form of a post card, *i.e.* " Mrs Murray will expect Marget Pow on Tuesday by the train which leaves Cupar at half-past two." Many's the time I've read it since ! That half-past two train hurled me into a New Sphere of usefulness (meanin' Edinbury), which I have never quitted syne.

But ye needna think I got all the road by the train ; no' very likely ! There was no Forth Bridge long ago, and we had to cross the Frith in the Burntisland boat. It was the first time ever I had been

on a steamer, and I mind I was terrified to move for
fear it would coup. Many's the watter I've sailed syne,
includin' the English Channel, the Frith of Clyde, the
Adriattic Ocean, and the Canal at Venice, and never
once been shipwrecked. I've been mercifully dealt
with, I must say that. But I've aye had a *pongshong*
for dry land (as the French say), and water's overdone
baith down the West Coast and over thonder in
Venice. And when you've cats carryin'—we aye
take Tatty with us to Kilmorag, and whiles there's
kitlings too—and Samson gettin' amongst your feet,
and the gangway that steep when the tide's low, and
the felly wi' brass buttons cryin', "Come along,
now; come along!" and flusterin' the folk;
many's the time I wish the land went a' the way.
And would you believe that they're chairgin' for
cats now! Plain cats! The very last time we
went down the watter, efter the luggage had been
weighed and paid for (3s. 6d. extry, if *you* please!),
here did Tatty no' let out the most fearfu' yell, and
her had sat in her basket a' the road to the station
like a pet lamb! "*A cat!*" says the weighin'-
chap, fair struck dumb—"one shillin'." Naethin'
but profiteerin', the auld sneck-drawer!

Miss Celandine says that I'm no' to put off time
tellin' about cats when I've not even mentioned
her birth yet. It's a funny thing, but when I'm
tryin' to recolleck the great events of my past life,
it's aye the wee things I mind the best. But nae
doubt birth is important enough too, and I'll mention here that the three young leddies was all born
at the usual age, and that Miss Celandine dared me
to tell the year *she* was born. It was an awful wet
day—I mind that—for we were washin' blankets,
and it was a job to get them dried. And it was
cranberry jam we were makin' the very day the poor
Colonel went away to the Boor War, leavin' me to
look efter his future widdy, and his bit bairnies.

I'll never forget the way he lookit at me when he shook my hand in the hall. He didna say " Goodbye," but just, " Take care of them all, Marget," in a queer, hoarse voice. My heart was wae for him ; and that cranberry jam didna geill, and it made wi' pure cane sugar and a'.

Well, when the Colonel's birthday came round, soon efter, Mrs Murray sent a present, and so did the bairns, and we decided to have the same dinner the Colonel always chose for his birthday, namely, mince, white turnips, with butter sauce, and a black-currant roley-poley puddin'. It was no' a dinner for company, but the bairns' Auntie Maisie was invited, and it was early, for them both to be there (it was afore Miss Celandine was born). Mrs Murray bad me draw a bottle of shampane wine to drink the master's health as usual. She was the first hersel', and she lifted her glass and wished her husband "A Happy Birthday and a safe return." Then Miss Maisie came next, and says she, " Many happy returns of the day to my darling Donald ! " (She was terrible set on her brither.) When it was Miss Isabelette's turn—they ca'ed her Isabelette for short, her poor mamaw's name bein' Isabel—it was discovered that she had drunk up all her wine, so I put water in her glass, and a wee drop of shampane on the top o't. " Long life to daddy," she cried, in an awfu' hurry to drink the wine afore the fizz went off it. Miss Jean askit her maw to make *her* water fizz, and then she sat lookin' at it, dreamy-like, but not a word did she say. " Come along, Jean," says her Auntie Maisie, " don't be all day about it ! "

Then the bairn lifted her head, and lookit straight at the pictur of the Colonel above the mantelpiece, and she says, " A short life and a happy one ! "

There was a queer silence fell on the room, like as if somebody was listenin', but it's a true say that " Hallowe'en bairns see far," and certain it is that Colonel Murray was killed in battle that very day.

No' long efter Mrs Murray died of a broken heart, when Miss Celandine was born ; and many a time I've said to mysel', thinkin' on that birthday pairty, " It's a sooth dream that's seen wakin'."

IV

IT was an awfu' miss to the poor weans no' to have father nor mother to guide them. Their grand-mamaw, old Mrs Scott at the Bield, did her best ; but it's weel kent that grannies aye spoils their bairns' bairns, and the three wee lassies were no' long in findin' it oot. When Miss Celandine was five she treated Mrs Scott as if she was a bairn of four, and backward at that ! I mind once when the auld leddy had undertaken to keep Miss Celandine amused while I was reddin' up the nursery, she started to tell her a story about hersel', and says she, " You know, Celandine, I was once a little girl like you——" and the bairn just gi'ed her a bit look and said con-temptiously, " Oh, granny, *don't* be silly ! " The poor auld leddy was dumbfoundered, and it put her story clean oot o' her head. But Miss Celandine aye said what she thought, and she was a perfeck pro-voke for askin' questions that naebody on this earth could answer ; for instance, " Why are radishes red ? " and " What was Adam and Eve's last name ? " And would her granny last till she was quite grown up ? And would she get takin' the cat to heaven with her ? And who would button her knickers if I didn't go ? Poor wee lassie ! it seemed to weigh on her mind, and one night she ended her prayers with, " And teach us to button our knickers." Miss Celandine says that a minister would no doubt have said, " And so replenish us

with heavenly wisdom and earthly skill that we may
be enabled to attach securely to our frail and sinful
frames the complicated garments wherewith we are
in mercy permitted to veil our mortal bodies." It's
mair like the thing; but Miss Celandine was a wee
lassie then—no' four year old. And she says now,
why am I no' puttin' in some of the *clever* things she
said ? I dinna mind them. And I'm no' to make
out that she was an infant progidy, for she canna
abide them. But she's certain that, considering
what a lot she's said in her lifetime, she must have
let drop many a pearl of wisdom. If she did, I never
lifted them. She'll just need to colleck her ain
pearls ; folks are usually mair interested in theirsels
than in ither people.

But there's one thing that I *do* mind, for many's
the time I've thought upon it since, in connection
with the weather—it's when we're confronted with
the weather that we feel our helplessness, so it is ;—
Miss Celandine had got a new toy donkey, and she
was out a walk with me trailin' it ahint her by a
string, for the first time. I'll never forget the way
the wheels squeaked ; it was fearsome ; the folk on
the Ferry Road were lookin' efter us wholesale and
retail. Unfortnitly a wee shower came on, and Miss
Celandine got uneasy-like. She lookit up at the
clouds and down at the donkey once or twice, and
then, when the rain got heavier, she stood stock-still,
and stared straight up at the sky, and says she,
"Now, now, God, that'll do ; do you not see that
you're spoiling my new donkey ? "

The way that donkey squeaked minds me of a
maist awfu' fright I got once, long syne. I was goin'
into the nursery in the dark, and I set my foot on
an animal of some sort that gave the fearfullest howl
that ever I heard in my life. My heart louped into
my mouth ; and, when I screwed up the gas, here a
rabbit lyin' on its back, that naebody had ever sus-

peckit of havin' a squeak ! It looked surprised itsel',
poor beastie ! The bairns was delighted when I told
them ; but naething less than jumpin' on its stomach
would make that rabbit squeak, its voice was that
powerfu' for its size ; I was feared I had murdered
the kitten.

I never saw bairns as set on cats as ours were ; it
would very near take a whole page to go over their
names—Leonora, and Tiptail, and Biler ; Bumfit,
and Maggie Lauder, and Jeremiah, and Santa Claws ;
Delilah, and Tibbs, and Bobs—but there was aye one
ca'ed Tatty, and I couldna undertake to add up the
kitlings she had. Miss Jean whiles ca's her " Mother
of Thousands," but I wouldna say that was exack.
I aye thought our bairns likit to go to Dunbar in the
summer-time for the sake of gettin' a walk in Cats'
Row. It's no' a genteel pairt, but what with the
pussies sittin' on the doorsteps, and the bairns playin'
about, and laddies fechtin' yin anither, and nets
mendin', and the smell o' fish, there's mair life nor
what there is where there's naethin' but rocks and
sea. But it's gone down—there's an awfu' odds on
it since the war ; it's adulterated like a'thing else.
It's still ca'ed " Cats' Row," but it's no' what it used
to be. I bought a pictur post card of it no' lang
syne, and lo ! the two principal cats in the foreground turned out to be baith dogs ! Just an intake.

V

MANY's the journey I've taken in my lifetime—baith
long, and short, and middlin'—but mebbe I've set
out for Dunbar oftener nor any other place. We
aye went there in the summer-time, when the bairns
was wee, for the sake of the fresh air, the house at
Kilmorag bein' shut up. But go where you like, the
platforms and the folk on them are just six and sax.

There's aye people hangin' on the last words of ither
folk—and them perfeck strangers—and payin' no
attention to their ain freens. It's funny what keen
they are to hear what's no meant for them ! It used
to make me mad to see our own housemaid, Merran,
no' attendin' half to the directions I was givin' her,
and the ither people round the carriage-door feared
to loss a single word I said.

Then, when the train moved, and everybody cried,
" Good-bye," and " Write soon," and " Love to
Maggie," etc., the meenit it was really off we a' sat
down sudden in the midst of a fearsome silence, and
examined yin anither, gey suspeecious-like.

It's a queer thing, mind you, that we a' start on the
journey of life withoot kennin' that we're away! Mebbe
it'll be the same when we start on our last and our
lanesomest journey—it wouldna be a bad plan either.

Naething parteecler happened for a long time efter
the bairns went to the school ; and then, all of a
sudden, when Miss Isabelette was just settin' out to
be a young leddy, at the age of nineteen, did she no'
go and get married ! She was aye one to do things
in a hurry, and nothing would halt her when she
once made up her mind. I was tellin' her the last
time she was here with her bairns (when she was
hearin' them say their prayers) about hersel' when
she was seeven year auld. She was extry sleepy one
night, and when she was half-way through her
prayers, she give a fearfu' yawn, and then she says
in a hurry, " And the rest's the same as last night, O
Lord ! " and with that she bounced into her bed, and
was asleep in a jiffy !

Miss Isabelette's freens aye ca'ed her marriage " a
perfeck Idle "—meanin' a fair romance—but she
never was one for idleset ; no' her. The way o't
was as follows : Her Uncle Nigel—her faither's
youngest brother—havin' died in the East of some
foreign disease, a freen o' he's, namely, Captain

Lindesay, wrote home givin' a beautiful history of
the sad event. Appearin'ly he was the only ither
white gentleman in the place. We decided that
Miss Isabelette was the proper person to answer the
letter, and thank the Captain for his kind attentions,
although Miss Jean had a neater hand-of-write (I
must say that), and she was firmer in the spellin'
too. We had an awfy work to get Miss Isabelette
to set to—she had an ill-will at writin' letters—but
if she had never written *that* letter, she might just
have been plain Miss Murray yet ; but wait till ye
hear ! At the hinder-end she wrott a long letter,
stickin' out her tongue at the kittle bits (as she does
to this day when she's drivin' her motor-caur, parteeclarly at the corners), and askin' how to spell a
word nows and thens. An' she aye said the same
thing when she was tellt, " I thought so, but it
looked queer." Nane o' us would she allow to see
the letter, and away it went, with an expensive
stamp on it. The Captain read it solemnly from
beginnin' to end, and says he to hissel', " *That's* the
woman I'm going to marry ! " Did you ever ? And
him had never set eyes on her, nor heard her voice !

Home he came, in a great hurry to see his sweetheart, and he took the precaution to bring a ring
with him. It was very near big enough for his joe
to put her wee heid through—outsize, it was—but
they got it taken in, and it looked fine, " like a
diamond in the sky," as the poet says. Miss
Celandine said it was lucky for the Captain that her
sister was pretty ; and so she was, with bonny blue
eyes and curly fair hair ; but beauty is deceitful and
favour is vain, as Solomon learnt from experience.

Miss Jean aye said she *knew* Miss Isabelette would
be married by the way she sang a song ca'ed in
Italian " Non mi voglio maritar," meanin', " I do
not wish to be married." Every verse ended with,
" No, no, no; no, no, *no* ! " louder an' louder, and

there were seven " noes " at the very end. And
efter singin' that song till the whole faimly was fair
sick of it, she went and married without a blush !
" There's naething for misdeeds but mends," as the
sayin' is.

VI

THE folks that writes what they ca' Autobiographies
must hae awfu' good memories ; but I nottice that,
when they're no' sure what to say next, they aye
put in a letter they've got from some freen o' theirs.
That's an easy way to make a book. It minds me
of a story-book the young leddies used to read when
they were bairns. It was ca'ed the *Fairchild Family*,
and every chapter ended with a prayer and a hymn.
Miss Celandine was mad at it ; she skipped every
one. The objeck of the work was to show how
easy folk could break the Commandments without
notticin', and the two young ladies in the book and
their brother managed to get through the whole ten
in the course of two volumes, and them just bairns !
It was an awfu' warnin'.

Miss Celandine says it's time I was tellin' about
me bein' converted when I was a lassie. No' me. I
dinna approve o' the folk that " thank God through
the medium of the newspapers." But I'll tell about
Mrs M'Curd and me goin' to the Revival Meetin',
for never will I forget it, and me left sittin' unconverted to the very end !

It was a leddy from the United States of America
that came to Edinbury no' very long syne to see if
she couldna convert the ne'er-do-weels, backsliders,
and ither unregenerate folk that canna be got to
enter a kirk door. So she took a hall, no' to put
them off it, like. It was ca'ed the Oddfellows' Hall,
and weel named, for the congregation was gey queer-
lookin'. Mebbe you'll wonder what me and Mrs

M'Curd was doin' among them. It was her. A
neebor had been tellin' her what a wonderful gift o'
the gab the leddy from New York had, and she was
set to go to hear her, and nothing would serve her but
she would ha' me to go wi' her, to keep her company.

We landed at the hall in good time ; there was
just three young leddies in afore us. There was a
row of wooden chairs on the platform, and a table
wi' a water-bottle and a tumbler on it ; it mun be
drouthy work preachin'. There was more folk came
efter us, and finally a row of leddies and gentlemen
(there was only three of the latters) come in by
a back door and sat down on the chairs ; the one
that preached was in the middle. And, mind you,
she did it fine ! It was a long discourse—I dinna
mind the text. Mrs M'Curd said there was *no* text ;
and she ca'ed it a dangerous innovation, and the
thin end o' the wedge, forbye. But mebbe no'
bein' in a pu'pit, let alone a kirk, was some excuse.
I was dumbfoundered, though, when the preacher-
leddy said that a' her dear sisters on the platform
had been converted through her instrumentiality ;
what a faimly ! Seeven o' them, an' a' grown-up !
Wise-like women too, and weel put on.

But wait or ye hear what occurred when the
sairmon was concluded. It ended with implorin'
a' the souls no' yet converted to see and be quick
aboot it. And then the leddy steppit forrit to the
very edge of the platform, and says she, " Will
anyone who has been converted here to-night stand
up ? " There was a fearfu' silence for a meenit, and
naebody seemed like to rise ; when, on a sudden,
the three young leddies near the front stood up
as one man. The Revivalist was real pleased, and
efter givin' thanks, she tried again. " Will anyone
who was converted last night stand up ? " And
up rose one o' the gentlemen on the platform as
quick as lightning. And, would you believe it, he

was her brither! And her never knew he was converted; that made nine o' a faimly. Efter that she tried "five years ago; ten years ago; twenty years ago," and who do ye think was one of the latters? Mrs M'Curd. And me never notticed the difference, though I kent her long afore that!

When it came to *forty* year ago the folk a' sat still, no' bein' inclined to let on that they could mind as far back, and Mrs M'Curd gave me a dunch with her elby. But I didna lift her. I was meanin' to rise at "fifty years ago," but the American leddy was discouraged with naebody risin' to forty year, so she gave out a hymn, and me still sittin' among the unconverted! I was black affrontit.

Mrs M'Curd and me very near cast out on the road home. She said I should have stooden up at twenty year ago, for if I was converted fifty year ago, then I was converted twenty year ago, and it would have been company for her. She's a grand head for theology, but she's easy annoyed if ye conter her, so I just said "mebbe," and dropped the subjeck, thankfu' to get away home, and it near ten o'clock.

VII

MISS CELANDINE says I better tell about all the grand places I've seen to fill up the book, like; and, when she heard that I had never been in Holyrood Palace in my life, she said it was scandulous, and she would take me hersel', and look up the catalogue and show me Riccio's blood. Poor young gentleman! Little did he think that he would attrack mair people to view the Royal Palace than mebbe anything else! But "murder will out," as the saying is, and the marks of the bloody deed has lasted well.

But I've been inside a palace afore, mind you.

Me and the young leddies bode in the Palatso Ster-
beeny in Rome for a whilie; it was up a common-
stair—a fearfu' downcome for a palace. Holyrood
is a self-contained house, stony-lookin' baith outside
and in; and draughty, I would jalouse.

The first objecks of interest we notticed outside
was a carving of a king on one side, and a serious-
lookin' fowl with a crown round its neck on the
other; and the first room we went into was the
pictur-gallery. It's a big place, with the portraits
of one hundred Scottish kings on the walls. They
were all pented by the same gentleman—a Mr de
Witte—and he just got two years to finish the job,
piece-work, like. Mebbe that was why he made
them a' much the same in the featurs—blackaviced,
lang-nebbit chiels they were, every one of them.
There was one with a extry thick black wig, and
two wee laddies were standin' starin' up at it when
Miss Celandine and me went forrit. "Sic a heid
o' hair!" says the one to the other, and away they
trotted hand in hand, puir wee lambs. Efter a while
Miss Celandine read out of the catalogue, "The
visitor probably will give but fleeting attention to
this collection," and she said she wished they had
mentioned it sooner, as she was only looking at the
pictures out of politeness, as they seemed to expect
it. But she got two fine names for Tatty's next
kitlings, i.e. Amberkeletus and Dornadilla; I doubt
I'll never be able to mind them. You would think
Dornadilla would be a female; but no' a bit; she
was just a gentleman like a' the rest. We stopped
a wee to look at a likeness of Queen Margaret. She's
no' a bonny woman—her hair wasna nice done, and
her body was yerked awfu' tight; but I understand
she was English, poor thing.

The next place we inspected was the Historical
Departments. Lord Darnley's bedroom had the
broadest bed that ever I saw; I doubt it'll no'

be turned *every* day. The curtains were made of
velvet, trimmed with fringe like withered seaweed—
a thing I never could admire someway. The grates
were outsize, plain black-leaded, but I was gled to
obsairve that they were a' fitted up with coal-saving
apparatusses : coals are an awfy price the now.
The guide-book said, " In the fireplace may be
noted some good Dutch tiles " ; but we couldna note
them without we had brought a telescope with us
on account of a string there was to keep back the
crowd. We noted a pictur of Lord Darnley and his
wee brother, though. They were baith dressed in
pure blacks from head to foot, and, if the pictur did
him justice, Lord Darnley must have been about
nine feet high.

It was in Queen Mary's Audience Chamber that
Miss Celandine went wrong in the catalogue, and
made me feel fair donner'd. When I asked her who
the gentleman depicted in portrait No. 1 was, she
threped down my throat that it was " Jane, Countess of Caithness." " Hoots ! " says I, " it's a man
with a beard." " I can't help that ; No. 1 is
' Jane, Countess of Caithness,' " was all she would
say. No. 3 was a collection of queer-lookin' tickets,
male and female, playin' theirsels on a green, near a
water. " What's No. 3," says I, " if you please ? "
And Miss Celandine finds the place and reads out,
" Lord Sempill ; the Honorable Marion Sempill ;
the Honorable Jane Sempill ; the Honorable
Rebecca Sempill." " Losh keep me ! " says I.
" Such a respeckable faimly ! " Miss Celandine
took a gliff at the pictur, and says she, " Perhaps
they were painted going in to bathe on Joppa sands."
But her attention was arrested, and when she tried
the catalogue at anither page, here did she no' find
that No. 3 was " Nymphs and Satyrs," and no' the
Sempills at all, decent bodies ! It turned out that
she was readin' the catalogue of the Tombs in the

Abbey Church, so she was. I'll no' easy trust her with a catalogue again! Anither sma' oil-pentin' that she informed me was "Mary Dunbar, widow of Lord Basil Hamilton," turned out to be a "Bacchic Scene" when we fand the right place: no' the same thing at all. The Bacchics had ower little on to please me. Not but what there was yairds of good dress material lyin' here and there, as Miss Celandine pinted out ; but what for did they no' put it about them, the gowks !

We were a long time of comin' to Riccio's blood, and, if you'll believe me, it's naethin' but a brass plate now ! The guide-book said there used to be " a dark stain, explained as being that of the Italian's blood," but nae doot it was a heavy expense gettin' it fresh pented every spring, and the brass plate would be mair economical-like. Penters are fair extortioners, that they are. But it was disappintin'. And Queen Mary's bathroom was outside, and no hot and cold water laid on— maist rideeclous !

We saw a great muckle cat playin' in the back-gairden, just like a common pussy, and I couldna help thinkin' that if Queen Mary had keepit a pet cat instead of a snufflin' wee spaniel, her blood would never have been " lapped by a dog," as the poet says.

VIII

MISS CELANDINE says I'm no' to forget to tell about thon war. No' very likely; it was maist annoyin'. I'll mind that Sunday as long as I live. It was a dark day, just *pourin'* wi' rain, and the young leddies came home from the forenoon church in a tacksie, fu' of the news. Appearin'ly the Kayser had cast out wi' mair nor one of his neebours, and it seemed likely that there would be a terrible stramash.

How the newspaper laddies got the news naebody kens, but anyway they were cryin' "Spesh!" the whole Sabbath day till nine at night, a perfeck inbreak on the Ten Commandments; little wonder there was a judgment. The servant lassies (and our Merran in the thick of them) were fleein' out every half-hour to get the latest news, and hearin' that things was gettin' worse and worse for their pains. About eight o'clock at night Miss Jean came daunderin' ben to see how I was bearin' up. I was takin' a read of my Bible to settle my mind like, and I pinted out to her that she would find the whole twenty-six letters of the alphabet, includin' x and z, in the seventh chapter of Ezra, the twenty-first verse. She took a whilie to find the place, but when she got it, she was pleased to see that it was quite correck—they're all there, mixed.

By Monday night His Majesty, King George, answered back, and proclaimed war on the Emperor of Germany—and him his first cousin! But there is folk that can agree better with *onybody* than their ain relations, so there is.

Co-evil with the war there was a fearfu' outbreak of knittin' of every known description—body-belts, kneekeps for Highlanders, cravats, helmets, no less (I aye thought helmets was metallick—mair like dish-covers), and socks by the thousand. And simulatinously there appeared in the *Scotsman* dizens of letters tellin' folk how to make them. And, if you'll believe me, there was a *gentleman* had the assurance to print directions for makin' a flannen body-belt. And how do you think it was to be fastened? "Gather together the loose material, and secure it with a safety-pin!" Did ever you hear such a feckless way of doin'?

The next thing to follow in the footsteps of the war was beads. Never in my born days did I see such an outbreak of beads! I aye thought they were mair parteeclarly conneckit with heathen lands, bein' worn for full dress by the inhabitants thereof. But the Edinbury folk was as keen on them as if they had been born black. The shop-windies was full of them—bead-chains, bead-bags, bead-purses ; wee beads on hats, and big ones round folks' necks —I was fair sick of them afore the war was ended. I'm no' sure whether beady eyes are on the increase or no' ; they used to be looked down upon in my young days ; but mebbe the war's made them quite the thing.

Efter that the short skirts came forrit, and never in my life did I see the likes of thon ! Up and up they rose like the risin' tide, leavin' half the responsibeelity to stockins and shoon. Nae wonder the formers rose to 25s. per pair, and the " foot-wear " (as they ca' boots in the shop-windies the now) was jist as dear. There was one day that I saw Mr Brown, at No. 17, and his lassie that's at the school comin' along the Terrace, and lo ! when they came near, the lassie turned out to be *Mrs* Brown, a grey-haired woman ! They say you canna put old heads on young shoulders, but you can put them on short petticoats, so you can. But I dinna like yon—it's no' needed.

One good effeck of the war was that it brought home Mrs Smith from Jerusalem for a whilie. She came to visit the young leddies for a two-three days, and many a grand story had she to tell. The Turks were sweir to let her away—she's a fine cheery cratur, and usefu'—and naething her freens could say would make them believe that she was a Teacher, or a Religious Order, although, mind you, she's a meenister's widdy, and bound to be mair or less releegious. At long last, when a' hope seemed past, the Turkish authorities decided that mebbe she would come under the headin' of " A Woman," and away she sailed from Jaffa with nae other recommendation ! It was lucky for her that they were right for once.

The first thing she asked for was a Finnan haddy and a bap (it was afore the baps became extinck), and efter that she felt she could enjoy a cracknel biscuit and a gless of Crabbe's green ginger cordial. Puir thing, she had been cut off from thae luckshuries for many a year, and oranges by the dizen will no' make up for the want of them—they're different someway.

IX

I AM about, in this chapter, to relate an incident which was youneek in my career, I'm thankfu' to say. It consisted of me goin' to the Opery, and Miss Celandine was the cause of it. She wanted to see an act they ca' *Fowst*, and Miss Jean no' bein' very well, she set upon me to go with her. She said it would be a warnin' to me no' to encourage the devil, and her too. So we went, mair for her sake than mine's.

The first thing we saw was the curtain—the very same as it was when we went to see *Hamlet*—but mebbe a wee thing dirtier. Then a good few gentlemen in private clothes, carrying fiddles, drums, flutes, sackbuts, salteries, etc., came in below and played a tune till it was time to begin. It was a gey grumblie tune ; I didna think much of it. When the curtain went up, here we sees an auld gentleman sittin' his lee-lane at a table, with a wheen queer-lookin' odds and ends on it. He minded me of the gentleman with the skull that we saw many's the time in Italy, in the pictur-galleries—a connection of the faimly, mebbe. He started to sing a song, withoot waitin, to be asked. " Many years have past me," says he ; but onybody could see that. He seemed annoyed at it, but an auld man like him might have had mair sense nor to let a'body ken what he was thinkin'.

When he had feenished, in flew a queer-lookin' ticket, dressed all in pure reds from head to foot. At first I thought he was meant for a lobster, but Miss Celandine said he was the devil; I've seen a lobster with an agreeabler expression, I will say that; but what I dinna like about fish is that you canna look them straight in the face—they're all profile, so to say.

I omitted to mention that there was a great big hole in the wall of the auld gentleman's room very like the one the mice made at the war, and I was thinkin' it was a peety if he had taken the house on a repairin' lease, when in flew a kind of a tablow. It represented a young leddy workin' a sewin'-machine with her foot. The auld gentleman was fair delighted with it, poor body, and away he went to tell the ither folk to come and see it. The first to arrive was a stout young gentleman dressed all in lilac; it set him no' bad. Miss Celandine said it was the auld gentleman made young; a perfeck haver; he was a full head shorter nor him, and twice as fat. But how could they expeck folk to understan' the story when they never took time to speak plain? No maitter what sort of a stramash was goin' on they aye stood up and sang a song aboot it; just a provoke. Many a time I've heard of sing-songs, but yon cowed a'.

Efter that we saw many a queer sight. Lassies wi' skirts shorter nor the Wacksies (if you'll believe me), and sojers dressed up like dandillies, and idle fellies playin' at the cairds in the very street. And every one of them could sing, mind you; I never heard as muckle street-singin' in my life. There was one felly gave us a song about a lass o' he's, and the bawl he gave at "I love her" was enough to deave a body; and the whole town listening! Miss

Celandine said he had likely been in the Navy as a megafone. If he was, I'll warrant he made thon auld scoundrel Fonnturpy hear on the deefest side o' his heid. I was glad when he went away home.

Efter that we saw a gairden, with a bonny wee house on one side, and a wall at the back, and a door in the wall, and a full moon in the sky. The stout young gentleman in lilac come through the door, and, the meenit he saw the flower-bed, he was that uplifted that he burst out singin'.

"Bounteous nature!" says he, and he lookit at the srubs as if he had never seen the like in his life. Mercy on us! Twa awfu'-like palms, as shankie as mine's, and a sun-flower stuck on one of them, by way of flourish! A young leddy dressed in light blue, with long yelly pleats hangin' down her back, come out of the house to see what he was goin' on about. She was a grand singer, and started the meenit the gentleman stopped to take breath. She was fine at doin' a shake—she minded me of a friend o' mines called Isabella M'Rorie that used to quiver equal to any opery-singer. Her auld faither was awfu' proud o' it. He used to cry, "Quiver, Isabella, quiver!" if she was singin' plain, so he did.

Margareet—that was the young leddy—went in-bye to do her hair. But appearin'ly she couldna see, owin' to the defence of the realm, so out she come to try if the moon was ony better, and she never notticed that the devil and the other young gentleman were stravaigin' about the gairden. "There's a time to gley, and a time to look straught." Miss Celandine says this was the time I fell asleep. I'm no' sure: I mind of seein' gentlemen with drawn swords, and I shut my eyes, for I never could bear the sight of cold steel; and mebbe I dovered for a wee, for the next time I took nottice I saw there was something far wrong. A gentleman was lyin' on the ground, singin' for all he was worth, and the young leddy in

blue was very near on the top of him. There was a
crowd of folk standin' round, askin' what was the
maitter, and no' a pollisman to be got, as usual!
How they settled it, I never made out, but anyway,
when the curtain was drawn up for the last time,
"the scene was changed," as the poetry says.
Appearin'ly the pollis had come forrit efter a', for
the young leddy had been clapped into a prison, in
a clean white nightgown nicely done-up: it would
be afore stairch rose to a perfeckly prohibutive price.
Her painful seetiation didna hinder her from singin'
though—loud and long—and in came the devil and
the stout young gentleman to see what was goin' on.
Then they all three sang turn about, and a' thegither,
and naething would stop them till they let the curtain down right in their faces. And thankfu' was I,
and it on the back of eleven, and the streets like
mirk midnight, and the cab-horse feared to put one
foot afore another, puir beastie! An' as for me
learnin' to resist the devil at the Opery, no' very
likely! *Onybody* would flee from a felly like yon.

X

WE'VE had what they ca' a "Raid" in Edinbury,
and a perfeck bedevilment it turned out to be. It
was on a Sabbath night too; and the Kayser lets on
to be a releegious man! Trust him! We were a'
away to our beds, and here at a quarter to twelve
precise did there no' commence such a bangin', and a
firin', and lightnin' coming down from the skies, and
guns shootin'—you never heard the like. We got
the bairns up (the three wee Lindesays from London
were stayin' with us to avoid raids), and away we
went down to the kitchen. Luckily the fire was in,
and Tatty and the three wee kitlings snorin' and
purrin' in front of it. Miss Celandine christened

them Korah, Dathan, and Abiram on the spot. The London nurse was mad at us for no' havin' a raid-cellar furnished ready. She said she was out of the frying-pan into the fire; and in Cavendish Square they had a commodious furnished cellar, and rugs, and sofies, and a lamp, and an oil-stove, and whisky and soda. But I never lifted her. I just said, dry-like, that we had a coal-cellar in the area, and a wine-cellar ben the house; but, when she saw me puttin' on the kettle to make a cup of tea for the young leddies, etc., she decided to stop where she was. It was just beginnin' to boil when the door opened, and in came Prothisa with her hair hangin' down her back and her eyes fair blind wi' sleep. Miss Jean had tried to waken her, but she was that sound that she thought it was better to let her sleep through it, if she could.

"Has this any connection with the war?" says she, glowrin' round the kitchen fair donner'd.

"Nane whatever," says I, kind-o' sarcastic, "just a sma' evenin' pairty."

With that there came such a bang and a crash that it dumbfoundered every one of us. The London leddy cried, "Ow!" wi' a screigh like a motor-caur; wee Miss Cielle stood in the middle of the floor, and stamped her foot like a fury, and says she, "Surely *we'll* do something now!" Then Kirsty she flew to the windy, and shook her neive at the sky, and bawled, "If I come ti ye I'll sort ye!" the very way I've seen Canongate mithers cryin' to their weans playin' in the gutter eight stories below, and just about as likely to be attended to. Miss Jean sat in my chair, gey white in the face, with Samson on her lap. Poor beastie; every time the bomms went off he whinged maist peetiful, and it was days afore his hair would lie down right. I was standin' petrifeed, with the big teapot in my hand, when I hears a wee soft voice low down (we were a' in the dark except

M

the fire and one caunle) and a wee soft hand touched
my elby, and Master Johneen says, " Would you like
to take my arm, Mrs Pow ? " That bairn aye minds
his mainners ; but when I took his airm, I found he
was just ditherin' wi' cold and fright ; so I hurried
to pour out the tea ; and I gave them a' hot drinks,
and let them help themselves to sugar, and eat far
ower muckle rich cake—and it the middle of the
night !

It was two o'clock the next mornin' or ever we got
away to our beds. The bairns was delighted ; they
had never been up as late in their lives. When Miss
Cielle bade her Auntie Jean good-night she said, " It's
been *nicer* than the Pantomime, because it's been
longer ! " And a' the road upstairs she was singin',
" Two o'clock and I'm not in bed ! "

The first thing we saw the next mornin' was the
doctor's wee blue caur fleein' round the corner, and
the doctor's golden heid shinin' inside like the risin'
sun. She came to see how Miss Jean had stood the
assault of the enemy. She had never been in her
bed hersel', but she had been a good whilie in a
cellar wi' her wee nevvy, Peter, her house bein'
seetiated in the centre of the disturbance. Poor
lambie, he quite enjoyed the variety, and when
there came a sort o' lull in the storm, he lookit up
at his auntie disappinted-like, and says he, " When
will there be another bang ? " And him just new
three year auld !

The English nurse let on to be dissatisfeed with the
raid. She said it was poor compared with the
London performances—no' near sae loud nor sae
long. But she didna make any objections when
she heard she was to go to Kilmorag with the faimly
—no' her—and she's a grand hand at makin' objections in the ordinar way.

In the efternoon Miss Jean advised me to go away
down to Raeburn Place for a wee bit change of air,

and to see how Mrs M'Curd was keepin' efter such
an awfu' night. She was lookin' fine. The folk in
the low flat invited a' the folk above (eight faimlies)
to come aside them for safety. The place was raither
crowded ; but they had a deal of agreeable conversation, and said many a thing they wouldna have
thought of in ordinar circumstances ; I felt that way
mysel'. We had our teas, and then Mrs M'Curd
offered to see me on my road home. We hadna gone
far when I notticed that her skirt was trailin' on the
ground. " What's wrong wi' ye, Eliza ? " I says,
says I. " Your gown's no' right on, surely ! "
" Mebbe I've no' fastened a' the hooks," says she,
and she fum'led round her waist for a whilie. But
when we set off again, it was still trailin' ahint her
like a train. Would you believe that the poor body
had lost a' her hips in a single night ! What with
the fright, and the strain of keepin' up a polite conversation in the mirk, and one thing and another,
she had grown perfeckly thin, and a' her skirts had
to be taken up two and a half inches ! Did you
ever ? And her had struggled for years to keep off
sugar, soup, cheese, and tatties with no visible
effeck ! When I told Miss Jean, she said, " Yet
grew she light, In a single night." That's poetry.

Master Johneen added a wee bittie to his prayers
efter the raid : he took a keek at Miss Jean through
his fingers, and then he said, causually-like, " And
You needn't bother about the Germans : Amen."

We thought when we got to Kilmorag that all
would be peace and goodwill. Naething o' the sort !
Here was a regiment of eleven full-grown sojers at
the pier-heid ! In the daytime they were quiet
enough, taken up wi' fishin', but when the gloamin'
fell they were fair ferocious.

One Sunday night Miss Jean wanted a letter put
in the post, and me and Miss Celandine went along
the road with it. Kirsty warned us that we would

be challenged, and told us what to say; but we forgot all about war, walkin' under the twinklin' stars, by the side of the lapperin' loch. Suddenly there was a fearsome rattle of fireairms, and a sojer cried, " Who goes there ? " and turned a light upon us, fit to blind us. I was struck dumb wi' surprise, but luckily Miss Celandine minded the answer, and " Friends," says she. " Your names ! " cries the airmy gent, fiercer nor ever. Miss Celandine could scarcely speak for laughin', and I thought she would have us both shot dead afore she answered, " Marget Pow and Celandine Murray." " All's well : pass on," says he, and then I minded who he was—the baker's laddie from Kildun ! But war's an awfu' leveller : " Be not a baker if thy head be of butter."

XI

EVER since Mr Askwhich put in the *Scotsman* that folk was respeckfully requested to practise economy, the way that Miss Celandine has carried on has been a fair provoke ! Set him up ! Tellin' *us* to practise economy that has never done onything else ! I would like fine to see into *his* kitchen, so I would.

And here's Miss Celandine sayin' that there's a silver linin' to every cloud, and that she's thinkin' I'll no' be near so likely to die of curvature of the stomach now that food's gettin' scarce. Did ever you hear the like ? And I'm to put water in the cat's milk when she's no' lookin'. But you'll no' cheat Tatty : she just put the end of her nose into it and sneezed, so she did ; and no' anither sup would she take till I put a wee drop cream amongst it. Miss Celandine ca'ed her a " bloated aristocrat," but Tatty never let on she heard her. And then Miss Celandine started to lectur' about the need-cessity of restrictin' the output of kittens—she

thought we would mebbe require to get kitten-cairds
—a perfeck haver. And when I said I would thank
her to get up out of my chair, and no' talk nonsense
(she aye sits in my chair, with Tatty on her lap,
when she comes down to the kitchen), she said she
notticed that I never *did* thank her when I said I
would, and that if all the hairs that Tatty shed on
folks' gowns was carefully collected, they would make
fur-lined coats to the Tommies. She's an awfu'
lassie.

I am no' denyin' that meat's a terrible price ; and
the pennyworth of cream has shrunk to what they
ca' an "irrejuicible minimium" ; and would you
believe that the greengrocer down the water had the
face to ask tenpence for a middle-aged cauliflower ?
Folks will need to caw canny ; but I dinna believe
in a' thae nourishin' soups that the papers say can
be made out of 1 oz. of split peas : "Boil thoroughly
in plenty of cold water ; strain through a colander,
and add pepper and salt to taste " ; no' me.

Miss Celandine has been readin' bits out of the
magazines about "substitutes," and she gave me
the maist awfu' fright the day—my blood fair ran
cold. And what do you think it was all about ?
She saw Tatty (decent cratur) eatin' a plain fly on
the windy-sole, and she gave the maist fearsome
squeel, and fell into my chair, pointin' speechless at
the poor beastie. "Mercy on us, Miss Celandine,"
says I, "what's the maitter wi' ye ? " I says, all in
a tremmle. "It is not generally known," says she,
as cool as you like, "that the common domestic fly,
plain boiled, with a little white sauce, is a perfect
substitute for roast beef." I was fair mad. She'll
have got it out of some of these daft-like books on
the *Nourishment of the Nation*. And she said that
she had notticed a thoughtful-lookin' spider on the
stair that would make a very pretty little *entrée* fried
with breadcrumbs, and a wee bit tomato on its tail.

Merran said that she couldna get on with her work, for Miss Celandine's conversation was makin' her feel the very same way as she does on the steamer, when the water's heisie. So away she went laughin', and no' five minutes syne she put her head in at the door to say that, if we was makin' sandwiches, we would mebbe like to know that a sheet of plain pink blotting-paper, gently soaked in cold water for three minutes, and dried in a kitchen towel, would be found a perfeck substitute for ham, and ordinary mustard might be used. Thenk-ye kindly!

But there's one thing I've notticed mysel'. An old skin hearth-rug with the tail hangin' on to it, and a mouth at the ither end, is a perfeck substitute for the fur things the leddies is wearin' round their necks—what they ca' " Chaste " in the shop windies. Many's the time I've wondered if they just lift the mat and put it about them when they're goin' outbye.

Miss Celandine's been out for a pound of apples for the curry, and she was wantin' to explain how I could do fine without them; but I just told her, there and then, that I was for no more of her savings and substitutes. So she sat very quiet for a whilie, and then she says, solemn-like, " Well, there's one thing for which I cannot find a substitute—no; not even an *im*perfect one."

" That's peculiar," says I dry-like; " and what might that be ? "

" It's just dear old Marget Pow," says she; and with that she bounced out of the chair, and upset the cat, and flung her arms about my neck, and fair choked me with kisses.

Miss Celandine is an awfu' lassie, but she has a kind of a way with her, too.

XII

Now that fightin's sae highly recommended, Miss Celandine's determined that she'll be mairried on a sojer. It was first a Cardinal she was wantin' (that was when we were in Rome); then she lifted her love to a Bassaleery, but she didna get him, I'm thankfu' to say. Since then she's just been lookin' round, like. But now she's announced that she's *set* to get a man afore she's a quarter-of-a-century old, and it's a sojer she's after—a private—naething else will content her. As a kind of first step she's told all the left-tenants, captains, kurnels, etc., that comes to the house that naething above a sargent need apply. Secondly, she goes to a meetin' conneckit with the church, and pours out tea, and sings hymns out of the same book as a Highlander—Black Watch. Nae doubt it'll be " Onward Christian Soldiers "; but he doesna seem to be very oncomin', for he's never been in the house yet, although we've had a good few douty swanes here at their teas.

Merran's away to make munitions. I dinna ken rightly what they are, but if they're as tough as her scones they'll do; and her currant-dumplin's were mair like bullets nor anything else. But I doubt it's just a first step to matrimony. We've got a lassie ca'ed Prothisa Black in her place; she's from Fife. But she'll have to be learnt everything, so we've engaged Mrs Shankie to come twice a week. She's a charwoman really, but she never admits it; she aye says she's goin' out " to oblige a lady." Mebbe that's what makes her feel no' sae obligated to exert hersel'. But she's a cheery body—just one eye and two teeth—and, naitrally, her man's a sojer. In private life he's a mason, though, when he's workin' —but that's no' very often. When I heard that he had been away to the war for a week, I says to Mrs

Shankie, " You'll be missin' your man," says I.
" Ugha," says she, grudgy-like, and then she gied a
hearty laugh, and she says, " But och, ye soon get
accustomed to it ! " I minded efter I spoke, that
onybody that had been habitted with Mr Shankie's
presence would get easy enough reconsiled to his
absence, and so I asked her if he had gone to the
Front yet. " No' him," says she scornfully ; " he's
just aye manewverin' about the country, pittin' aff
time."

The next day Mrs Shankie came, I thought she
looked awfu' dowy, and she wasna long of lettin' out
why. " He's back ! " says she. " Mercy on us ! "
says I, " what for is he back already ? " So she
tellt me that it was his feet that had brought him
back, for they were that way blistered that he
couldna walk. And what do you think was the
cause o' the disaster ? The poor felly had on a
pair of socks a kind leddy had knitted for him, and
here had she no' put a piece of po'try that she made
up hersel' in the inside of one of them ! Mr Shankie
never notticed it till he was on the march, and it
rumpled up inta a wee hard ba', and he walked on
till he was a perfeck lameter. I thought it would
mebbe be a kind of prayer, and I wondered when
Mrs Shankie said it was advisin' him no' to run away
from the German hens. " They'll be wild, the hens
thonder, will they no' ? " says she. I tried to mind
seein' hens goin' about in Germany, but, as far as I
could recolleck, they were a' cooked when they got
my length. So she recited the po'try, which was as
follows :

> God bless the folks,
> That wears these socks,
> And may they never run
> Before a German hen.

" Hoots, wumman ! " says I, " it'll be ' Hun ' : hens
are that nervous it's no' very likely that they would

attack a big man like Maister Shankie, and him armed from head to foot ! "

She's ill to convince—dour-like—and she wanted to thriep down my throat that Hun was the German for a hen ; and I couldna say but what it *might* be, for there's naething too queer for foreigners to ca' the plainest things, but it'll be a warnin' to Kirsty and Prothisa no' to be puttin' papers of *no* sort in the socks they're kniittn' for sojers ; poor fellies ! they've enough to put up wi' withoot that.

XIII

THE day Miss Celandine and me inspected Holyrood Palace we came home up the steep brae that ends opposeed Regent Terrace. It's a kind of a gairden, and we sat down on a seat to get a bit rest. There was a good few bairns playin' about, and Miss Celandine was that diverted listenin' to their conversation that she wrott it all down when she got home. She says I'm to put it in here, and I'm to call it " War News : delayed in transmission," because the wee bairn that started the discussion had a heavy stammer.

No. 1 (*two feet high by two and a quarter broad, comfortably seated on damp grass ; bursting with information, but impeded by defective utterance*).—" Ma faither is a—is a—is a tellitolial."

No. 2 (*with inexplicable bitterness*).—" He is no' ! "

No. 1.—" He is so."

No. 2 (*with positive fury*).—" He is no', I'm tellin' ye ! "

(*Complete collapse of No. 1, and sudden cessation of hostilities.*)

No. 3 (*tactful young lady, breaking an awkward silence*).—" Mine's lays mines in the sea."

No. 2 (*sceptically*).—" Whit kin' o' mines ? "

No. 3.—" Jist mines."

No. 2.—" What for ? "

No. 3.—" Jist for mines."

No. 2.—" Where dis he put them ? "

No. 3.—" Thonder " (*pointing vaguely in the direction of the North Pole*).

No. 2.—" Havers ! "

No. 1 (*arousing suddenly from a state of lethargy*). — " Ma faither — ma faither — ma faither is a tellitolial."

No. 2.—" Yur a leear ; he's a fruiter."

(*Repulse and temporary withdrawal of No.* 1.)

No. 3 (*more tactful than ever*).—" Puir wee tot ; she means a ' torryterrial.' Div ye no', dearie ? "

CHORUS (*as one man*).—" She dis nut ! "

No. 4 (*in a superior tone*).—" My daddy has gone away to fight."

ELIPHAZ, THE TEMANITE (*with gloomy satisfaction*). —" He'll get killed."

No. 4 (*cheerfully*).—" Ugha ; he's a preservist."

ELIPHAZ (*unconsciously associating ideas*).—" He's a sweet yin. Whae's he gaun tae fecht wi' next ? "

No. 4 (*airily*).—" I dinna mind his name the now ; he's a Jairman gentleman."

No. 3.—" His name's Kayser, but they call him ' Ananias ' for a by-name ; it's in the papers."

ELIPHAZ (*as one reminded of an old friend*).—" Oh ay, Ananias ; I mind him in the Testament ; he was an awfu' leear, and they wound him up and carried him out and buried him."

No. 4.—" Ay, that's him ; I kenned he was a Jairman gentleman."

ELIPHAZ (*not without hope*).—" He'll get killed too if he disna watch hissel' ; he's no' ower particular what he says whiles."

No. 1 (*who has been husbanding wind for a final effort*).—" Mafaither'satellitolial ! "

No. 2.—" Aw, haud yer whisht, Jaisie; ye're a prood wee besom."

No. 6 (*elderly young lady, whose hair is tied up with wilted crape*).—" My father has gone to heaven."

> (*Horror-struck silence, followed immediately by disorderly retreat of the entire company, dragging the daughter of the Territorial in the rear, singing, " in accents of that unknown tongue," something which sounded like " Lool Bedania.*")

When the bairns were a' away home Miss Celandine and me sat quiet a whilie enjoyin' a fine view of the Canongate, includin' the kirk and the kirkyaird. We read in the guide-book that " the ancient motto which is graven round the figure of King David's stag bearing the Holy Rood upon the burgh seal was *Sic itur ad astra*, meanin', ' This Way to the Stars.' " Seemingly they had the motty in their minds when they built the houses, they're that high !

We got into the Portobella caur near the jail, no' many folk bein' in it. There was a stoutish leddy sittin' next to me with one o' these wee dogs they ca' Peekineases in her airms. Appearin'ly it was sufferin' from cronick bronkitties, it was breathin' that heavy, and its eyes was fair startin' oot of its heid, puir wee cratur.

A decent-lookin' woman came in with a laddie about five year old. The bairn was awfu' taken up with the animal, and efter starin' steadily at it for a whilie, he turned to his maw, and says he, " Mither, that's a *dug* ! " " Ye're no' to say ' dug,' " says she, affrontit-like. " It's no' ' dug,' it's ' *doag*.' " " ' Doag,' " says the bairn, real biddable ; and then he lookit up in his mother's face, and says he, " But it's *like* a dug." And that's just about as much as onybody could say for it, thinks I to mysel'.

XIV

WE'RE told in the Scriptures that we're to take no
thought what we're to eat nor what we're to drink,
but it takes a lot of gentlemen to control the food
appearin'ly! But I must say they're thorough:
there's no' a day passes but what they change one
thing or another. If it's a shilling's worth one week,
it's tenpence the next, and there was a whilie it was
one-and-three, no less! There's a chief Live Stock
Commissioner—he's name is Mr M'Dougall; and
no sooner are the puir beasties killed but they need
a Dead Meat Supervisor to attend to them—Hunter,
he's ca'ed. Then there's a Chief Meat Agent, but
I'm no' sure what kind o' meat that'll be—beef and
mutton likely. Three gentlemen ca'ed Divisional
Food Commissioners come next: they'll cut it up.
And that's no' the whole o' them; there's five
more! But it's an awfu' work to feed the whole
nation by hand, like. They've never made out to
control the fish seemin'ly, for it's a fearsome price:
it's kind o' slippit through their fingers mebbe.

I could get on fine masel' if it wasna for the meat
cairds, and parteeclarly the instructions. But what
with fillin' in name and address at E, and syndin'
it; "also at B overleaf"; and makin' the butcher
attend to C and D, it's a fair provoke. And Miss
Celandine's been pointin' out to me that it says on
the back that if I die or join the forces the caird
must be returned *at once* to the nearest post office,
or dropped in a pillar-box. Set them up! And me
dead! But she says she'll do it hersel' if I'm no'
able: she's a sensible lassie. She's new come home
from the Front. Her uncle, the general, got her a
place in a hospital "somewhere in France," as the
ministers that writes letters to the papers ca's it.
She was to be an orderly! Sad's her fate! I could

have told them she never could mind to put a thing in the right place. But they keepit her for six month, and then she heard that the Wacks had skirts a full inch shorter nor hers, and home she came post-haste to join *them*. She said she preferred kiltie regiments, and her faither was a kiltie, and the neatest thing about her was her ancles ; and so now she's one of the lassies she ca's " the wee Wacksies," so she is. But she often runs in to see Miss Jean, and me, and Tatty, and the kitlings : she sits on the edge of the kitchen-table, sweein' her legs, and lets on to be helping me with the meat caird, etc. We just need four o' them now that Merran's mairried, but, if you'll believe me, here anither yella paper come this very day ! " Application for Ration Books " is the name o' it. There's " Read Carefully " at the top, and when you've read 1*a* and 2*b*, and a' the rest of the directions, you'll mebbe find out that there's no' a thing about you in it. But what between lodgers, and bairns, and temp'ry visitors, and laddies under eighteen at mid-night, and boys born between midnight 30th June 1900, and ditto 1905 (there'll be a good few o' them !), and persons *normally* livin' in the house, it's perfeckly bewilderin'. There's a bit about " cows belongin' to any member of the household " ; but there's none o' us keeps cows or sheep, I'm thankfu' to say. Miss Celandine says that, for rationing purposes, Tatty would probably come under the heading of Household Cow. A perfeck haver ; but Miss Celandine is aye on the nonsense. She's been tellin' me that there's to be an exhibition of a' the folk with what she ca's " the slightest pretensions to ombongpong," and me and Mrs M'Curd'll be in the front row ! She's a daft lassie, and whiles I'm thankfu' when she has to rin away back to her work and give me peace to do mines.

I thought she was away this morning, when back

she come and stuck her head in at the kitchen-door, and says she, solemn-like, " Jean wishes to know if you subtract two stroked coupons from one plain one how much more meat can we have this week ? " I was tryin' to add it up, but I never was good at the countin', and I was thankfu' when she said she couldna bide anither meenit.

The shoppin' takes a fearfu' time. If you see a thing you're needin', you'll mebbe think you've just to go in and buy it ? My certy ! They look at you up and down, and round and round, and then the lassie behind the counter goes away to the back of the shop to consult wi' anither gentleman, and back she comes and says, " *No jam*," and it starin' you in the face in the windy ! A leddy was tellin' me that " the highest authority " is just anither name for Ananias : but there's mair Annaniasses nor him, I'm thinkin', parteeclarly in the grocer line. The very tea is ca'ed a drug now, if you please— " comes under the Drug Act "—and you might just as weel ca' the whole of the substitutes " shams " and be done with it. Here's Miss Celandine back ! She says the Government is going to release a large quantity of Giraffe tripe, and does it come under the heading of " offal " or " onnal " ?

I'm awa' out.

XV

WE'VE had a grand supper-pairty for Tommies, accompanied with tea and coffee. There was twenty-three sojers includin' a Naval gentleman that got hissel' invited on account of bein' a kind of cousin o' the young leddies. Miss Celandine introjuiced me to the Black Watch corporal she's been pourin' out tea for at the kirk. He's a tall felly, no' bad lookin', but what for do they make

their kilts sae scrimpy ? The front width would
need a full quarter o' a yaird mair in it to be respectable, so it would. But there's plenty of material
in the pleats, and the way they keep them flat is
wunnerful. I notticed that Miss Celandine didna
say the corporal's name ; but the queer thing was
that I kent his face, although I never saw him afore !
And there was a kind-o' glimmer of his name in
my heid, every time I looked at him, although I
couldna mind it right—it was what they ca' a " high-
fennated " name like Finnan-Haddock or Graham-
Murray—but no' just exackly either the one or the
other.

Efter the supper was past we had music baith
vocal and instrumential. The corporal gave us a
song to a real bonny tune. Miss Celandine says
the first verse was :

> Call me while the lark is sleeping,
> Ere Flora fills her dewy cup ;
> The festive beetle homeward creeping
> Before the early worm is up.

He'll be a good riser, likely. But Miss Celandine's
the very opposeed. She's a grand sleeper ; it's an
awfu' work to get her up.

The Naval gentleman gave us the true history of
the entrance of Liberia into the war—no' *Siberia*,
that's a different place a'thegither. The way of it
was as follows, namely : When His Majesty's ships
went away to Africky (what to do they ken best
theirsels), in course of time they came to the place
ca'ed Liberia. And the Admiral, bein' a real sociable
gentleman, invited the President and a twa-three
mair to come to their dinners on board his ship. So
they came, sure enough ; and efter the dinner, the
ship's band played to them. They were grand
players, and the President liked it fine. The next
day came a message to the Admiral to say would he

allow the band to come ashore and play to the people
of Liberia on dry land. So away they went in a
sma' boat, airmed with brass instruments, one each,
and a man wi' a drum forbye. You'll mebbe have
heard that " Music has charms to soothe a savage
breast " ? Well, if you'll believe me, the band
played that soothingly to the Liberian Nation that
they declared war on Germany there and then !
Little did the Kaiser think that such an innocent-
like thing as a tune or two would cook his goose
with the Republic of Liberia ! But you never can
tell.

Efter that we had a fine cheery song with a chorus.
I dinna mind the name o't, or the tune either, for
I'm gey like the man you've heard tell of that didna
ken " God save the weasel " from " Pop goes the
King " : but the gentleman sang it beautiful. Then
we got a grand surprise. The corporal coaxed a
wee drummer-laddie to give us a recitation (it seems
he's celebrate for it), and here did he no' stand up
and repeat Miss Celandine's Poem from beginnin' to
end ! I'll put it in here, for she'll be pleased to see
it in print, and it's no' likely she'll get an Editor to
take it. She's tried mair nor once, and they aye
send it back with compliments :

I looked far back into other years, and lo ! my wistful gaze
Descried, as in a dream, a butcher's shop of pre-war days.

It was a stately edifice with windows left and right,
A plate-glass door stood open, and within, oh, what a sight !
Ox after ox, and sheep on sheep, were hanging in a row,
While cutlets, and a nice lamb's head, lay smiling down below.
Oh ! for the sirloins that were there ! and oh ! the juicy chop !
It was a dream—but *what* a dream—a pre-war butcher's shop.
A lady entered on the scene—a fair and well-fed dame ;
The civil butcher, swift to serve, gave welcome to the same :
And with her came a tall brown dog that sniffed about the floor,
And found some bits of suet there, and fondly looked for more.
" A middle cut," the lady said, "well-hung ; about ten pounds."
Such was the word she spake, and sweet to memory it sounds.

The scene was changed.—It was a shop with one small lonely roast,
A pot of ferns, some sausages, and twelve eggs at the most :
And puddings black and white were there, and potted head so cold,
A small (but most expensive) hen, and a bunny uncontrolled.
With slow, reluctant step there came a lady through the door ;
She seemed, somehow, to feel as if her shopping were a bore.
The butcher was preoccupied ; the lady had to wait ;
And when, at last, her turn arrived, she truly was irate.
" Well, Mr Smith," she boldly cried, " were I but once more free
From registration's hated bonds, I'd leave thy shop and thee !
These coupons would I scatter wide to every breeze that blows——"
She paused for breath ; and what she got for dinner, goodness knows.

The scene was changed.—Not very much ; still whitewashed were
        the walls,
And still the floor was saw-dusty, where soft the footstep falls ;
The potted head was going strong, the ferns were growing green,
The eggs were just like pre-war eggs, the beef was red and lean.
And yet once more that lady came (the same that came before),
And, at her heels, the same brown dog that scavengered the floor.
I knew that queenly form again, though ravaged of its fat ;
I knew the face ; I knew the hair ; I also knew the hat ;
I knew the voice—the voice with which she argued with her foe—
I knew a lot—but I admit the end I did *not* know.

The scene was changed. (But stay ! methinks I mentioned that
        before,
It almost seems I may have heard those words in days of yore.)
With trembling voice the lady spake, " How much have I to get ? "
The clerkess, with a haughty toss, said, " One and twopence yet."
" Then I might have a bone for soup " (the lady thought aloud) ;
" Or else a pound of tripe." Alas ! she was no longer proud.
The butcher found a marrow-bone, to lay before the dame :
She gazed on it with loving eyes ; her mastiff did the same—
Then made one dash, secured the prize, and bolted by the door—
The bone was gone ! Gone to return, ah ! never, *never* more !

Snatch'd by a dog ! Go think of it in silence and alone ;
Then weigh against a pound of tripe the glories of a bone !

XVI

PEACE broke out suddenly on the eleventh of
November 1918, and upset all our prayers. At first
it was just what they ca' an " armistice "—a kind of

a substitute for peace—but we're habitted wi' substitutes now, and it did no' that bad. The real thing began at the Midsummer Term, on a fine dry day. The folk crowded to the kirks to give thanks, and to hear what the ministers had to say on the subjeck. Would you believe that there was a kew standin' outside the church round the corner ? Me ! I wouldna stand in a kew to hear *ony* man preach : I canna abide thae luminaries. But I went with the young ladies to the church they worship in, on a Thursday—just to encourage them, like. It was well filled, I will say that, but just you bide a wee, and I'll warrant you'll get a pew to yoursel', and one for your umberelly. We started with singin' " God save our gracious King." I've heard thon tune afore. But I never heard a drum thumpin' and rum'lin' along with it ! It's no' needed—just a caper. Efter that there was a good few prayers, and then the minister gave out a hymn. I dinna mind the words—the hundred and oddths it was—and efter that came the sermon. I was gled to get a sit down. But the music was no' near done : there was anither set-to *efter* the sermon. Two laddies sang a song ca'ed " O Lovely Peace," and if they said it once, they said it twenty times. But they didna get started baith thegither, someway, and the wee one was just at " O " when the ither one was singin' " O lovely, *lovely* peace," over and over again till the wee yin could make up on him. But they managed to stop at the same time, poor wee fellies, so they did.

At the very end of the worship, when the collection had been gathered, and a', here did they no' sing what they ca' the Tedium ! It was a bonny tune, too ; but I was like to drop, and thankfu' was I when it ended, and we got away home to our dinners.

The end of the war was the sign for a grand outbreak of faimly affection in high circles. Compli-

ments have been fleein' in every direction ; but the
Germans are no' speakin'—no' yet anyway : there's
a kind o' a dryness between them and a good few
ither folks.   But the rest o' the nations are a' for
peace and goodwill, includin' Americky.   It minds
me of the old song about Queen Victoria going to
pay a visit to the King of France :

> And syne he kissed her on ae cheek,
> And syne upon the ither ;
> And he ca'ed her his sister dear,
> And she ca'ed him her brither.

There's been a deal o' that kind of carry-on ; I just
hope it'll last.

Miss Celandine says she heard the ghost of a
German band last Setterday night ; but I doubt it
was just the Salvation Airmy, takin' a tune to
theirsels.   " There's as good fish in the sea as ever
came out of it," but the latters is easier come by.

One of the queer things that were brought forrit
by the war was a Tank-bank ca'ed Joolian.   Miss
Jean got me persuaded to put five pound in it ; but
if there's a thing I canna abide it's goin' to a bank,
parteeclarly since yon time I got stuck in the
whirligig at the door.   What for can they no' make
things mair convenient ?   Half of the gentlemen that
transack the business are cocked that high up that
the maist ye can see of them is the crown o' their
heids, and ye can only see that from a distance, like.
An ordinar-sized woman like me has to stand on her
toes to get the pass-book hoisted up to them, and ye
never ken if it's the right man that's got it or no'.
And when they're done with it they take good care
to hand it over just when you're no' lookin' ; and
then they tap with it on the top of the wall ; it's
maist annoyin'.

The ither gentlemen that sit ahint a counter very
near as broad as it's long are just about as bad : but

you can *see* them—I will say that. But it's mebbe no' a'thegither advantageous, for they can see you; and they like fine to see you tryin' to push a pound-note over a slope of polished wood like Greenland's icy mountains. And they watch you countin' your money wrong; and they cry directions to you, and pint out the wee mistakes you make, for the whole bank to hear. And if you dinna understan', they come out of their compartment and speak to you outside the counter—a perfeck affront. But I didna go to Joolian mysel': Miss Jean put in my money for me, and thankfu' was I.

XVII

WE'VE had Duncan M'Neil to see us. He's leavin' the Army through lossin' his airm at the Front, and he's got the promise of a pension, but he'll have to fill up the form first.

It's no' easy fillin' up a form; I've aye kent that. No' that I've had muckle to do with it mysel'; but syne I used to get a money-order through the post, and I never could mind whether it was me that was the " payee " (as they ca' it) or the ither man. Poor felly! I lent him five pound twenty-nine year ago come Martinmas. He just needed it for a month, he said, or mebbe no' sae long, as a temp'ry accommodation like. But he's never made oot to get it a' paid back yet. He's very likely dead and buried by this time. But, if he is, he never let on.

It's no' me, though, that's got a form to fill up the now—it's Duncan, and he's terribly taken up about it, for anither sojer has been tellin' him a' the questions he'll need to answer, and he's feared he'll loss his pension if he canna pass the examination right.

I gave him a good tea to hearten him; and Miss

Jean and Miss Celandine came ben to see him : he was gairdner's boy at the Old House when the young leddies was just bairns.

" What kind of questions do they ask, Duncan ? " says Miss Jean ; " they surely won't be so very difficult to answer ? "

" No' difficult, mem ! " says Duncan, wi' a kind-o' a snort—" no difficult ! The very first yin is ' date of marriage ' ! Figure that ! ' Date of marriage ' ! It's like their impidence ! "

" Ye dinna mean to tell me, Duncan M'Neil," says I, " that ye dinna mind when ye was mairried ?"

" Och ay ; I ken fine when I was mairret," he says ; " it was the year efter the hen-house at the Manse was pented green " (Duncan was a penter to his trade); " but if ye think that'll serve *them*, wumman, ye're muckle mista'en. Rab Thamson tellt me that naething less than the exack day and the exack month 'ull satisfee *them*—set them up ! "

" Was it winter or summer ? " says Miss Celandine, tryin' to look awfu' intelligent.

" I dinna mind. I was pourin' wi' sweat," says Duncan, cast-down like.

" Then it was summer ! " cries Miss Celandine, quite triumphant.

" It was naething o' the sort, mem " (it's little use contradickin' Duncan M'Neil) ; " it was a cold sweat. Ye'll mind that Leeby but to be mairret in the Peliscumpalian Church on the ither side of the Loch ? Weel, no suner was I standin' afore the meenister, and Leeby by my side, than he up and says (efter a few introductory remarks), ' Willst thou have this woman to be thy wedded wife ? ' says he, loud out, an' a' the folk in the kirk listenin'. ' Weel, sir,' says I, ' ye see Leeby's that set on it '—and I was preparin' to gie him the real facks o' the case, when Leeby gave me the maist awfu' dunch wi' her elby, and, says she, in a fearsome whisper, ' Say " I

will " to the gentleman.' So I said ' I will '; and,
no' five meenits efter, the meenister said, 'I per-
nounce thee to be Man and Wife.' I aye kent that
I was a Man ; and weel I wot that Leeby would
never rest till she was a Wife ; but he needna have
made it the clash of the countryside, and I was
pourin' wi' sweat, summer or no' summer."

"And what is the next question ? " says Miss
Jean ; she's aye sympathisin'.

"Weel, mem, they start on the bairns next, and
they need to know a' their names, and when every
yin o' them was born."

I would have thocht ony man would have re-
membered when his first-born was put into his airms ;
but no' Duncan M'Neil.

"Jamie's the oldest," says I, to give him a lift,
like. But the maist he would say was that anyway
Jamie was born afore any of the rest : he's cautious.
He minded his oldest lassie's name easy—it's Maggie
—and he was sairtain she was older then Leeby (she's
the third) ; but they needna try to get exack dates
out o' Duncan, nor names either : he's yin o' thae
folk that canna mind them.

However, efter he had thocht a whilie, he re-
colleckit perfeckly that the fourth o' them—there's
sieven a'thegither—was either a lassie or a laddie ;
and the twins was the next two ; and he couldna
mind exackly when *they* were born, but it was either
before or efter Leeby got her black silk, and about
the same time that Jamie had the fit. And it was
efter Tit (they ca' the twins Tit and Tat for bye-
names) got the better of the wheezles that the Baby
cam' forrit ; and he's name is Duncan ; and he was
born no' that long ago. So, efter a', if they put in
the parteeculars that Mr M'Neil mentioned, the form
will no' be empy : it'll do him credit, so it will.

XVIII

I'M gettin' raither uneasy about Miss Celandine and the corporal in the kilt. He's been comin' to the house, and they're ower chief now for my taste. There was one night, no' long syne, when he took ten meenits by the kitchen-clock to say good-bye. And when I went upstairs, causually-like, here was the corporal standin' starin' at a pictur on the wall ; and Miss Celandine with her back to him gazin' at the lobby-clock for a' she was worth. " You may weel look at the clock, Miss Celandine," says I ; " it's past ten, and if the gentleman doesna hurry he'll be clappit inta irons the meenit he gets back to the Barracks, so he will."

" But I've got an extension of leave to-night, Mrs Pow," says he, real pitiful-like. " I'm off to the Front to-morrow, you know."

" Weel," says I, " you're jist like a' the rest— ' Give them a fish and they'll take a whale,' as the proverb says," and, with that, I bad him good-bye, and left the two their lane.

I didna see Miss Celandine again that night, but the next mornin' I thought I would give her a warnin', so I told her a story I heard about a corporal's wife. I dinna mind right what the beginnin' o't was, but I think she was likely applyin' for something that sojers' wives was entitled to. And the gentleman says to her, " Your husband is a corporal, isn't he ? " " Corporal ! " says she, wi' a perfeck bawl. " I dinna ken whether he's a corporal, or a wastrel, or a mongrel, but I ken fine he's a scoundrel ! "

But Miss Celandine's no' easy turned, and she jist gave a bit laugh. Then I pinted out the perils of war, and read her out a bit that a Chaplain wrote, namely : " The life of the soldier is one of great hardship ; not infrequently mingled with moments of real danger."

But she didna lift me, and " He that winna be coun-
selled canna be helped." It's queer, though, that I
never see the kilty corporal without bein' minded of
somebody I've seen somewhere, and there's a name
comes inta my mind like " tumty-tumty," so it does.
Mrs M'Curd thinks he'll likely turn out to be a Prince
in disguise ; she's romantic whiles, is Eliza.

There's been a great furory about garden-plots
lately owin' to the fearsome price of pitaties and
ither vegetables. Miss Celandine's got one at Comely
Bank, and she's real proud of it. She had me hauled
away down to the foot of the Orchard Brae to see it.
The cabbages was the most prominent featur of the
display—the shanks of them are that long that they
minded me of stunted palm-trees ; and the tatties
are wee, *wee*. But Miss Celandine is quite pleased,
and we had a work to keep her from goin' " on the
land," as they ca' it. She was mad when she fand
out that the Agricultural Leddies had no skirts whatever—just top-boots and peenies—she was sairtain
she would have set the costume fine. But the worms
and the ear-wigs put her aff it ; she canna bide them
—parteeclarly the latters ; she flees at the sight of
them. It's wonderfu', mind you, to see what an
effeck uniforms has upon the female mind. Mebbe
now they've got them theirsels they'll no' think so
much of them on the menfolk. There's all sorts—
blue, and yella, and grey, and a bonny shade the
same as the Fleein' Corpse, and buttons by the
dizen, and wee jaikets and long jaikets. But there's
one thing they've a' got the same, *i.e.* skirts like
kilts ! Many's the time I've thought on Emily, the
young leddy in *The Fairchild Family* that broke the
whole ten commandments as a warnin' to ither
bairns. She was mebbe the worst of the lot—the
sort of rake of the faimly—and when she was
goin' the pace (at the age of twelve or thirteen),
here did she no' get a new frock " fully displaying

the ancles." *Ancles!* Her grandchildren are likely
fully displayin' their knees, and naebody either up
or down! But Emily didna get off so easy. As
far as I mind, she fell inta the pig-stye when she was
caperin' on the wall, showin' off her ancles, and I'll
warrant her skirt was let down two or three inches
efter that.

But there's an awfu' odds on books for bairns
now: they're no' near sae serious, and the picturs
are bonnier. I just had three wee bookies when I
was a lassie, and I've got them yet. They belanged
to my mither afore me, so they're no' exactly modern.
The one the young leddies liked the best when they
were wee was ca'ed *The Little Monitor, or Good
Examples for Children: Calculated to Form Their
Minds, and Lead Them to Virtue*. I'm no' sae sure
about formin' their minds, but many's the laugh
they had at the stories. They were peculiarly
sudden-like. The one ca'ed " Temperance " starts
wi' the words: " Oh! what beautiful fruits and
what nice wine on the sideboard! Yet these aimiable children ate nothing but dry bread. It was
mamma's order, and she was imprudent in exposing
her children to such temptation." " That's one for
' mamma,' " Miss Celandine aye says, when she's
readin' to the little Lindesays: it's queer what fond
they are of the " Miffis Pow books," as they ca'
them. When it comes to "Aminta is a little glutton,"
they crowd round their auntie, cryin', " Let's see
Aminta! " and then they roar and laugh at the
pictur; and little wonder! Aminta's nose and
mouth and chin are jet-black; I doubt she had been
at the treacle, instead of confinin' hersel' to dry
bread like the ither " aimiable children." And I
dinna think Pussyfoot would think much of a story
ca'ed " Temperance " bein' illustriated with a pictur
of two quart bottles of wine—no' him!

There's a story ca'ed " Courage," and it starts

just the same sudden way, as follies : " Francis and Amelia were on the water in a boat, which their parents, by mistake, had left in their way." " That's right—blame the parents ! " cries Miss Celandine ; and then she asks the bairns all round where ought the parents to have put the boat ? And she ends with tellin' them " on the top shelf of the wardrobe in the back bedroom."

" Modesty " is a great favourite with the children —no' the virtue exackly ; I doubt it's ower auld-fashioned for the present day—but the story. It begins wi', " These are little Charles and Louisa, whom they are crowning." " They " is an auld gentleman in a black suit like skin-tights ; nae doubt it would be the fashion then ; but he's no' a nice-lookin' gentleman.

The two other wee books is *The Book of Beasts for Young Persons*, beginnin' wi' an elephant—no' a sootable pet for young persons at all ; and *Twenty-Eight Divine Songs for the Use of Children*. The best known one is, " How doth the little busy bee," but, as Miss Celandine aye mixes it up with " Delight to bark and bite," Lady Lindesay says the bairns is no' to be learned it wrong.

The last time Miss Celandine gave me the " Miffis Pow books " to put back in my kist, she says to me, " Take good care of them, for I know my children will enjoy them immensely—especially the twins ! " Did you ever ?

XIX

It's naitral when folk are gettin' on in life to look back and ponder on the wonderfu' changes that has come to pass in the last fifty years or thereabout. There's hardly a shop left in Princes Street, Edinburgh, but what has been altered and renuviated

since first I set foot in the town ! And I'm thankfu'
to say that they've discontinued a'thegither the habit
of drownin' witches in the Nor' Loch. But I mind
an auld body at Carldoddie tellin' me, when I was a
lassie, that when she was goin' to her first place in the
town, here did she no' land at the West End at the
very meenit when a crowd of folk was tryin' to drown
a witch ! It was an awfu' reception to get. It's
a mercy that witches appears to be extinck now ;
and there's naethin' left of the Nor' Loch but a
fountain that lets out a whiffle of water nows and
thens, when there's grand folk bidin' in the town, and
the man that attends to the water happens no' to be
on strike. But mercy me ! there's no' a workman of
no sort, from waiters to grave-diggers, but what takes
a bit strike to theirsels when they're that way inclined. Appearin'ly work's no' the blessin' it used
to be considered. And what with some shops shuttin'
airly on Tuesday ; and ithers closin' at one 'clock
on Wednesday ; and the lave o' them puttin' up the
shutters on Setterday efternoon, it's a fair torment
to get your shoppin' by. I'm aye thankfu' now when
Christmas is past—the shops are that throng. It's
mair kept in Scotland nor what it used to be when I
was young. We aye kept Singin'-e'en in Fife, and
New Year's Day, but there was no' muckle nottice
taken of Christmas. Then all of a suddent Christmas
cairds came forrit, and Christmas presents. Ye'll
see the shop-windies just crammed wi' shortbread
cakes with grand devices on them made o' sugar.
" Ye ken wha frae " is a favourite motty ; but the
folk that sends their freends that style takes good
care to put a wee bit paper inside to tell that it was
them that sent it. It's as weel to " mak' siccar," as
the Black Douglas said.

But it wasna till I was at Brighton for Christmas
time that I kent how it was kept in England. Lady
Lindesay had a furnished house in Chesham Place,

and me and the young leddies paid her a visit. We
arrived a full fortnight afore Christmas Day, but the
carol-singin' had begun, and it went on, mair or less,
till Christmas Eve. One company of singers would
come in at the top end o' the street bawlin', " 'Ark
the errol aingils sing," and anither set would come up
from the seaside singin', " Wile shepherds watched
their flocks by night," and when they met in the
middle of the street, just about opposeed our house,
there was the maist awfu' rippat ! The way they
argle-bargled and scandaleezed one another was
fearsome. And thankfu' were we to pour oil on the
troubled waters in the form of coppers.

Then there was folk that played on cornets, flutes,
salteries, etcintera, and they played no' that bad ;
but the tune was gruesome. They aye came when
I was in my bed, and tooted away that slow and
waesome that it gave me a melancholy sinkin' in
the inside of me, so it did. At the hinder end I
askit Miss Jean if she kent what the tune was
ca'ed, and she said it was " The Mistletoe Bough."
It didna sound like it : I was fair sick of it afore
Christmas came.

What a cairds I got that year ! The bairns sent
me one each, and Merran sent a grand one with a
sprig of heather glued on inside, and the words :

> Oh ! yer company to share
> At this jolly Christmas season ;
> Oh ! to grip yer haun aince mair,
> But we maun abide by reason !

She was aye a sensible lassie.

Mrs M'Curd didna forget me. She sent me a
handsome caird depictin' five well-fed-lookin' owls,
graduated sizes, sittin' in a row on a tree mair nor
half asleep, and underneath, printed in gold, was the
well-known words, " Should auld acquaintance be
forgot." Her and me is auld freends, but I never

saw an owl but once, on the road by the river near Springfield.

XX

CHRISTMAS DAY at Brighton was a reglar Feastable what between the Church, and the roast-beef of old England, and the plum-pudding, and crackers for the bairns, and a Christmas tree in the drawing-room efter dinner. There was a present for every one in the house on it, and mines was a dress kep—white lace, with a bunch of velvet pansies at the side— very genteel. They all said it set me fine : it was a sootable endin' to a real happy day.

When I was young there was a habit of giving what they ca'ed " sentiments " at supper-pairties, and a favourite one was, " May the evening's diversions bear the morning's reflections." I dinna think bairns are liable to refleck much on what they've been efter yesterday, like, but mebbe the three wee Lindesays had eaten ower many sweet things on Christmas Day, for the next day they were neither to haud nor to bind. It was a pourin' wet day, and they didna get out, or mebbe their tempers would have held up better. Miss Cielle was the first to give way : she's gey fiery, like her poor grandpapaw, the Colonel. Master Johneen was buildin' a grand bridge on the carpet with a new toy his grannie had given him, and Miss Cielle came flyin' into the room— she's aye in a hurry. So she caught her foot in the arch and nearly fell on her nose. Then she flew into a passion and kicked the whole edifice down. Master Johneen is the sweetest-tempered bairn you ever saw, but he's serious-minded too, and he lookit up at his sister (he was kneelin' on the floor), and advised her to say, " Get thee behind me, Satan." And with that she bawled, " Get thee behind me, Satan ! " and

gave Master Johneen such a thump in the middle
that he tumbled right over on his back! He was
astonished-like for a meenit, and lay still, and then
he began to laugh so sweet and cheery that Miss
Cielle couldna help but laugh too; and then she
hauled him up, and gave him a kiss, and went away
gey an' hum'elt-lookin'.

There was peace till tea-time, Miss Jean bein' in
her bed, and the ither two with their mamaw. But,
when they came to their teas, nothing would serve
them but they would toast bread, and I would butter
it to them. So they all stood round the fire, as close
as they could get, with cheeks like red roses. And
queer-like toast they made; but I buttered the best
of it. At last Miss Jean held up a slice that had just
a wee bit of brown at one end, and all the rest was
white with black strokes on it where it had come
against the bars. I said I wouldna waste butter on
it, and then the question arose which of them was
to get it to eat dry? Miss Jean got the first chance,
and I asked her whether she would eat it herself or
give it to Master Johneen? She swithered a wee,
and then she gave it to her brother. But the meenit
she heard him crumshin' it her heart failed her, and
she burst into such a roar that Lady Lindesay came
fleein' up the stair in terror. She couldna understan' what it was all about; and then Master
Johneen, with his mouth cram-full, says, " Oh, baby,
baby! say ' God loveth a cheerful giver,' " and, with
that, the pour wee tot said it, with the tears pourin'
down her cheeks, and a mouth like the De'il pu'in'
heather. Lady Lindesay couldna keep from laughin'
at the bairn's face, but she told Master Johneen that
he had the maist aggravatin' selection of texts that
ever she heard, and she would thank him not to be
so free with them. I was gled when they were a'
safe in their beds, so I was.

It seems that it was the bairns' grandmamaw, auld

Lady Lindesay, that taught them to say, "God loveth a cheerful giver," and they're grand at it when they're pairtin' with things they're no' carin' aboot. But there's mair nor them like that. Miss Celandine says she feels fine and cheerful when she puts the least she can afford in the alms-bag; and the folk that sets out for the kirk on the Sabbath Day, with one penny each in their pocket, dinna look downcast. I heard of a young leddy once that said she couldna go to the kirk because she had naething less than a threepenny in the house! And the folk that lived in the big house on Carldoddie Brae aye sent to the grocer every Setterday night for a shilling's worth of small change. It's no' respeckable. You'll never keep a minister on that, and them celebrate for lairge faimlies too!

XXI

WE'VE got Miss Celandine settled at last, and I'll no' deny but what it's a weight off our minds. It's the Corporal. He's no' just exackly turned out to be a Prince in Disguise, though; but he's the eldest son of Sir Donald Coleridge-Burton (I kenned fine it was a name like Finnan-Haddock), and his mither was one of the Hays of Pitlossie—Fifeshire folk, like me. He's his mither's drawn pictur—the "handsome Hays" they're aye ca'ed in the districk. Mebbe it's no' such a stylish down-sittin' as the Roman Cardinal or the Bassaleery would have been; but "A bird in the hand's worth twa fleein' by," and the ither two never lookit the road Miss Celandine was on, as far as I could see.

When she came ben to announce the engagement, as soon as the Corporal was demobbolized, she brought him wi' her. He was holdin' her hand (he's an awfu' tall felly—out-sized, like) and they were baith fair beamin' with joy.

" Well, Marget Pow," says Miss Celandine, " she's
got him ! "

That was aye what I used to say when the young
leddies lent me a read of a love-story. I likit them
to end right ; so I used to ask afore I started the book,
" Does she get him ? " And latterally, Miss Jean
aye said when she brought a book, " She gets him ! "
So that was what Miss Celandine was eludin' to.
And then the Corporal put his airm round about her,
and lookit at her with the lovelight in his eyes, and
says he, soft and low, " And *he* has got *her*," and afore
ever I kent what I was doin' I was sittin' in my big
chair, greetin' like to break my he'rt ! I doubt I
was thinkin' on the Kurnel and Mrs Murray. Auld
folks are easy upset. But I'm real pleased, mind
you ; it's a very sootable alliance, and I was aye
feared Miss Celandine would do something daft, and
then take the rue. She was terrible camsterie when
the Corporal was in the forefront of the battle :
" A'thing angered her, and the cat broke her heart."
Would you believe that she called Tatty a " can-
tankerous old crocodile " one day just because the
decent cratur was annoyed at bein' interrupted when
she was sortin' her back hair ! But, now that her
jo's safe home, it's a' peace and goodwill, and Tatty's
" little sister cat " and a' the rest of it.

We've been away seein' the Prince of Wales
towering through Canada at the Cinema. Thon's
a wonderfu' sight ! We saw the very train he started
in comin' into the station ; and his paw and his maw
seein' him away ; and the engine-driver in a fearfu'
twitter for fear he would upset the royal train. But
maistly a' the folk seemed to be in a nervish state—
trembly-like—feared, nae doubt, for ony ill happenin'
to the Heir to the Throne. He was calm-like hissel',
though ; an' awfu' active dink wee felly, as the Fifers
say—meanin' precise. We saw him in four different
suits. First he was a Naval gentleman, and then an

officer in the Airmy, and for a wee while he had on a plain tweed suit and a light felt hat. It was when he went boatin' that he was dressed like a scout—thon's no' neat—no' the thing for a real Prince at a'. I thought he would have had three long white ostrich feathers on the crown of his heid, parteeclarly when he was colloguin' wi' the Red Indian Chiefs, and them dressed to the nines for the occasion. But we only saw the Prince of Wales's feathers once, stuck on the front of a motor-caur.

The Canadians are quick folk, and the Prince seemed to be in a fearfu' hurry the whole time he was away. One meenit you would see him on a platform, readin' a speech off a paper wi' his mouth wide open, and the next meenit he was inta a caur in a jiffy, and off! His principal business, seemin'ly, was to lay wreaths on monuments, and inspeck guards of honour, and pin decorations on veterans : it was the same wherever he went : gey tedisome, I would jalouse. I notticed that he had a ring on the pinkie of his left hand : it'll likely be the fashion among the Nobility.

Miss Jean told me a queer thing about a deaf-and-dumb bairn that was taken to see a Cinema Play. She had been learned what they ca' " lip-reading," and here did she no' understan' every word the folk in the Play were sayin'. It was a downcome for them that had their hearin' to be tellt by a deaf-and-dumb bairn what was goin' on.

XXII

THERE's been a bit in the *Scotsman* ca'ed " The Old Made Young," and Miss Celandine's been advisin' me to renew my youth like the he-goats and rams that the Paris doctor has been tryin' his tricks on. He says " he has made them frisk like kids and lambs." But friskin' is no' the only differ between youth and

age ! I've seen auld folk frisky enough on Singin'-
e'en or at a weddin', but they calmed down the day
efter, so they did. It would ill set me to be fleein'
about the house, waggin' my tail, like, so I'll just
conteenue to be " Auld Marget Pow " to the end of
my days, thenk-ye : I wouldna like to be beholden
to a monkey for the prolongation of my earthly
career ! But there's a minister has found out a
better way nor that to keep young, and I'm in a
poseetion to give you all parteeclars concernin' the
method, for I was at the tea-pairty when he announced
his discovery. It was in a church hall—a fine big
place—and the occasion was the birthday of the
minister. But there was nine ither leddies belongin'
the church that all had been born in the same month
(it happened to be Feb'uary), and so they settled
that they would give a birthday-tea to all the mothers
in the congregation. And I was invited to it acci-
dental-like—a sort of a complimentary invitation—
through me knowin' a party that knew a leddy that
had a friend that worshipped in the kirk. And a
fine tea it was, I can tell ye ! Birthday-cake, and
scones, and cookies fair squirkin' wi' jam, and every
one of us got a bunch of snowdrops to stick in our
buttonholes, and they lookit fine. Then there was
music and singin', and, efter that, the minister got up
and made a speech. It was in the middle of it that
he eluded to his discovery about how to keep folk
young. He bad us obsairve what fresh-like the Nine
Leddies that was born in the same month as hissel'
lookit (and one of them was a grandmither, no less !),
and then he informed us that his assistant had added
up their ages (he would get them from the censor),
and they came to five hundred ! But, when you
divided them by nine, they were all under sixty—
just fifty-five, and odds ! It's a cheery way of lookin'
at the subjeck ; and Miss Jean pinted out on the road
home that, if me and the young leddies were added

up and divided by three, we would just be forty; and, even if we threw in Mrs M'Curd (she's older nor me), we wouldna be more nor forty-seeven! But, though we're taught in the Scripturs to bear one another's burdens, I doubt the burden of years is no' sae easy shifted : it'll be the kind that every man must bear hissel', mebbe.

But I mustna omit to mention that the minister said anither good way of keepin' young was to take an interest in young folk ; and he told us that his bairns had been at a tea-pairty at the house of one of the Nine ; and, when they played at hide-and-seek, where do ye think *she* hid ? In the kitchen-boiler! There's suppleness for ye !

Finally we sang " O God of Bethel ! " to the usual tune. There was a wee lassie about eight year auld, with a bonny innocent bit face, standin' in front of the minister ; and she fixed her eyes on his face, and never took them off it while she sang the paraphrase a' through without a book. I never saw a mair adorin' look on a bairn's face. And, someway, the sight of her minded me of anither wean, just about the same age, that we saw in a great big church in a foreign city. (I'll no' let on where it was for fear of the censor ; but, anyway, we're no' goin' *there* again.) It was at a Children's Service, and I'll warrant there was a thousand bairns at it ; I never saw as many in my life. And the little lassie that the Scotch bairn put me in mind of wasna kneelin' with the rest in the body of the kirk : she was standin' her lane in an open space inside the big door, with her wee thin hands claspit on her breast, and her e'en shut, and her face turned towards the altar. She was poor-like—they were all that—but she was a perfeck pictur of worship, and it was easy to believe that " of such is the Kingdom of Heaven." It's a mercy in these times of fechtin' and general ill-will to re-colleck that there's innocent weans all over the world,

and that they're much the same nae matter what
country or kirk they belong to.

It was in that same church that we saw two wee
tots—laddies—come in hand in hand. They lookit
about them, and then they accidentally turned their
backs on the altar (it was an awfu' distance away)
and jennyflected simultaneously to the statue of an
auld King that was likely no better than he should
have been !

We've been keepin' Armistice Day, and I was out
for onions, etc., when the gun fired from the Castle
to announce that the two-meenits' silence had begun.
I heard on the deefest side o' my heid, I can tell ye,
for I was just at the corner of Castle Street. And
then there fell such a silence and a stillness as never
had been heard afore in the very middle of a workin'-
day : it was real solemn. The folk in the street a'
stood still, and the very caurs stoppit. I saw a lassie
that was just gettin' into one when the gun fired, and
there she stood with one foot up and one foot down
the whole time. Someway the snow on the ground
made the scene mair impressive ; and while we were
a' holdin' our breath, like, a pibroch sounded far, far
away, the only thing that broke silence. I couldna
help wonderin' if the great army of dead warriors we
were thinkin' on heard the voice of silent stillness,
and what it said to them ?

XXIII

THE wedding-presents are arrivin' for Miss Celandine
wholesale and retail, and Prothisa is that taken up
helpin' her to admire them that she disna nottice
fuff under the beds, and thrums on the drawin'-room
carpet, the way I would like. And the motes and
the flichters are a' over the house owin' to the peat
we're usin' to save the coals. The constant strife

wi' dirt that a mysterious Providence has ordained
as the principal occupation of no' a few of the dwellers
on this earth, parteeclarly the womenfolk, is a dis-
pensation that's never been satisfactorily explained.
It's where it a' comes from that baffles me! And
when you think on the airmy of house-maids, kitchen-
maids, scavengers, bootses, laundry-maids, windy-
cleaners, etcintera, that's fechtin' with dirt day efter
day, and year efter year, ye may well wonder what
the world would be like wantin' them. I doubt dirt
is just of the same natur as original sin or innate
cussedness; but mebbe the " higher criteckism," as
they ca' it, can explain the maitter better nor me.
No' that I hold with they new-fangled notions. I'm
told that they're castin' doubts on Job bein' a real
man! If it's true, they dinna ken muckle about
human natur. There's many a gentleman like Job
that'll bear the extermination of their freens and
relations with fortitude, but when it comes to gettin'
boils theirsels they turn the whole house upside
down, so they do. Yon's a real man.

I've notticed on my way through life what a deal
of our time is taken up with waitin'—waitin' on ither
folk mair parteeclarly—sweeps, and painters, and
plumbers, especially the latters when they're needin'
something they havena brought with them, and
traivel away back to the shop to get it. There's no'
such a thing as " Orders Punctual Executed " now,
though many's the time I've read it above the
sweep's door in Princes Street: he'll can take *that*
nottice down now, I would jealouse. And if the
painters promise faithfu' to start work on Monday
first, you may be thankfu' if you get them on Friday
fortnight; but a'things changed since that weary
war. So Miss Jean took me to a grand concert to
cheer me up, like. I'm no' very sure whether it had
the desired effeck; it was an awfu' noise. All the
leddies and gentlemen played at once, maistly on

fiddles ; and sometimes it was fearfu' loud, and sometimes it was that low that you could scarcely hear it. It was when it went low suddenly that I heard a voice sayin' quite clear, " Where *does* Lady Brierly get her hats ! " I kent fine, for I saw the hat no' far away, and the leddy too, but I never let on for fear of disturbin' the concert : but it's no' a bonny hat—I will say that.

When we got home it was very near six o'clock, and here Miss Celandine came flyin' to meet us to tell us she had got anither present—" the best of them all," says she. She wouldna tell us who it was from for ever so long ; but at last she let out that it was a pure white kitling, and then Miss Jean and me both guessed at once " from Tatty ! " Mind you it's the first ever we've had without a single black hair, so Miss Celandine says of course it's for a wedding-present for her ; and it's to have a rose-pink ribbon round its neck at the marriage, and it's to be ca'ed " Humphrey," efter Mr Coleridge-Burton. But, mind you, she generally ca's *him* " Haddy ! " And would you believe that one day when I was in the drawing-room helpin' to unpack a new-come present, here did I no' hear Miss Celandine introducin' her feeongsay to a grand lady by the name of " Mr Findhorn Haddock ! " And the leddy held his hand high up, and says she, quite calm, " Delighted ! Have we met before ? Your name seems quite familiar to me." I was thankfu' to get out of the room, but no' afore I heard a' the company laughin'. I ken fine Miss Celandine will never let down on me that I thought her sweetheart's name was something like Finnan-Haddock.

XXIV

THERE's some advantages in old age; I'll no' deny
that; but mebbe they're no' sae easy seen as the
advantages of bein' young. When you're young you
say " soon," thinkin' on the grand things you're
goin' to do. When you're middle-aged you say
" some time." But, when you're auld, like me, you
say " never." On the ither hand, there's " anxieties
of to-day that fade into nothingness to-morrow."
That's a true say. I've seen the time when I would
have been like to drop if anybody had stoppit me on
the street and tellt me that my hair was comin'
down : but now I just say " Thank-ye kindly, mem,"
and stick the preens firmer in, and never take a red
face nor onything. That minds me of a young leddy
that Lady Lindesay told me about—a great freen o'
hers. She was in Paris when the Huns was drawin'
awfu' near, so she thought it was time for her to go
away home. She had miles to walk to the station,
and two kind Belgian women went with her, and helped
her to carry her bag, etc. They were that polite that
they *would* insist on walkin' ahint her, which was no'
what she wanted at a'. Well, Lady Lindesay went
to meet her at the London station, and welcomed her
home, and showed her to the tacksie that was waitin'
on them. And then says she, surprised-like, " Laura,
do you know that there are two white tape strings
hanging down below your coat ? " " Strings ! " says
the Paris leddy, and she jerkit them round, and lookit
at them, fair stiff wi' horror, " and those two tidy
Belgians walked behind me the whole way to the
station ! " Lady Lindesay assured me that her freen
was mair upset by the strings than by the Huns.
And when she got safe home and her mother said
to her the next day, very near greetin', " Laura,
the Germans are advancing straight upon Calais ! "

" Well, mamma," says she, as cool as you like, " did you expect them to sit down ? " That's young folk—they're easy annoyed wi' trifles, but they take disasters very calm, I will say that.

When I was young mysel' I never seemed to think I would be auld some day, if I was spared. I was kind-of surprised when the conductors on the caurs started to hist me up the step, and folk stood up to let me sit, and poked hassocks to me in a strange kirk. But it's when ye begin to loss your faculties, and your head grows through your hair, and you canna mind things the way you used to do, that you feel the awkwardness of eld. Miss Jean comforts me, when I've forgotten anything, wi' a piece of po'try out of a book she's aye readin'. It's ca'ed " The Diary of an Old Soul," and the words is as follies, namely :

> and I can well afford
> All to forget, so thou remember, Lord.

It's very nice and consolin', nae doubt, but when it's a cauliflower for the denner, or tea-bread for the efternoon, I would prefer to ha' minded it mysel', so I would.

The Old Age Pensions has reconsiled no' a few to the rapid flight of time. Some poor bodies wearies for the day when they'll be " threescore years and ten." But it's safest to " Be aye the thing you would be ca'ed," as the proverb says, and the woman that shifted her age five year back when she was wed, rued the day when she was seekin' her pension.

We're gettin' on fine with the preparations for Miss Celandine's marriage ; she's to be all in pure whites, and the same lace veil that Lady Lindesay had on, ower her heid. The ribbon for the kitling's neck is in the house—rose-pink—and Tatty's is forty-second tartan, no less ! But she doesna like bein' dressed up, decent cratur, and I'm hopin' she'll no' have it all licked and chewed afore ever the company arrives.

I'm gettin' a new gown for the occasion from Miss Celandine ; it's to be black silk—the kind they ca' " mervello "—and it's to be made full and longish, " durnay cree," as the French folk say, meanin' real stylish. The bonnet's to be black lace, but the bow's no settled yet. There's many a one would say it would set me better to be thinkin' on my latter end ; but Miss Jean pinted out to me last Sabbath that it was just efter St Paul said, " I am now ready to be offered, and the time of my departure is at hand," that he minded Timothy to bring the cloke that he left at Troas with him when he came (it would likely be his waterproof) ; and he didna hesitate to tell on Alexander the coppersmith either. Mr M'Duigald's discourse that day was on the subjeck of clothin'— " Be clothed with humility " was the text, and I couldna help thinkin' it would take a deal of it to make up to some fashionable leddies for the garments they dinna put on nowadays. But I was thinkin' on my own weddin' costume too ; I'll no' deny that : and mebbe it would have been sootabler if I had been settlin' what I would put on when I start on my last and lanesomest journey. There's folk that's been feared all their lives for the day they never saw. And there's ither folk that think that, when they die, they'll go bouncin' straight into heaven, and they'll find their freens and relations sittin' in the front row waitin' on them. I'm no' sae sure : there's degrees : but mebbe " If we canna preach in the kirk we can sing mass in the quire," as the auld Scotch proverb says. With which solemn words I will now conclude.

P.S.—The bow's to be lilac, with a silver edge— very genteel.

EPILOGUE

Should you ask me, whence these havers ?
(Which, I know, is most unlikely),
Whence these stories and traditions,
With the Edinburgh accent,
With the flavour of Auld Reekie,
With the tinkle of the tea-cups,
With the lapper of the water—
Of the water " down the water "—
With their somewhat doubtful grammar,
And their more than doubtful spelling ?
  I should answer, I should tell you,
" From the fairest of all cities—
From the royal town of Edwin,
Swept with winds from every quarter,
Where the sea-gulls swoop and waver.
From the lone hills of Argyllshire,
Scented with the blooming heather,
Musical with many waters,
Where the tender gloaming lingers
Till the night has kissed the morning.
They are printed as she wrote them,
She the writer—Powsie-Wowsie."
  Should you ask where Powsie-Wowsie
Found these tales, these perfect havers ?
(With a rare desire for knowledge),
I should answer, I should tell you,
" In the haunts of men and women.
In the cosy, fire-lit kitchen,
In the ways of little children,
In the common talk of Nature.
  All the pussies sang them to her,
Sang them purring on the hearth-rug ;

Tatty fat, that ancient mother,
And the beauteous one—Delilah ;
Granville Barker told his story,
Granville, better known as Samson ;
Sparrows chirped their little legends
Pecking at the kitchen-window,
And she heard them, and she told them,
The Narrator, Powsie-Wowsie."

If still further you should ask me,
Saying, " Who was Powsie-Wowsie ?
Tell us of this Powsie-Wowsie,"
I should answer your inquiries,
In well-chosen words, as follows :—
" Look her up in handy *Who's Who* ?
Under ' P ' perhaps you'll find her ;
Is the date of birth withholden ?
Then be sure she's somewhat olden.
Nothing said of noble forbears ?
Then *noblesse* does not *oblige* her ;
And her favourite amusements—
Could they just be talk and laughter ?
If she is not there in *Who's Who* ?
Then unknown is Powsie-Wowsie."

Ye who love the Scottish accent,
Love the proverbs of the people,
And the olden-time expressions,
Half-forgot for want of using,
Which recall the days of childhood
And the sweet familiar faces,
Listen to these simple legends,
To these tales of Powsie-Wowsie.

Ye whose minds are clear and powerful,
Who believe that, in all ages,
Every Scottish heart is Scottish ;
That, in even English bosoms,
There are longings unsuspected
For the homely Northern language,
For the words they comprehend not—
Listen to this humble story,
To this tale of simple people.

Ye, who sometimes, in your journeys
To and from the crowded city,
Passing through a noisy station,
Pause by some attractive book-stall
For a while to muse and ponder
On the titles of the volumes—
Of the volumes price one shilling—
Writ with little skill of book-craft,
Homely stories, but each chapter
Full of hope that, some one reading,
Might be moved to healthful laughter ;
Full of heartbreak, when the reader
Yawns with weariness unfeignèd ;
Full of all the unseen pathos
Of the real and the ideal—
Stay and read this final chapter
Of the life of Powsie-Wowsie.

BOOKS *published by* THE MORAY PRESS

By
COLIN MACDONALD

Published at **6s.** *each (post free* **6s. 3d.**)

ECHOES OF THE GLEN
MACTALLA NAN GLEANN

HIGHLAND JOURNEY
SÙIL AIR AIS

To be published in Autumn 1947
(*Price* **7s. 6d.**)

CROFT and CEILIDH
CORRA CHAGAILTE

From *The Inverness Courier* :

When Colin MacDonald published his first book, *Echoes of the Glen*, we considered it to be such an important contribution to the story of social life in the Highlands, with its vivid and faithful portrayal of the characteristics and daily living of the Highland people, that in a leading article on Highland matters we recommended everybody interested in Highland problems to read it and take it to heart. The same may be said of *Highland Journey*, for nobody who wants to understand the Highlands and the Highland people can afford to neglect it.

From *The Observer* review of *Highland Journey* :

One may learn more of the people and problems of the north-west from this book than from a dozen that deal mainly with its glamour.

THE SCOTTISH NATIONAL WAR MEMORIAL. With an Introduction by Sir Ian Hamilton, G.C.B., D.S.O. The volume contains 46 whole-page illustrations, most of which are in colour. Throughout the Memorial the artists and craftsmen have employed colour which is an essential part of the beauty they have created. Without colour it is impossible faithfully to portray that beauty. In this book this has been done in print for the first time. It is a book which will appeal to all Scotsmen and Scotswomen throughout the world, leading them, as it does, step by step through Scotland's Shrine. Royal 4to. Boards with cloth back.
15s. (Postage **6d.**)

HELEN DREVER

THE LURE OF THE KELPIE and Other Tales and Legends. A selection of the best fairy tales from the Highlands. Illustrated by Mildred R. Lamb.
7s. 6d. (Postage **4d.**)

TALES OF THE SCOTTISH CLANS. Illustrated by A. Mason Trotter. **7s. 6d.** (Postage **4d.**)

W. MACKAY MACKENZIE

THE SECRET OF FLODDEN. A critical study of the battle. Illustrated. **5s.** (Postage **3d.**)

ALISTAIR MACLEAN

HEBRIDEAN ALTARS. Translations of prayers and runes collected throughout the Hebrides from the original Gaelic.
7s. 6d. (Postage **4d.**)

AMY MURRAY

FATHER ALLAN'S ISLAND. Island lore and folk-song gathered in Eriskay. With music. **8s. 6d.** (Postage **6d.**)

DAVID RORIE

THE LUM HAT WANTIN' THE CROON.
6s. (Postage **4d.**)

J. B. SALMOND

WADE IN SCOTLAND. An historical and topographical study of Wade's Roads. Fully illustrated.
(*New Edition in Preparation.*)

THE OLD STALKER AND OTHER VERSES.
5s. (Postage **3d.**)

PRINCE CHARLIE'S COUNTRY

A series of one hundred and one full plate photographs of that part of the Scottish Highlands associated with Prince Charlie's wanderings.

With an Introduction and a Running Commentary on the Pictures

BY THE ARTIST

DONALD B. MacCULLOCH

16/-

ON TINTOCK TAP

A collection of Scottish Lowland and other Folk Tales, retold for Young People.

BY

MARION LOCHHEAD

Illustrated by Mildred R. Lamb.

7/6

SHEEP DOGS AND THEIR MASTERS

Being a history of the Border Collie, together with some notes about the men who have developed the breed.

BY

JOHN HERRIES McCULLOCH

Illustrated.

6/-

Forthcoming Moray Press Books

MOIDART AND MORAR.

Its Romance and Story. By WENDY WOOD. Fully illustrated with Drawings by the Author and with Photographs.
8s. 6d.

LETTERS FROM SHETLAND.

Being a series of letters written to a friend dealing with the varied activities of life in the Shetlands. By PETER A. JAMIESON. Fully illustrated from Photographs. **8s. 6d.**

From the Ettrick Press

ALL AROUND SCOTLAND.

By ROBERT J. DRUMMOND, D.D. With 15 Illustrations from Photographs. **7s. 6d.**

LEAVES FROM THE LIFE OF A COUNTRY DOCTOR.

(CLEMENT BRYCE GUNN, M.D., J.P.)

Edited by RUTHERFORD CROCKETT. With a Foreword by JOHN BUCHAN. **7s. 6d.**

THE PEAT-FIRE FLAME.

A comprehensive collection of the best folk-tales of the Highlands and Islands of Scotland. Illustrated from the Author's Photographs. By ALASDAIR ALPIN MACGREGOR.
15s.

WILSON'S TALES OF THE BORDERS.

Illustrated with Pencil Drawings by J. Thomson. A selection of twenty-two of the best stories from *Wilson's Tales*, with an Introduction by THOMAS HENDERSON.
10s. 6d.